IT'S NEVER TOO LATE

HANNAH LYNN

PAPER CAT PUBLISHING

ALSO BY HANNAH LYNN

Standalone Feel Good Novels

The Afterlife of Walter Augustus

Treading Water

A Novel Marriage

The Complete Peas and Carrots Series

Peas, Carrots and an Aston Martin

Peas, Carrots and a Red Feather Boa

Peas, Carrots and Six More Feet

Peas, Carrots and Lessons in Life

Peas, Carrots and Panic at the Plot

Peas, Carrots and Happily Ever After

The Holly Berry Sweet Shop Series

The Sweet Shop of Second Chances

Love Blooms at the Second Chances Sweet Shop

The Lonely Hearts Book Club Series

It's Never Too Late

Lessons in Love

Text copyright © 2023 Hannah Lynn
First published 2023

Published by Paper Cat Publishing

ISBN: 978-1-915346-13-1

Cover design by Wonderburg Creations
Edited by Carol Worwood

To my choir ladies,

CHAPTER 1

*F*leur slowed her pace and gazed down the row of mismatched buildings. A clear blue sky stretched out above her, broken only by the slightest white tufts of cloud, while spring blossoms burst into colour in the green patches of land that were dotted in front of the Church and Visitor Centre. On a day like today, it was easy to see why Maldon had stolen her heart so easily. There was something about the irregularity of the shops that made it so endearing, from the pink walls of Mrs Salisbury's Tea rooms to the dark-stone brickwork and balcony of Moot Hall. Sometimes, the whole town seemed so new and intriguing, it felt impossible to believe she'd moved there almost two months ago. At other times, it was like she'd been born there.

Smiling to herself, she continued her walk up the High Street, only to stop again as she felt her phone buzz in her bag. For a second, she stared at the name on the screen and her hand hovered above the green telephone symbol, but then she changed her mind and hung up instead. She would speak to her later.

Ever the overbearing older sister, Annelise had been ringing constantly, trying to persuade her to throw an over-the-top birthday bash on her encroaching, big four-zero. No matter how much Fleur insisted it wasn't what she wanted, Annelise would not drop the subject. Given what a wonderfully relaxed day Fleur had spent so far, the last thing she wanted was her good mood ruined by her sister's well-meaning but constant badgering.

After dropping her phone back into her bag, she continued towards the last of the morning's errands, picking up her prescription from the pharmacy. Wanting to get in and out as quickly as possible, she hurried to the back of the long and narrow shop, only to stop before she reached the counter.

"This is disgusting. You understand that? An absolute farce. I want to speak to your line manager. Now."

The man speaking — or rather shouting — towered over the petite pharmacist. While Fleur could only see the back of him, the impression she got was definitely hostile. His shoulders were pushed back, his stance wide, and if she had to place a bet, she would have said his arms were locked across his chest. Yet despite this, the little woman placed her hands on the counter between them and spoke with measured calmness.

"Sir, *I* am the duty manager here today. I am very sorry about the mix-up with whoever you spoke to on the phone. I will get onto our suppliers immediately and see if I can get a rush delivery for tomorrow, or I can ring up our branch in Chelmsford. They're a much bigger store, so I can see if they have what you need in stock. Then you could collect it from there, if that's easier."

"Easier?" the man snorted. "What would have been easier is if you'd done your job properly in the first place."

Fleur's skin prickled at his tone as she moved towards the counter, awaiting her turn to collect her own prescription. She wasn't the only one. Several people were now queued up behind her, though she soon realised she was in the unenviable position of being closest to the action. And it was making her more and more furious with every passing second.

"You mark my words," the man continued. "The moment I get out of here, I'm going to be straight on the phone to your head office and putting in a formal complaint. About this store and about you."

"That's it," Fleur muttered. With jaw set, she stepped forwards and tapped the man lightly on the shoulder. "Excuse me," she said.

As he turned to face her, she stepped back, partially because of the lack of room, but also so she could get a better look at this infuriatingly rude man. Flecks of silver dappled his dark hair that was trimmed into a perfectly straight line. From the back, this had given the impression of age, which was why she was surprised that the person who turned to face her was only slightly older than she was.

"What do you want?" he snapped, his unbridled aggression and piercing glower now focussed on Fleur; yet he didn't intimidate her. When she'd worked in London, she'd come across arrogant men like him so many times she'd lost count. She cleared her throat and pushed back her shoulders.

"I can see that you're upset, but I'm sure that whatever has happened, this lady —" she paused to scan the name tag pinned to the pharmacist's uniform, "—*Grace*. I'm sure that Grace is doing her very best. She's been nothing but polite and helpful and, to be honest, your attitude here isn't doing anything other than holding up a queue of people, many of whom I'm sure have places they need to be. So perhaps, rather than causing a scene which is, quite frankly, a waste of all our time, you could accept one of the solutions Grace has offered, and let us all get on with our day."

Considering what she would have liked to have said, Fleur thought she'd been very restrained and polite and hoped that the man would get the message. She waited for a response. With his gaze fixed on her, he straightened his spine and a deep crease formed on his brow, as if he were utterly confused by her presence there. He tilted his head to the side, quizzically.

"I'm sorry. Do I know you?"

It was the first thing she'd heard him say at a normal volume, and the unexpected question meant it was her turn to look confused. She took a moment to study the man more closely. He was dressed smartly enough to have worked in an office with her in London. His suit was just on the right side of fashionable and well cut, and he was about the right age that she could even have known him growing up or perhaps he'd been the boyfriend or spouse of one of her work colleagues, and yet she couldn't place him from anywhere.

"I don't think so," she said, after a moment.

"No, neither do I," he sniffed. "And though it might be wrong of me to judge, I presume from your flowery attire that you do not work here, meaning that this conversation is also absolutely none of your business. So how about you take a step back and let me deal with this?"

Fleur was utterly dumbfounded. She stood, jaw slack, as the man turned back to face the counter again. In that moment, a thousand thoughts flew through her mind. *Flowery attire?* Admittedly, there were flowers on her blouse. Colourful clothes were something she'd embraced since leaving London. After all those years in plain, constricting office attire, she enjoyed having fun with what she wore. But the sartorial attack wasn't the only thing that had got to her. The way he'd looked down his nose at her set every one of her nerves on fire. She'd met hundreds of men like him in her life. Middle-aged males who assumed the presence of a Y-chromosome, combined with a moderate degree of attractiveness, meant they felt justified speaking to people — and in particular women — however they wanted.

Before she could second guess herself, Fleur was moving.

"Actually," she said, as she planted her feet in the small gap between the counter and the obnoxious man. "This *is* my business. And not just because you're delaying the wonderful morning walk I had planned, but because bad behaviour is *everyone's* business. And yours is nothing short of a teenage, school-yard bully. Now, rather than throwing you out, as *I* would have done, Grace kindly gave you the available options. So please, for the love of God, before I am forced to escalate the situation to a level that I don't think any of us want, give her an answer and leave, so the rest of us can get on with our day."

Fleur wasn't oblivious to the fact that the entire shop had gone completely silent. Had she shifted her line of sight ever so slightly, she would have seen nearly a dozen people staring at them, waiting with bated breath. This was something she didn't realise, however, given that her eyes were locked on one place. The icy hues of Mr Moody in front of her.

He sniffed, the muscles along his jaw twitching slightly as his eyes narrowed.

"Fine then. Just get out of my way," he snapped.

With another side-step, Fleur shuffled back to her place in the queue. It was the man's turn to clear his throat this time as he spoke to Grace, the pharmacist.

"Ring the Chelmsford branch," he said. "I guess I'll just have to miss my afternoon meetings."

A moment later, he turned on his heel and left, without so much as a glance in Fleur's direction.

CHAPTER 2

"*W*ell done, love." A hand on Fleur's shoulder brought her back to the moment. "That was a good thing you did there. Standing up to him like that. Now, you're next, aren't you?"

"Next?" Fleur said, with a vague sense of dissociation, before realising that the woman was referring to the queue. "Oh, yes. Yes, thank you."

As she moved to the spot in front of the counter, the pharmacist smiled kindly.

"Thank you for that," Grace said, taking the prescription that Fleur was holding out. "You didn't have to do that."

"I'm just sorry you have to deal with people who behave in such an appalling manner."

Grace cocked an eyebrow, implying this was a far more frequent occurrence than Fleur could have imagined.

"People get quite upset when things don't go their own way. I do understand. Medication is important."

"But it's not your fault. They shouldn't take it out on you."

"I know, but people don't always think rationally when they're stressed. I've learned not to take it personally."

"Then you're a bigger person than me," Fleur said truthfully, tapping her card on the machine as Grace handed her the white paper bag with its distinctive green cross. "I hope that the rest of your day goes better."

"Thank you. You too. Have a good day."

As Fleur dropped the small package into her bag and left the pharmacy, several of the queueing customers met her eye to offer smiles or even tapped her on the arm. Yes, there were definitely more good people in the world than bad, she thought to herself, stepping outside onto the pavement.

Given the drama at the pharmacy, she decided to opt straight for the age-old and proven method of addressing all issues, cake.

There was no shortage of places to find a decent slice of gateau in Maldon. There were coffeeshops with quaint wooden beams that sat directly on the High Street and several smaller, but no less excellent, establishments tucked away down alleys and side streets. There was even a waffle bar, with every topping you could hope for, although that tended to be packed out by families with young children. But Fleur knew exactly where she was going.

The walk down the High Street was exactly that. Down. The hill was a continuous slope that flattened out only when the shops began to thin, closer to the waterfront. This was the part of town where she lived. When she reached the bottom, she took the turning past St Mary the Virgin Church, with its iron grave markers, stained glass windows and silvery-grey spire that dominated the skyline. She'd heard that the building was even more impressive inside than out, and she had every intention of attending one of the choral evenings. That was another thing on her to-do list, along with getting some curtains which fitted her windows properly and perhaps even forming some friendships in the town.

Getting to know people had been at the top of her list for weeks now, but it was easier said than done. Working mainly from home meant there were few opportunities to make friends with work colleagues at the London office. And although her hours were flexible, any daytime get-togethers on offer locally seemed to revolve around baby groups, and any evening gatherings appeared to be aimed at twenty some-things who could still drink more than three glasses of wine without suffering a pounding headache and an inability to function the following morning. There were dating apps, of course, but she'd swiftly learned she would not find the type of friendship she was looking for on one of those. It was just so tricky to form something organic at her age.

As she took the final narrow pathway, she stopped and paused, staring out at the view. High tide was always impres-sive. The estuary filled to the brim, sailing boats with their perfectly straight masts spearing up into the sky, their halliards jangling with a soft chime. Beyond the river, marsh-land stretched out, the rugged landscape a home to wildlife and a myriad of birds. Egrets were Fleur's favourite. There was something so graceful and yet unassuming about them. That day, though, there was no sign of the slender, white birds, although a family of swans was at the water's edge, pestering tourists for bread. After one last look at the view, she headed to the Waterfront Café.

Dog walkers, young families and many others tucked into hot food and drink outside. She weaved her way through the tables, pushed open the solid wood door and was immediately hit by a wonderful aroma. The smell of freshly baked bread mixed with warm, homemade cakes eddied around her, and an instinctive smile grew on her face as her nostrils filled with the scent of quiches and pies, strong enough to make her mouth water. In the two months she'd been in Maldon, she'd eaten at the Waterfront Café nearly a dozen times and everything she'd chosen had been delicious, from the sandwiches to the salads and everything else in between. The only problem she'd had was limiting herself to one slice of cake per visit.

Inside was unusually quiet, with only three tables filled, meaning she had her pick of seats and chose one with a view out onto the water. At that angle, the river was a pale grey, though it constantly darkened and lightened as clouds crossed in front of the sun. A small sailboat was drifting lazily, its bright-white hull gleaming, while a flock of seagulls squalled and circled above it. She was still busy staring out at the view when a voice brought her back to the moment.

"I was wondering if I'd see you today," the woman said, placing a paper menu down on the table. "It's been a couple of days. I was worried you'd got bored with the quiet life and headed back to the big city already."

Fleur chuckled politely. "No, I've just been busy with work, that's all. Although, you seem quiet this morning," she said, gesturing to the empty tables.

The woman — who Fleur had only recently learned was named Gemma — raised her eyebrows. "You should have been here an hour ago. I was run off my feet. My chef called in sick and one of the waitresses is down with a sickness bug."

"I'm sure you did a great job of managing it all," Fleur replied.

Gemma wasn't just a waitress; she was the manager and had helped Fleur on her first visit by giving her directions to the big supermarkets on the outskirts of town. She was one of those people whose age was almost impossible to guess. As the job dictated, she dressed somewhat plainly in black trousers, a white top and flat shoes, but judging by the funky-coloured eyeliner and tattoos on her wrist, Fleur suspected she was younger than she'd first appeared.

"That's very sweet of you to say," Gemma replied, "Although you might not think the same had you seen me earlier. Now, the specials are on the board, except for a frangipane tart that's just come out of the oven. But we're out of the vegan chilli and the steak-and-ale pies, I'm afraid. There was a rush on those this morning."

"Thank you. I'm in the mood for something sweet anyway, so that's fine with me."

Gemma took a step away from the table. "Well, I'll leave you to look through the menu. Double-shot latte, right?"

"Thank you, that would be perfect."

While Gemma retreated to the counter to fix her drink, Fleur scanned down the list. Carrot cake was always a guaranteed winner, although the double-chocolate gateau sounded divine. But with the warmer air, perhaps something less heavy would be a better choice. Like lemon-drizzle cake.

She still hadn't decided when Gemma reappeared.

"One double-shot latte," she said, placing the drink down in front of her. "So, what have you decided?"

With one last look at the menu, Fleur pursed her lips.

"I'll have the frangipane tart. That is almond, right?"

"It is. And I think you've made a fabulous choice. I'll just fetch that for you."

"Thank you."

Then, with the steaming coffee in front of her, Fleur reached into her bag and pulled out her current book.

Reading alone in a café was never something she'd done while living in London. Just the idea of being seen out in public, casually enjoying the words as if there was nothing more urgent to be done, would have caused her to feel twitchy. That wasn't the way life was in the big city. You were supposed to be busy all the time. Rushing from place to place, consumed by an overfilled schedule. As far as she was aware, the only reason coffee shops had tables and chairs there was so people could sit while their laptops and phones charged.

But Maldon was different. It may have only been an hour from London, but the pace of life was so different. You could see it in the way people would stop and chat when they passed one another on the street. Or the way a group of friends could stretch out a morning coffee into elevenses with cake and then sometimes even an early lunch. Which was why she didn't feel in the slightest bit conspicuous sitting there with her book in front of her. At least she didn't until Gemma reappeared with her frangipane.

"You're reading that?" Gemma placed the thin slice of cake down on the table. "What do you think of it? No, don't tell me. You haven't got to the end yet, obviously. How close are you? Have you found the—sorry, I just really want to talk about this book to everyone."

Previously Gemma had only spoken to Fleur about the daily specials or the weather and therefore this outburst was quite unexpected. She perused the cover while contemplating her answer.

"I've got about four chapters left to go," she said. "And I still don't have a clue who the murderer is, which I guess is a good thing. But if I'm honest, I'm worried I'm gonna be disappointed by the ending."

"You won't be," Gemma answered immediately. "Or at least I wasn't. I was certain I knew who did it, but it fooled me. We're doing it as part of my book club, and we're divided. Particularly because of the second chapter."

"You mean the part about the cat?"

"Exactly." After a quick scan of the room to check no one needed her attention, Gemma pulled out a chair and sat down opposite Fleur. "I get why the author did it and everything, I just think it was a little ..." she paused, searching for the right word.

"Unnecessary?" Fleur suggested.

"Yes. Yes, that's it. Don't get me wrong; I love the rest of it. But I knew exactly what was going to happen. It's the only bit of the book that's predictable, though."

"You're more on the ball than me if you found any of it predictable," Fleur said. "There's been at least a dozen twists I didn't see coming." As she looked down at the book, Gemma suddenly jumped to her feet.

"Sorry, look at me here, chewing your ear off and you wanting a bit of peace."

"It's fine. It's nice to chat to someone about books. I really don't do it that often anymore. I was in a book club myself once, but that was years ago. Maybe I should see if I could find something like that again."

Gemma's face lit up. "You should join ours," she said. "You'd love it, and you're already reading the book we're discussing at the moment."

Fleur shifted in her seat slightly. She'd forgotten Gemma had mentioned it was a book-club book, and now she was worried it looked like she was angling for an invitation. But it would definitely help her meet new, likeminded people and the offer seemed genuine.

"I don't know, I mean I'm not a particularly fast reader," she said, wanting to give Gemma a way out.

"Me neither. But it's only one book every two weeks, and there's never anything too taxing. No War and Peace or anything like that. I love it. It's a chance to get together and gossip. And they really are a great bunch. A real mix of people."

Fleur desperately wanted to say yes. But something was stopping her. "Are you sure?" she asked.

"Of course, I am," Gemma replied, with a grin. "Now let me write down the address for you. The next meeting is tonight."

CHAPTER 3

Fleur checked her outfit in the mirror for the third time in as many minutes. She'd gone back to her gingham-patterned heels, paired with a green dress but was worried it was a little too much. It wasn't only the colour, but the heels themselves. When she'd worked full-time in London, she'd had no problem tottering around on four-inch stilettos, utterly stable. But now she had somehow lost the knack. On days when she went back to the office for team meetings, she often opted for flat pumps. After all, it wasn't like she was in a senior position anymore. But she enjoyed dressing up, and it felt good to be going out to meet people. Then again, she'd have to walk there and back, and the hill wasn't exactly made for heels. As she stared at her reflection again, she wondered if perhaps it wasn't just the shoes that were a mistake but going to the Book Club.

More than once, she'd considered messaging Gemma to decline the invitation. But what would she say? Something had suddenly come up? That she'd changed her mind in the four hours since she'd seen her? She couldn't even lie and say she hadn't finished the book, as Gemma had been there at the coffee shop when she'd turned the final page and dropped back into her chair with a sigh. No, she would have to go now but not until she'd got her footwear sorted.

As she stood debating, her telephone rang. Given how few people called her nowadays, she knew exactly who it must be. Annelise had sent several messages after she'd ignored her phone call earlier in the day. Knowing her sister as she did, Fleur couldn't put it past her getting in her car, driving to Maldon and banging on her front door, if she didn't pick up soon. So, steeling herself against what was about to come, she accepted the call.

"Fleury, you know you haven't answered my messages in days. I was worried something was wrong. I nearly got the train up to see you."

"Thank God Maldon doesn't have a station," Fleur replied, not quite sotto voce. "Sorry, I've just been so busy with work."

"Really? Too busy to reply to a single message? You know, if you don't get birthday invites out soon, people will be booked up."

"And what a shame that would be." This time, Fleur made no attempt to lower her voice.

As much as she loved her sister, they lived entirely different lives. The words *budget* or *money troubles* weren't in Annelise's vocabulary. Spa breaks and weekly massages were on her list of essential activities. Her children's nanny was an absolute necessity, and their five-bedroom, London town-house was worth more than Fleur was likely to earn in a life-time. As such, the idea that someone would pass up an opportunity to throw themselves a party was simply unthinkable.

"You only turn forty once," Annelise continued, ignoring Fleur's less than positive attitude. "And I know you might not feel like it, but you deserve to celebrate. You deserve to treat yourself."

"I do treat myself," she insisted. "But being stuck in a room full of people I haven't seen for the best part of ten years, all talking behind my back about why Robert and I got divorced, while I pay for the drinks, just isn't my idea of fun."

As Annelise's voice crackled down the line, Fleur instantly regretted bringing Robert into the conversation. The last thing she wanted was for her to think that the divorce was still playing on her mind. That would definitely be her cue to leave the kids with the nanny and come rushing to her side. So, before her sister could say anything else, Fleur cut across her.

"Look, I'm really grateful you called and everything, but I'm on my way out. Can I ring you back at the weekend?"

"You're going out? With people?"

"Yes, with people." Fleur wasn't sure whether she should be offended or laugh at the surprise in her sister's voice.

"Where are you going?"

"Nowhere, if I don't get off the phone. I'll tell you about it at the weekend. I better get going, though. I don't want to be late. Love you."

"Love you too."

She hung up the call and let out a long sigh. Talking to her sister could be exhausting. She knew she only meant well, but how she thought Fleur could want a birthday party after the last two years she'd had was beyond her. Especially the type of party Annelise would throw.

No, she planned on spending her fortieth some way that would relax her, maybe a day trip on one of the narrow boats that weaved around the nearby canals. Or an overnight stay somewhere like the Cotswolds. That was much more her style.

As she reached down to replace her phone in her bag, she did a double take. The Book Club was due to start in twenty minutes and she still hadn't got anything to take. The last thing she wanted to do was turn up at the home of someone she didn't even know empty-handed. Throwing caution — and the possibility of a twisted ankle — to the wind, she decided on the patterned heels, then dropped her phone and book into her bag and hurried out of the door.

CHAPTER 4

The Book Club was meeting at a house on Market Hill. While there were lots of attractive roads in Maldon, Market Hill was one of Fleur's favourites. As the name suggested, it weaved all the way from the top of town to the river front, but it was the houses lining it which so appealed to her.

The houses, which perched precariously on the steep incline, were every pastel shade, from buttercup yellow to the palest lavender, could be found adorning the mismatched buildings. Most butted right up to the pavement, some with bay windows, others flat fronted. But there were one or two magnificent mansions, hidden behind large stone walls, with only the top stories visible from the road. If she was ever to buy a house in Maldon, Market Hill and the surrounding streets would definitely be her first choice of location.

Before crossing over the mini roundabout, she made a quick left into the supermarket. The question of what to take someone she didn't know was rolling through her head as she instinctively headed towards the wine section. This was always her go-to when she visited people, but as she put a bottle of white and a bottle of red into her basket, she was struck by the thought that these people might not drink alcohol. "They could all be teetotal," she said to herself, staring at the bottles. Or recovering alcoholics. That would be the perfect way to make a terrible first impression.

Changing her mind, she put the bottles back and headed over to the soft drinks, only to hesitate again. When did people ever take soft drinks to someone's house? She never had. It would look like she was turning up at a children's party, not a sophisticated adult gathering. Scrapping that idea, too, she headed down the cake aisle.

Everyone likes cake, she thought, about to pick up a large chocolate specimen, only to spy one next to it with the label *gluten-free* in glowing colours. *Is gluten intolerance on the rise?* she wondered. Possibly, and given how many people she knew in London who suffered from it, it seemed likely someone in the Book Club would, maybe even the host. She would look like the worst guest possible bringing a flour-filled cake to their house. Fleur's mind spiralled with possibilities. Maybe she could take the chocolate cake and something else, gluten-free, too. Although neither would be any good if there were vegans.

By the time she left the supermarket, her hands were weighed down with bags. The problem was, there was no one-size-fits-all solution. A cheese platter was no good for the vegans, biscuits no good if someone avoided wheat. Crisps were okay but hardly substantial or sophisticated. Every option threw up a new issue, and so she'd done the only thing that felt sensible at the time and covered all bases. Now, though, as the straps of her cloth bags dug trenches in the palms of her hands, she couldn't help but feel she may have gone a little overboard.

The extended shopping trip meant she was running far later than planned as she power-walked down the hill. Light spots of rain hazed the air. It had started drizzling hours ago when she'd left Gemma at the café, but it still hadn't properly rained. It would likely stay like this all night, she considered, ignoring the dampness building on her sleeves.

When she reached her destination, a smile spread across her face.

"Wow," she said aloud, staring at the house in front of her.

It was the type of place that could appear in a country-living magazine or perhaps in a watercolour, the type they sold in touristy shops. Despite being later than intended, she couldn't help but take a minute to study the façade. Most of the house was painted a delicate baby blue with the front door a contrasting dark green. Hung on it was a handcrafted wreath, though rather than being made from dried flowers or pinecones, it was constructed of brightly coloured pompoms. Anyone who had something like that displayed on their door couldn't possibly take themselves too seriously, she hoped.

Fleur mounted the step, carefully balanced half the bags there and lifted her arm to clasp the door knocker. *Of course, a house like this would have a door knocker*, she thought. A common doorbell would have looked entirely out of place. The one she'd owned with Robert had a door knocker. A novelty one in the shape of a cat, which had been there when they bought the place. At the time, she'd told him it was a sign they should get a cat. Of course, they should, he'd said as he kissed her on the threshold of their new life. Not yet though. One day. One day … another promise he had broken.

With her fingers through the wrought-iron loop and her mind still floating around memories she wished she could forget; she was just about to knock when the door swung open. Given how she was already precariously balanced with shopping at her feet, the sudden movement caused her to topple forwards. All she could see was a pair of legs. Legs in neatly pressed trousers that she was about to tumble into until, by some miracle, a hand caught her by the shoulder and pushed her upwards. With her feet righted, she dropped back onto the pavement, resting her hands on her thighs as she recovered her breath from the shock of the near fall.

"Thank you; I'm so sorry," she said, her heart racing.

"I think it was simply a case of bad timing," the man said.

The voice was enough for Fleur's head to snap up. Deep and gravelly with perfect enunciation, it was one that could command the attention of a room full of people with very little effort. And she'd heard it before. Looming above her, a pair of icy, blue eyes stared down. Eyes that she recognised, although it took her a moment to realise why.

"You," she said, as the puzzle pieces fell into place. "You're the one from the chemist this morning."

There was no denying it. That peppered hair. The square jawline. Now she'd said it, she was a hundred percent certain that the man standing in front of her was the very same one she'd confronted less than twelve hours earlier, in the pharmacy. And now here she was, standing on his doorstep.

For a split second, he looked at her contemplatively, before his lips twisted slightly.

"I remember. Yes, this morning was rather stressful," he said.

Fleur baulked. If that was what he considered an apology, he was sorely mistaken. Not that she required an apology, of course. Unlike poor Grace, the pharmacist. She was about to say as much, when he spoke again.

"Are you delivering food?" he asked, with a nod to her bulging bags.

"No, I'm here for the Book Club."

"And you decided to do your weekly food shop beforehand?"

She gritted her teeth. It didn't matter how much she wanted to meet new people or had looked forward to joining a book club, there was no way she could stand to be near this arrogant man for a second longer. She opened her mouth to say she wouldn't be staying, when Gemma's voice called out from the hallway.

"Fleur! Come in! I was just telling everyone about you. Come in."

The weight of the bags pulled down on her hands as she hesitated. Her gaze momentarily flicked up to the man from the pharmacy. How the hell was she going to tell Gemma she couldn't stay without coming across as rude? She could hardly tell the truth. She was wracking her brain for a suitable excuse, when the man spoke again.

"As enjoyable as I'm sure your night will be, I have to leave," he said.

"You don't go to the Book Club?" she asked, hope lifting her voice.

"No, I do not," the man scoffed.

He was staring intently at her, as if he were waiting for a reply, though she couldn't imagine what he thought she might say. "Would you mind moving, please, so I can get by?"

"Oh, yes, sorry," she said, stepping aside while simultaneously cursing herself for apologising to him. What the hell did she have to do that for?

Without a word of thanks, he stepped down onto the pavement and made his way up the hill towards the town centre, leaving Fleur well and truly dumbstruck. The anger that he'd sparked in her at the pharmacy was well and truly reignited. For a second, she contemplated running after him and asking what exactly his problem was, when a voice spoke.

"Well, are you standing there all night, or are you going to come in?"

Her eyes moved back to the doorway. She had momentarily forgotten that Gemma was waiting.

"Oh yes. Of course," she said then, taking her heavy carrier bags, she stepped into the house.

CHAPTER 5

leur wasn't even close to getting over the shock of seeing Mr Pharmacy Man on the doorstep of the Book Club, let alone processing the rather rude manner in which he'd spoken to her and left, when she was faced with a new shock. If the front of the house belonged in a country-living magazine, the hallway should have been in some fantastical period drama. The mosaic tiles on the floor, which formed intricate flower patterns, were polished to a gleaming finish, and the walls were painted a deep peacock green that would have been dark had it not been for the variety of pale-pink paintings in gold frames that hung there. It was opulence without garishness, and Fleur was even more certain she would love whoever lived here.

She removed her flamboyant heels as Gemma waited at the end of the hallway.

"You're the last one to arrive" she said. "Why don't you sit down in the living room with the others, and I'll get you a drink. What do you fancy?"

"Actually, I brought a few things," Fleur gestured to the bags she was holding.

"I guess you should come and put those in the kitchen first, then."

As she had expected, the kitchen looked like it belonged on a Pinterest board. The walls were the same dark peacock, though here their colour was lifted by the white cupboards and marble surfaces. A large island unit stood in the middle of the floor and an Aga at the back, where a woman with long, grey hair in a plait was currently stirring a large pot.

"Dee, this is Fleur."

The lady turned from the stove. At a best guess, she was in her sixties, but she had an ageless quality about her. A makeup-free face with glowing skin and a smile that brought a mass of welcoming creases around her eyes.

"Fleur is the lady at the coffee shop I told you about," Gemma said before switching the introduction around. "Fleur, this lovely house belongs to Dee."

"It really is beautiful," Fleur said, crossing the room to greet her host. While she'd been going in for something between a handshake and a hug, Dee went straight for a kiss on both cheeks.

"Welcome. We are so glad to have new people join us."

"Thank you. It was kind of Gemma to invite me." As Fleur stepped back, she noted the aroma. "What are you cooking? It smells amazing."

Dee smiled broadly. "Oh, it's nothing special, but you know how these things work: the host always provides the food. Unfortunately, this soup needs at least another half an hour to thicken up and the bread maker hasn't pinged yet, so we'll go and chat about the books first. Still, you need a drink. Make yourself at home. Alcohol is in the drawing room, or I've got plenty of hot drinks if you'd prefer."

As Fleur took all this in, her offering of wheat-free donuts and salt-and-vinegar crisps suddenly felt rather studenty compared to homemade soup and rolls.

"I didn't know there would be food. I brought some nibbles," she said, lifting the bags up.

"It's my fault. I didn't tell her the host normally cooks," Gemma said, apologetically. "I should have mentioned that."

"It's hardly a problem." Dee said, bringing some plates and bowls out of a cupboard. "You can never have too many nibbles. I, for one, like a biscuit while we're chatting. Here, why don't we put some out?"

A feeling of warmth spread through Fleur at the sight of Dee sorting out her hodgepodge of food. This was what she'd missed since moving to Maldon. Since before that, even. People who you could be at ease around. People who wanted to make you feel good.

"I think we should leave this one here for now?" Dee indicated the bottle of wine Fleur had dropped into her basket at the last minute. "There are already two bottles open. Anymore and we'll forget what book we're supposed to be talking about. Now, I'll just give this soup one last stir. Gemma will show you the way. I'll just be a minute."

Fleur followed Gemma, although the need for a guide felt somewhat superfluous given the constant stream of chatter coming from behind one of the doors.

"After you," Gemma said, her hands full of Fleur's purchases.

With butterflies akin to a first day at a new school, she pushed open the door to the drawing room.

"Yay! Snacks!" someone said, jumping up and grabbing a plate out of Fleur's hand.

"Thank God. You know we're not going to eat for ages.

Food always takes at least an hour longer than Dee says it will."

"I think her bread maker is faulty, actually. I've been telling her that for months now. It sticks on ten minutes for at least half an hour."

"Are those chilli crackers? I love chilli crackers."

It was impossible to follow the thread of a conversation as chaos enveloped Fleur and the warmth she'd felt from Dee in the kitchen now multiplied tenfold.

"Guys, let Fleur get into the room." Gemma pushed herself in forcefully. "Fleur, grab one of the spare seats."

"But don't take the armchair," someone else said.

"No, the armchair is purely decorative at the moment. Why she hasn't got it fixed yet, we have no idea."

It would have been tough enough taking in what everyone was saying in any location, but the decor of the room had Fleur well and truly distracted. The peacock had been dropped here, in favour of a deep magenta, and a large, abstract oil painting with gold leaf filled the wall opposite the window. The remaining walls were chock full of books, and now that it had been mentioned, she could see how the armchair in question was propped against the wall.

Having been relieved of her bowls of nibbles, Fleur took a seat next to a young girl of around twenty, who she vaguely recognised.

"We should probably do introductions," the girl said, "although if you're anything like me, you won't remember. I'm terrible at names. I'm Sophie, by the way."

"Sophie works in the coffee shop with me," Gemma said.

"That's why you look familiar," Fleur replied.

"And I just drink lots of coffee there." The comment came from the only male in the group. He was sitting on the edge of a sofa and, along with Sophie, appeared to be one of the youngest members. His shoeless feet sported socks covered in miniature dinosaurs, while he wore a dark green V-neck top and thin-framed glasses at the end of his nose. "I'm Graham."

"Graham and Sophie," she said, trying to keep track of people as they were going.

"I'm Maria."

A lady, of similar age to Fleur, introduced herself next. From the volume at which she spoke, she got the impression Maria was someone who didn't like talking that much. Which could be, she considered, because of the way she looked. While it was a tough thing to judge, she was almost a hundred percent positive she had never seen someone so unassumingly beautiful in all her life. With jet black hair and bright blue eyes, Maria looked like she should spend her evenings in swanky roof-top bars with film producers or sitting on yachts having her Champagne flute refilled, rather than at a local book club. Not that there was any chance to ask what it was she did, for the introductions were still going.

"Jules." A woman on one end of a chaise long raised her hand.

"Nina," came from the other end.

"And I'm Eunice."

Sitting next to the beautiful Maria, Eunice was by far the most elderly of the group. Though her posture was quite good, a walking stick was propped up next to her on the arm of the sofa. Her white hair was complemented perfectly by bright-red earrings and a black dress which had oversized matching red buttons down the front. Fleur would never be so rude as to ask anyone's age, but a rough guess put her at eighty. She was about to ask the standard question of how long they had all been meeting there, when Dee walked in.

"So, are all the introductions done?" she said, before turning to Fleur, at which point her smile turned to deep horror. "Has no one poured you a drink yet? What can I get you? Wine? Red? White? Rosé? Bubbles? G and T?"

Fleur's mouth moved wordlessly for a moment.

"Oh, wine, please. Red wine. Thank you," she said. No sooner had she spoken than a glass was found and hastily filled.

"So, this is us," Gemma said, as Fleur took her first sip. "Welcome to the Lonely Hearts Book Club."

"Lonely hearts? As in romance?" It wasn't that she didn't read romances but given that the book she'd been reading when Gemma invited her was a thriller, it was a little confusing.

"As in we're all hopeless in love," Nina replied, only for her eyes to suddenly widen in fear. "You're not married, are you? Or in a committed relationship? You can stay, but we'd have to change the name of the club. Or you'll just have to pretend you're single."

"Umm, no." Fleur was slightly taken aback by the question. "I'm definitely hopeless in love too."

"Phew," Nina sighed with visible relief. "I feel much more comfortable being surrounded by romantic rejects. Other than Eunice, that is. She's a technical exception."

Fleur shifted her attention to the old lady, who was currently picking at the edge of one of the cakes she'd brought. When she saw that all eyes were trained on her, she popped the cake back on the plate.

"Married for thirty-six years but widowed for the last twenty-seven. So technically single. Just like everyone else here."

"Wow," Fleur replied, doing a quick mental maths sum. Sixty-three years since she'd been married. That meant the youngest she could possibly be was early eighties, and there she was, still enjoying cake and a glass of wine with friends.

"I have a boyfriend," Sophie piped up. Several pairs of eyes rolled, including Graham's.

"Who is nowhere near good enough for her. Believe me, as much as she likes to pretend otherwise, Sophie is as unlucky in love as the rest of us," Gemma said.

Fleur couldn't help but feel rather sorry for young Sophie who pouted, although she did nothing to defend her situation, and given how closely they worked together, she suspected Gemma had reason enough to make her claim.

"Right, that's enough nattering," Dee said and lifted the book she'd been holding at her side. "Are we all in agreement that chapter two was phenomenal?"

CHAPTER 6

*N*ormally, Fleur would find herself the one talking. Since her divorce, her old London friends had struggled to find things to chat to her about, and as much as she disliked being the centre of attention, she enjoyed awkward silences even less, so often filled in pauses in the conversation with anecdotes about her week or things she'd learned on a documentary channel. Not that she could remember the last time she'd gone out with them. The messages in the group had all but dried up. Maybe they'd set up a new one, without her.

That night, however, those old friends were a million miles from her thoughts as she sipped on her wine, content to watch and listen to the others. Breathing in their energy.

"You must be joking? You can't possibly think what she did was right with the way he treated her. She was crazy."

"She was trying to protect him, that was all."

"If she was trying to protect him, she would have told the police everything she knew in chapter four."

Emphatic gesticulations accompanied almost every statement, and more than once, Dee took to her feet to reinforce her point.

"If she'd told the police everything she knew in chapter four, the book would have ended there!" Nina said, slamming her fist down on the arm of her chair.

"Exactly, which is why I don't think the plot works."

"It's a brilliant plot."

"If you ignore what happened in chapter four, you mean."

Gemma leant in and whispered to Fleur. "Things can get a little heated."

"I can tell. I'm worried someone's going to get hurt."

"It's never got that far, although Eunice did have to take Nina outside for some fresh air once when we were discussing Louise Ross's latest."

Even when Dee announced that the soup was ready, the conversation didn't stop. From what Fleur could tell, it was Maria on one side of the argument, with Sophie and Graham on the other.

"Right, time to move this to the dining room," Jules called above the chaos. Finally, the volume dipped.

"Jules is a teacher, if you didn't work that out," Gemma said. "When she has to use her teacher voice, you know we're getting really loud."

"I'll remember that," Fleur laughed.

As people filtered out, she noticed Eunice and Maria still sitting on the sofa. Attempting to be helpful, she picked up Eunice's walking stick and handed it to her.

"Can I help you up?" she asked.

The old woman bit down on her lip before exchanging a sideways glance with Maria.

"Actually, it's not Eunice's walking stick; it's mine," Maria said.

A rush of heat flooded Fleur's cheeks. "Oh, I'm sorry. I didn't realise."

Maria smiled. "Why would you? But if I could accept that offer of helping me up, that would be great."

"Of course. Of course." She bent her knees and offered her arm. Up close, Maria was even more beautiful than she'd first thought, and Fleur couldn't help but wonder why she needed a stick to walk, but it hardly felt appropriate to ask.

"Thank you," Maria said, as she took the stick and balanced her weight with it. "A drunk driver struck me on a pavement while I was out walking."

"Oh." Fleur wasn't sure what else she could say.

"I find it easier to tell people straight away. It stops them wondering. It was a long time ago, and I was very lucky. Things could have gone a lot worse."

There was a sincerity in her tone. An ease that emanated from her. Just like with Gemma and Dee and every other person in the Book Club, Fleur got a great feeling about Maria. They could be friends, she thought. She would like them all to be friends.

Not wanting to leave the old woman alone, Fleur turned back to Eunice, who was currently holding her phone in her hand. The sparkling device was far newer than the one she possessed, though at that moment it was beeping angrily.

"Everything all right, Eunice?" she asked.

A second passed in which the beeping became even louder, and Fleur wondered if perhaps she'd unknowingly set off some alarm, but before she could ask, Eunice had shoved the phone deep into her bag, muffling the sound though not silencing it completely.

"That bloody thing. I think the battery's playing up. It keeps making that noise for no reason."

"You've been saying that about your phone for as long as

I've known you," Maria said. "Why doesn't Henry take you out and buy you another? Or get one online? I don't mind ordering you one, if that's easier?"

"I'll get it sorted at some point. But I've got better things to spend my money on than a new mobile. Like books. Now this soup better be good." Eunice rose to her feet. "She's kept us waiting long enough."

In the dining room, Fleur was too preoccupied with the ornate chandelier and various paintings to concentrate on the food.

"I think this might be the poshest book club I've ever known," she said to Nina as they sat at the extended oak table.

"It's only posh at Dee's house," Sophie said. "Gemma and I take our turns in the coffee shop, and Nina has it at the pub. Maria's is nice but not like this, though."

"And I get pizza in," Jules said from across the table. "Trust me. There's nothing posh about that."

Fleur imagined everyone crammed into her living room. The open-plan arrangement meant there would be enough space, but she'd need to move the sofa against the wall and half of them would have to sit on dining chairs or cushions. And there certainly wouldn't be room for them to all sit down like this to eat. Still, pizza would work if Jules hadn't called permanent dibs on it. Then again, perhaps she was getting ahead of herself. She hadn't even been invited back yet, let alone asked to host.

At some point, the chatter turned from the book they'd just read and onto what the next fortnight's pick was going to be.

"Can we have something light?" Sophie asked. "A romance. Or comedy. Or a romcom? Something where no one dies?"

"I thought we were picking from the spreadsheet," Nina said. Fleur had learned that she was a librarian, and she could hear it in her tone so clearly, she almost chuckled. "I made a spreadsheet with all the suggestions people sent me. Although as Eunice was the only one to send me any, it means it would be her pick."

"Eunice has only just had a pick," Dee said.

"Because she was the one who sent me her choices so they could go on the spreadsheet."

It reminded Fleur of break time at school, when everyone would debate who should go in goal at football. Not that she ever played.

"No one wants the responsibility of running the Club," Gemma explained, talking under her breath so that only Fleur could hear. "The problem is, it means no one is in charge of selecting books, so we have this discussion every fortnight. I'll be honest, I'll read anything, so it doesn't bother me. Normally it ends up going to a vote. Once people can decide which books we're voting on, that is."

Considering all the effort they went to with the food, this felt like an incredibly haphazard way of doing things.

"Why don't we all put the book we'd like on a piece of paper and pick one out of a hat?" Fleur said. "You have some paper, don't you, Dee?"

"Of course."

"But what if more than one person chooses the same book?" Sophie said. "Then it's got more chance of being chosen."

"That's fair enough if more people want it, isn't it?"

A murmur of agreement rolled around her.

"Great. Okay, let's get this done then."

Ten minutes later and much to Sophie's delight, a romcom had been picked. Less delightful, however, was the fact that the evening was drawing to a close.

"I better get off." Jules was the first to mention leaving.

"Austin is probably still awake. My lodger is babysitting him, and she lets him get away with murder."

"I should probably be going, too," said Nina.

And with that, everyone began to gather up their things.

"So the next meeting is going to be at mine, right?" Graham said, as he picked up his bag. "I'll make a risotto."

"Sounds good."

"Fabulous. You want a lift home, Soph?"

Fleur watched the friends chatting away and bidding each other goodnight, happy to let the moment wash around her. It may have taken a little while, but whether through fate or good luck, she had found herself a group of people she could really see herself being close to. When the first bunch had left, she turned to her host.

"Thank you, Dee. I really enjoyed myself and the soup was delicious."

"Are you off too? Thank you so much for all the snacks. That was very kind."

"I'll walk you out," Gemma said, "unless you'd like help tidying up, Dee?"

Dee brushed the comment away with a wave of her hand. "Don't be silly. It'll all go in the dishwasher. I'll show you out."

"No need. You stay here."

After exchanging hugs with her, Fleur and Gemma made their way to the front door.

"Thank you for inviting me," Fleur said, hugging her new friend.

"Don't be silly. Thank you for coming. You'll join us at Graham's next time, too?"

"Absolutely."

With her bag on her shoulder, Fleur opened the front door, only to be hit by a rush of cold air. She stepped back, the front of her cardigan covered in drops of rain.

"When did that start?" she asked, shocked by the storm that was blowing outside.

"No idea, but at least the plants will get a decent drink," Gemma replied.

Fleur nodded, though she was only half listening as she rifled through her bag for her umbrella. She tended to leave one in the bottom for days like this when rain came unexpectedly, but as she rummaged in the depths of the fabric, she began to worry she hadn't this time. Finally locating it, she looked up to find Eunice standing beside her.

"Where did you park, dear?"

"Oh, I don't have a car," she replied. "It's fine though. It's not far."

"Don't be silly," Eunice said, waving her hand in the air. "You don't want to be walking anywhere in this. My Henry will give you a lift."

"Henry?"

"He's my nephew. Great-nephew, actually."

"I really don't want to be any trouble."

"What nonsense," Eunice said, looping her arm through Fleur's. "It's no bother whatsoever. And I'm not taking no for an answer. He's got plenty of room in that flashy car of his. He might as well make use of it."

"Only if you're sure he won't mind," Fleur protested, although as she spoke, the more a lift felt like a lovely idea. The rain was pelting down so hard, she could see it springing up from the puddles on the pavement.

"Really, it's not a problem. You can ask him yourself now."

Fleur followed Eunice's line of sight through the door to where a man was stepping out of an oversized vehicle, with a large golf umbrella over his head which obscured his face, but she didn't need to look for long to know exactly who he was.

When he reached the doorway, he lifted the umbrella up and met her eye.

"Fleur, this is Henry Pierce. Henry, this is Fleur Fisher. We're going to give her a lift home."

"You're Eunice's nephew?" she said.

CHAPTER 7

$\mathscr{F}$leur felt like the strangest third wheel in history. Eunice had insisted that she take the front seat right next to Henry. It was — as she had said — a truly massive car, some kind of four-by-four and probably a very expensive one, judging by all the dials and buttons and the touchscreen sat-nav that spoke to them the moment they got inside.

"How was Book Club?" he asked, throwing his aunt a quick glance as he started the engine and making it perfectly clear exactly who the question was aimed at.

Eunice leaned back in her seat.

"It was lots of fun, as always. Dee made her soup, and Fleur here brought a delicious selection of nibbles."

"Well, I hope you didn't eat too many of them."

Fleur's jaw dropped. Hearing a man say what a woman should eat in any circumstances was absolutely disgusting, but the way he'd spoken to his aunt made every muscle in her body tighten. She was ready to say as much, when he spoke again. "Where is it you need dropping?" he asked, offering her the most cursory of glances.

"Me? Oh, North Street. It's at the bottom of the—"

"I know where North Street is," he cut over her.

She forced herself to take a deep breath. The rain was hammering down on the windscreen so hard that the street-lights were blurred. But if he said one more word, she was going to get out and walk. Judging a person on first impressions may not always yield an accurate picture, but three meetings in and she was certain of one thing: Eunice's great-nephew, Henry, was an arse.

She forced herself to smile and turned back to Eunice. "Are you from Maldon?" she asked. "Did you grow up here?"

"Oh, no. I moved here after I got married. Henry was born here though, and he recently moved back. Which reminds me, I haven't actually introduced you two properly. You've got a lot in common. Fleur's just moved here recently, too, Henry."

"I don't think both of us moving to the same place counts as having anything in common, Auntie Eunice," he said, his eyes still fixed on the road. "Besides, I'd hardly call two years recent."

Everything about this man made Fleur want to slap him, but Eunice was trying her best to make small talk, and she felt so sorry for her. After all, it wasn't her fault she had an arrogant arse as a nephew. And she could still hear the muffled tone of the old woman's phone beeping away. Forcing herself to be the better woman, she gritted her teeth and tried again.

"What is it you do, Henry?" she asked, already picturing him in some soulless, money-grabbing line of work. A property developer, perhaps.

"I'm a lawyer."

She suppressed a smirk. Of course, he was.

"What type of lawyer?"

It felt important to check. After all, if he was a human-rights lawyer working for impoverished families in desperate situations, then she might have to reconsider her opinion, only slightly, of course. As it was, she could have laughed aloud at his answer.

"I'm a divorce lawyer."

"Wow." She wasn't sure what else she could say to this. She couldn't imagine that it would ever be at the top of any child's dream-jobs list, but then perhaps his ambition had been to drive around in a car the size of a small plane, and if that was the case, he'd succeeded.

Silence descended. The drive from Dee's house on Market Hill to North Street should have taken no more than three minutes. But the downpour meant that they were crawling along with the wipers going at double speed, and traffic at the mini roundabout at the top of the hill was at a complete standstill. It was possible the lack of conversation would have felt even worse if the rain wasn't so loud and there weren't so many cars beeping their horns. But it felt almost stifling, and clearly Fleur wasn't the only one who sensed it.

"I've asked Henry to join the Book Club," Eunice said, her voice unnaturally jovial. "Several times, in fact. He's refused so far, but I'm determined I'll get him to a meeting soon."

"Are you a fan of reading?" Fleur asked, not because she was interested in any way what he might enjoy, but because she was still thinking of how awful this was for poor Eunice. "What kind of books do you like?"

"Not the type that your club reads."

"Wow, that was judgemental." The words came out before she could stop herself, but once said, she realised she had no intention of apologising. After all, it wasn't just her he was insulting. It was every person in the Book Club, his great-aunt included. With the car still stationary, she doubled down. "So,

Henry, what exactly are these book types we read that you're so disparaging of? Because from the one meeting I've been to, the group seems to have an exceptionally varied taste from all sorts of genres and time periods, not to mention fiction and non-fiction. And given that you haven't actually attended a meeting, it seems to me that you're just being rude for the sake of it."

In the back of the car, Eunice choked back a laugh. "I knew I liked you," she said. "Henry is what we at the Club call a *book snob.*"

"I am not a book snob," he said, with notable petulance.

That one sentence and Fleur could see it all. The young boy, living with his middle-class parents in their large, detached house, throwing tantrums whenever things didn't go his way.

"I simply refuse to waste time on predictable plots and badly written prose. And whilst, no, I have not technically attended the Book Club, I have seen examples of the romantic nonsense Auntie Eunice has brought home with her, and to be honest, I'm amazed it hasn't already melted her brain."

Never had a man rendered her mute so frequently. Once again, Fleur found herself lost for words. How anybody could be so openly narrow minded and derogatory was beyond her. Thankfully, the car was moving again now. It would only take a couple of minutes until she was home. But she wasn't letting this go. Not a chance.

"Just taking a step back and ignoring the fact that some of the greatest literature published has *predictable plots*, even if we were reading nothing but *romantic nonsense*, as you so like to call it, what is the problem with that? There's nothing wrong with people wanting something to pick them up a little, to lose themselves in and make it feel like they're the ones finding true love."

"Apart from the fact that it utterly skews real-life perception. Books like the romantic trash you're talking about are the reason I have a job, because people believe these ludicrous notions of love and soul mates and other such juvenile constructs they watch in films and read about."

"You're saying love is a juvenile construct?"

"No, I am saying love doesn't exist."

Fleur sat back in her seat, truly stunned. Surely, he had to be winding her up. Maybe he just had an incredibly dry sense of humour. Though he didn't look like he was joking.

"You can't be serious?" she said, needing to confirm what she had just heard. "You don't believe in love at all?"

"I don't see why you're behaving so indignantly about this. It's no different to not believing in Father Christmas or the Tooth Fairy. They're all equally fictitious figments of the imagination. Now, which number house are you?"

She had been so full of outrage that she hadn't even realised they'd turned onto her street.

"Just up the end," she said, although her mind was still locked onto what she'd just heard. "Surely you've been in love at some point in your life?"

Henry scoffed. A sound she now assumed was his most frequent form of communication. "Love, or what you think is love, is just a surge of chemicals. Dopamine and adrenaline, flooding the system for the sole purpose of procreation."

Fleur could feel her jaw hanging open, but she couldn't bring herself to close it. In the back of the car, Eunice let out a deep sigh.

"This is what I have to work with, Fleur. Honestly, he drives me to distraction, but once you get past this vexatious exterior, I can promise he's got a good heart underneath it all.

Vexatious. That was the perfect word to describe the man, Fleur thought as she alternated her gaze between Eunice and

Henry. How this woman who had been happily married for thirty-six years could be related to this egotistical git who didn't believe in love was beyond her. It was the most bizarre thing she could have imagined.

"Is this the right place?" he asked, his voice pulling her out of her thoughts. He'd parked up just a short way from her house, so close there wasn't any point getting her umbrella out.

"Yes, this is great, thank you," Fleur said, before turning back to Eunice. "And thank you for such a lovely evening."

"I'll see you again at the next get-together?"

"I'm looking forward to it."

Then, with one final glance at the divorce lawyer who didn't believe in love, she climbed out of the car and made a mad dash for her front door.

CHAPTER 8

*T*he wipers were working at full speed again, battling the rain as Henry U-turned in the road. Fleur's reflection had already disappeared from his rear-view mirror.

"So?" his aunt said, as they turned back onto the High Street.

"So what?" he replied, trying to act ignorant. He'd known her plan from the minute she'd suggested giving that awful woman a lift home, despite the fact her house was in the opposite direction to theirs.

"She's a lovely girl. Really sweet."

"She's opinionated and utterly obstinate," he countered before he could stop himself.

When he glanced in the mirror, his great-aunt's lips were pressed tightly together in a smile.

"You know, that reminds me of someone," she said.

He didn't try to suppress his disdain. "Honestly, we're not going down this route again, are we?"

"What route?" she replied, with feigned sincerity. "All I was saying was that she was lovely. She's obviously got her own mind, which is a good thing, but she was nothing but absolutely charming all evening. And she's single."

"You do surprise me."

If Henry had been a better person, he would probably be more patient with his elderly aunt. After all, she meant well even if she did always stick her nose into his relationships. But since he'd moved back to Maldon, it had become ridiculous. Every week, she was trying to set him up with someone.

"You said the woman at your hairdresser's was charming, remember? And the one who worked at the bank. And Maria."

"Maria is a sweetheart. Far too good for you."

"Undoubtedly. But according to you, every other woman in Maldon could be my perfect match."

Eunice let out a loud grunt, which seemed less than fitting for a lady of her maturity.

"If you actually went out with one of them, you might find I'm right. I mean, is there really anything that terrible about going for a drink with someone? You might even enjoy it."

Henry held back the deep sigh that was about to leave his lungs. To be fair, it had been at least three weeks without them having this conversation, and he should have known his aunt could never go long without trying to play matchmaker. But Fleur? If the romance book thing wasn't bad enough, the way she'd taken it upon herself to address him in the chemist, when he was clearly under a lot of stress, showed just how unsuited they were.

Deciding it was better not to reply, he turned into Eunice's driveway, cut the engine, stepped out and opened her door. He'd hoped the fact they'd arrived back without him offering any reply would be enough for her to understand he didn't want to get into this again. Apparently, that wasn't the case. The second they stepped through the front door, she started at it once more.

"I just don't understand why you're so against having a woman in your life. Or a man. You know I wouldn't mind at all if you wanted to bring a nice gentleman home to meet me? I'm not one of those homophobe type old people you get."

"I know you're not," he said, wondering how long his aunt had been thinking about his sexuality. "I'm just not at the right place in life to meet anyone."

"Because of me?"

This was not a great question to have to answer. Eunice was part of the reason he couldn't have anyone in his life, but she wasn't the only one. With work the way it was, he just didn't see how he could ever give over the time required to make a new relationship work.

"Yes, because of you, Auntie Eunice," he said, taking her coat and hanging it up for her. "You have ruined me for all other women. How could anyone possibly hope to compete? You know you'll always be the number one in my life."

He suspected that there was a good number of women, her age and younger, who would be flattered by such a comment, but Eunice was not one of those. She turned around to face him, scowling.

"Yes, well, I shouldn't be. You know, *I* might be happy on my own, but that's only because I've already had my life. What little free time you have shouldn't be spent with an eighty-year-old woman. You should be out there, having fun."

"Auntie Eunice?"

"Don't you Auntie me. If I'd have known that you'd lock yourself away and ruin any chance of meeting someone, when you moved here, then I would never have let you."

"Let me? I think you'll find that, as a forty-two-year-old man, I'm perfectly capable of making my own decisions."

"Bad decisions, yes," she agreed, as they went into the

kitchen. "Not all marriages end like your parents' did. You must realise that."

"Actually, no I don't," he said, checking his phone and noting the beeping had stopped, before flicking on the kettle. "Forty percent end in divorce. And that doesn't mean the ones which don't are happy. Yours was a rarity."

"I don't care about the statistics; I care about you." Grabbing the stick she refused to use outside of the house, she walked over to him.

"Henry, as much as neither of us wants to admit it, I won't be here forever. I need to know that someone's going to be around to take care of you when I'm gone."

"I don't need to be taken care of. Unlike you," he said, turning the tables and matching her scowl. "I know you heard your phone beeping. You're lucky I didn't come down there."

She waved away his comment, like she always did. "I had it under control, didn't I? And I'm sorry, I don't believe this nonsense about not needing someone. We all need a little taking care of now and then. Please, just think about it. Think about putting yourself out there. For me?"

She had him backed into a corner, the way she always did with this conversation. And he hated lying to her, when he had absolutely no intention of doing anything about it. But this was Auntie Eunice, and the last thing he wanted was to be stuck at loggerheads with her all night. He needed to get home and look over the case notes for the morning's meetings.

"I will think about *putting myself out there*," he said, with a resigned sigh.

"And going for a drink with Fleur?"

At that, he put his foot down. "Trust me, Fleur and I are not a good match."

"I think you're wrong."

"Eunice—" Henry said, warningly.

"Fine." She waved her hands again. "But you better not be saying this just to get me off your back. I want you to go on a date by next Book Club. Otherwise, I'm taking matters into my own hands."

The woman was insufferable. If it was anyone else, he would stop speaking to her until she agreed not to badger him anymore. But this was his Aunt Eunice, who had taken him in every time home had become unbearable. Who had offered him stability when life with his parents had been anything but stable. At the end of the day, if pretending he had gone out with someone in the next fortnight was what it took to make her happy, he could do that.

"Fine," he said. "I'll go on a date before the next meeting. Now, can we finally drop the subject?"

CHAPTER 9

*a*s was always the case, the weekend flew by for Fleur, her time filled with exciting tasks like cleaning the bathroom and emptying the washing basket. Though, strangely, she enjoyed these jobs now or, at least, far more than she had done when she and Robert were married. Back then, housework had felt like a chore. Things she had to get done on top of her actual job.

She could never pinpoint exactly how it had happened, but by the time she and Robert had been living together a month, their roles in the household had somehow been assigned. Robert put out the bins, ironed his work clothes and did the drying up — before they moved house and got a dishwasher. Fleur did the cooking, the washing up — which then turned into the loading and emptying of the dishwasher — the clothes washing, the vacuuming and mopping of floors, cleaning the bathroom, doing all the ironing except Robert's work clothes and any other miscellaneous jobs that would crop up during the week.

Given that his hobbies included long-distance, off-road running which would result in a sodden sports kit twice a week, and the fact that he was prone to a late-night fry-up, Fleur wasn't oblivious to the uneven division of labour, but it was only when they separated that she realised just how much she had done for him.

Now, it was her choice which part of the house she cleaned each day and whether she was going to iron at all. Now, she listened to music or podcasts as she waltzed around with a vacuum, singing along or laughing. As such, she didn't mind two hours spent rearranging the kitchen cupboards or wiping down the skirting boards, particularly on rainy, grey days, when being outside just wasn't something she fancied. That weekend, it had hammered down with rain day and night, so it was unsurprising that by the time Monday rolled around, her tiny flat was utterly pristine.

But as much as she wished otherwise, she couldn't shake Henry from her mind. Every time she thought she was clear of him, a love song would pop up on the radio and he would spring back into her head with his pompous attitude and condescending manner. How could he not believe in love? People risked their lives in the name of love. They died for love. Plays and poems and thousands of films and television shows had all been written about it. Even reality TV had homed in on it now, drawing in thousands of viewers watching complete strangers in their quest for true love. It was real. It existed, and to think otherwise was just downright stupid.

As grey as the weekend had been, Monday was stunning. Clear blue skies had gleamed through her windows all day, and she was desperate to get outside and go for a run. As it was, all she could do was open them as far as possible and let the sounds from the waterfront drift in. It was a day of back-to-back online meetings, hanging up one call to get straight on to the next. This was one aspect of working remotely she wasn't a fan of. It was great when you got to set your own schedule and sit filling in spreadsheets from a table in a little coffee shop; it was less fun when you had to spend your entire day glued to your desk. Thankfully, the meeting with her line manager, Paul, was her last of the day. After that, she'd be free to get out of the house.

"Congratulations on your numbers last month," Paul said. "You know, I didn't think you'd top the previous one. I should have known you'd prove me wrong."

"Thank you," she replied, already knowing where the conversation was going.

"You know, there is definitely a position available for you higher up, and we'd all love it if you'd consider it. You'd have to interview, of course, but honestly, I think you'd be an obvious candidate for any promotion going. Have you looked at the email I sent out on Friday?"

"Thank you." Fleur fixed her smile. "But honestly, I'm not in the right place for a promotion just now. It's not what I'm after. I'm happy where I am at the minute."

"You'd be a real asset to the team."

"I'll think about it," she lied.

"Good, I'm glad. We'll chat later in the week. Have a good evening." And with that, he hung up the call.

Letting out a long sigh of relief, she pushed down the lid of her laptop. The truth was, she had no intention of applying for any other position at all higher up in the company. Not now, possibly not ever. It wasn't that she didn't enjoy working for them and it was no secret that those above her thought she was grossly over-skilled for the role she was currently in, but that had been her choice, and the idea of being a manager again made her skin crawl. She had been there before. Suffered the weight of responsibility on her shoulders and the constant anxiety of whether she was making the right decision, along with the added stress that the divorce had piled on top of her—she shuddered at the thought. It was a mystery to her how some people thrived in high-powered jobs and kept their sanity intact.

And just like that, Henry was back in her thoughts again. Of course, he would manage the pressures of being a lawyer. He was likely gunning to be made a partner too, assuming he wasn't one already. The kind of ruthlessness his job required probably went hand in hand with not believing in love, and from what she had seen of him, he gave little weight to good manners or compassion, either. Yup, she could see exactly what type of lawyer he would be.

Frustrated that she was once again thinking about him, she clicked her neck from side to side while stretching her arms above her head. She was done thinking of him for the day, just like she was done thinking of work. What she wanted to do now was unwind in her favourite way possible. With a run.

Running wasn't something that had come naturally to Fleur. As a child, she'd hated P.E. She was the kid who'd forget her kit so that she could miss the lesson or ask her mother to send in a note saying she'd twisted her ankle and couldn't play netball. But as she'd got older, something had changed. Living in London, running had been a way to see more of the city she loved. She could easily lose a whole hour jogging around the parks and along the banks of the Thames, slowing her pace as she weaved between tourists or crossed one of the multitude of bridges. Just one thing had dampened the pleasure slightly. Robert.

Unlike Fleur, he took his running incredibly seriously,

always training for marathons or ultra-marathons or extreme, super-sporty, ironman-type things. He found his pleasure competing in the sort of event where he would exhaust his body to such a point that he'd need to buy little glucose sachets from the pharmacy to take with him, just to keep his sugar levels up long enough to complete the race. Bizarrely, he could never understand why she wouldn't join him. But now that pressure was gone, and by running in Maldon, she'd found an even greater love of the sport.

The waterfront was her favourite place to jog. It didn't matter where she went or what the weather was like, there was always something to see amongst the collection of boats docked there, and the breeze that whipped through her hair was always so fresh and clean, it was like pure energy for her muscles.

Dressed and ready to go, she was just about to pick up her keys when, at that exact same moment, her telephone rang. She stared at the name. Annelise. Of course, it was Annelise. No doubt ringing to ask whether she'd put together a guest list for the birthday party she so desperately didn't want. For a moment, she continued to stare at the phone buzzing around on the sideboard, before taking a deep breath and turning around. She would speak to her sister later and without giving it a second glance, she headed out of the flat, slamming the door behind her.

Her side street quickly joined the High Street, where she turned uphill. It was a steep warm-up, past the pink walls of Mrs Salisbury's Tearooms and the Moot Hall with its pillared entrance. When she reached the mini roundabout at the top of town, she headed left, past the secondary school. This long downhill stretch was a great place to pick up some pace before she began to weave her way through the housing estate towards the promenade park. This large area stretched along the riverfront and offered everything a family could possibly want. There was a magnificent park, with a climbing frame in the shape of a pirate ship, and water play where children could run around between the constantly changing fountains. There was even a skate park. For the adults, there were plenty of places to grab some food, and occasionally, a mobile bookshop would be set up on a cute little trailer, though she had not yet worked out exactly what the opening hours were. If she were to have a family, this would be the type of place she wanted to do it. Although time was not on her side when it came to that, which was why she had given Robert the ultimatum in the first place: start trying now, or it was over. That hadn't gone the way she'd expected.

With a shake of her head and an increase in speed, she pushed her ex from her mind. He didn't belong here in Maldon and certainly not on a run with her. This was her time.

When she reached the duck pond, she was suitably out of breath. Here was a great place to stop. Quite often, she would have put a five-pound note in her pocket to grab a drink at one of the cafés, but she'd been in too much of a rush to think about that today. So, forcing herself to keep going, she continued up the slope and finished the loop home.

For a minute, she stood there with her hands on her knees, waiting for her pulse to slow, before reaching into her pocket for her keys. With her hand lost in the depth of the fabric, she paused. They weren't there. She checked again and then pulled the pocket inside out. There were some remnants of tissue, where one had obviously gone through the wash, a fifty-pence coin and two bobby pins, which was remarkable considering she couldn't remember the last time she'd used them in her hair. But definitely no keys. Tracing her mind back, she tried to work out where she could have dropped them, only to recall how Annelise had rung at the very moment she'd gone to pick them up. She'd left the flat without evening thinking about them again.

"Crap," she said, as the realisation struck her. She was locked out.

CHAPTER 10

The good thing about living in the upper flat of the house was that it offered Fleur a lovely view out over the estuary without the nuisance of noises above her head. There were no issues with rising damp, either. The less positive side of it was getting yourself in when you were locked out.

First, she tried her downstairs neighbours. She knew from passing comments that they were friends with the landlord, and the overly optimistic part of her hoped they might have a spare key. Worst-case scenario, they'd have the landlord's number so she could ring and ask him to let her in. But after several rings on the doorbell, followed by a couple of loud knocks, she ascertained no one was at home.

Standing on the pavement, she pondered the situation. A good deal of cloud coverage was now masking the sun which, combined with rapidly cooling sweat from her run, caused her to shiver. It was a far cry from the heat she'd faced in the flat earlier that day.

"Of course!" she shouted.

She'd had her living room window open all day because of how warm it was. Without pausing for breath, she raced around the house. Reaching the back garden, she was confronted by both good news and bad. The good news was that her living room window was wide open, and being the most sizeable one in the flat, she knew she'd have no problem getting in through it. The bad news was that she had to reach it.

While the front offered a bay window that would have been relatively easy— if a little disconcerting — to climb up on, the back offered no such convenience. Even if she'd possessed the upper body strength to climb up it, one quick tug on the plastic drainpipe told her that was a no-go. Determined not to be beaten, she looked around for other options.

As the tenant of the upstairs flat, she had no claim on the garden, though she looked out on it from half her rooms and already knew that it was separated into three sections. At the far end was a worn and crumbling shed, which sat behind an area that had probably once been the lawn but was now a mixture of overgrown bushes and mud. Then, nearest the house, was a small patio with a cast-iron table and set of matching chairs.

"Okay, let's see if this'll work," she said, looking at the outdoor furniture. Galvanised by the dropping temperature, she gripped the edge of the table to drag it toward her. "Crap!" One small tug had caused it to start toppling to the side. She somehow kept hold of the metal as she ducked down, grabbing the rest of its weight before it could fall over entirely. Only then did she notice the pile of bricks that had been used in place of a broken leg. "Okay, time to rethink."

It took far longer to move the table back onto the bricks than it had to topple it off them, and afterwards she was still no closer to getting into her home. As she cast a gaze around, in search of any other options, her eyes landed on the shed.

I'd let someone look in my shed if they were locked out and needed a ladder, she justified to herself as she picked her way through the overgrown weeds and grass. It was fair to assume her downstairs neighbours were no gardeners, and the state of the shed further confirmed this. The once-green paint had peeled off in flakes, and the door was holding on by just one hinge, although despite that, there was still an open, rusted padlock still in place.

"I'll get you some chocolates, if you have one," she said, as she opened the door.

Stepping inside felt like walking onto the set of a horror movie. A smell of damp and varnish filled the air while cobwebs clung to every corner and crevice, so thick they were near opaque. Rusted paint tins were stacked haphazardly upon each other, and several of them had leaked so that the various nuts and bolts that had spilled from upended tool-boxes were covered in puddles of dried paint. Amongst the array of tools, of which there were plenty, were saws, hammers and wrenches, all in varying states of disrepair. And there, propped against the back wall, stood a ladder.

"Please don't let there be rats. Please don't let there be rats," she muttered, as she picked her way through the debris.

Generally speaking, Fleur didn't have a problem with animals. Not in the slightest. For a short while, she had owned a dog, and the chickens at her allotment had brought her so much joy, it had near broken her heart to leave them. But there was something about rats she just didn't like. Whether it was their eyes or their tails or their twitchy little noses, she couldn't say, she just knew that being in close confines with one was not on her to-do list.

Wishing she could squeeze her eyes shut but knowing that

would likely end in disaster, she reached in, grabbed hold of the ladder and yanked at it. While it didn't budge immediately, a small amount of jiggling was all it took to dislodge it from its holdings, before she pulled upwards, and — taking numerous cobwebs with her — heaved it out into the garden.

Considering the state of everything else in the shed, it was in surprisingly good nick, and after a strong tug on each rung, she was confident it would hold her weight. Feeling far more optimistic about this option than she had about the wobbly garden table, she carried it over to the patio and propped it against the wall. It was the type of ladder which had two sections and was currently at its shortest. Despite having never used one like it before, it took less than a minute to find the catches and figure out what to do. A few moments later, Fleur was standing at the bottom of a fully extended ladder which finished less than a foot below her open window.

"Perfect," she said. "I can do this."

Despite her initial confidence, she was far more nervous than she'd expected. She checked the bottom of the ladder was secure several times, before finally deciding to place one of the patio chairs against it, just as a precaution. Though this didn't eradicate all the nerves, the first few steps were fine, but once she reached the top of the ground floor, a feeling of vertigo that she'd never suffered from before kicked in.

"You can do this," she said, as she forced herself up the next two rungs. It didn't take long until she could get her hands into the open window, and then she was standing almost level with it, ruminating on the best way to get off the ladder and into the room.

Her biggest fear was that the ladder would topple backwards, and so after only a minor deliberation, she heaved herself up and flopped onto the window ledge. From this horizontal position, she wriggled forwards, feeling like the front part in the world's weirdest wheelbarrow race. There were undoubtedly more elegant ways of getting in, but she wasn't worried about that. She was only concerned about not falling back out of the window. She inched further in, until finally tumbling forwards, landing with a thump on her carpet.

"That could've been a lot worse," she said, as she brushed down her running trousers and stood up. Noting the smears of mud now on the carpet, she kicked off her shoes to ensure she didn't trample any more into the flat.

She was in the hallway, about to put the shoes back on so she could go down and replace the ladder, when the door buzzed. One thing she'd really liked about this flat was the buzzer system. A small screen was next to her front door so that she could see who was waiting for her downstairs. Then she could either open the front door from where she was, simply tell the postman to leave the package outside or not answer at all.

It was a reasonable assumption for her to assume that it was a delivery driver calling up, given that they were the only people who ever did. However, when she looked at the little screen, her eyes widened in surprise. She blinked a couple of times, as if the image might be distorted, because while the people standing outside were in uniform, it was not that of a delivery company.

"Hello," she said, pushing her finger onto the button so she could communicate with them.

"Hello ma'am. We've been informed about a break-in. Can we come up, please?"

CHAPTER 11

Fleur stood at the entrance to her flat as the police officers climbed the stairs. She had considered going down to let them in, but then worried that it might look like she was trying to escape or that she was somehow being confrontational. So now she was just standing and waiting, and somehow that felt even worse.

"Good afternoon, madam." The police officer at the front was the first to speak. With a closely shaved head and a light-gingery beard, he looked only slightly younger than her, while behind him, a female officer was turning in a circle, as if she was worried someone was about to jump out on her. "As I said, we had a call about a possible break in at this address."

"Here?" she said, only for a sinking feeling to settle in her stomach. "I think that was me."

"That was you?"

She could feel the heat colouring her cheeks.

"Yes. Sort of. I broke in. Well, the window was open."

"You broke into this flat?"

"Can you break into your own home? I didn't technically

break anything other than my downstairs neighbours' table, and in my defence, I think that was broken beforehand."

"Sorry." The police officer lifted his hands in the air, to stop her. "I just need to clarify. Are you saying there was a break in or there wasn't?"

"There was, but it wasn't a real one. I locked myself out."

"You locked yourself out?"

"Yes. But I'd left the living room window open. So, I climbed inside that way."

He stared at her for a minute, and his lips twisted. Generally, she considered herself fairly adept at reading people's expressions, and had she been forced to guess, she would have said that the officer looked somewhat amused. Unlike the one behind him.

"Have you heard of locksmiths?" she said, pointedly, her eyes still scanning the place suspiciously.

"Yes, of course. But to call a locksmith, I would have needed my phone. And my phone was next to my keys."

"Fair point." The male officer glanced at his partner with a slight smirk. "And so, you just climbed onto your neighbour's table?"

"No, well, I tried, but it was broken. Then I looked in their shed and found a ladder. I guess you could call that the breaking and entering part, but it was already unlocked. In fact, I was just about to go downstairs and put it back in the shed and then go and grab them a box of chocolates to say thank you for letting me borrow it."

"Not that you gave them much choice," the female officer remarked.

Fleur didn't reply. Despite the coolness of his partner, the policeman was no longer attempting to hide his amusement.

"If you're going to give them chocolates, how could they complain?" he said, as his lips twitched and eyes glinted.

"Do you need anything from me?" Fleur asked, suddenly feeling very aware of the seriousness of a police presence in her home. "Do you need me to prove I live here? I have a bill I can fetch with my name and address on it. And the ladder is still up against the wall, if you want to corroborate that part of my story."

"No, it's fine, thank you," the female officer said. "We just needed to follow up on the report. It's all good. I can see everything is in place here."

"Oh, I don't know. I think I might need to see this ladder," said the male officer. "You came in through the living room window did you say? Is it through there?"

Fleur nodded, stepping back to make room for him to pass.

"Jack, we don't have time for this."

Ignoring his partner, Jack continued down the hall.

For a second, she wished she'd tidied up before going for her run. Her jumper was strewn over the back of the sofa, and she'd left the flat in such a rush she hadn't even tidied away the plate she'd used for lunch. But then, why would she have? It wasn't like she was expecting the local constabulary to come knocking on her door.

"Is this the window you climbed up to?" Jack asked, leaning out. "That's a pretty good height."

"I made sure the ladder was secure."

"I can see you did that with the chair." He was mocking her again. That much was obvious. But it was playful and the way he was smiling at her was almost as if they were friends. "To be honest, I'm impressed."

"At least that's something," she replied.

Fleur nearly gasped at the sound of her own voice. Was she flirting? With a police officer? The thought horrified her. She was pretty sure that people got into serious trouble for behaviour like that, although Jack didn't look like he was about to give her any form of reprimand. She wondered what he might say next, when he called to the officer who was still standing in the doorway.

"Officer Stanton, I think we're done here. We should head downstairs."

Officer Stanton nodded and turned towards the staircase, although rather than following her, as Fleur expected him to, Jack stopped and looked straight at her, before pulling out a notepad from the top pocket of his jacket.

"I could write my number down for you, you know, in case you get locked out of your flat again?"

Fleur considered the offer.

"To be fair, if I'd had my phone on me, I would have called my landlord, so I'm not sure your number would be of that much help."

Jack's lips pursed as he suppressed another smile.

"Perhaps you could use it for something else then, like, I don't know, if you'd like to go for a drink."

"A drink?"

It was then that it hit her: Jack was flirting with her, too. And not in an accidental manner but full-on. A hot flush flooded her face as she attempted to clear her throat. It took several sharp coughs to manage it properly.

"A drink might be nice," she said.

"Good, well, I look forward to hearing from you. And maybe I should take your number, too? Just in case?"

CHAPTER 12

*F*leur was lying on her sofa, the Book Club's pick of the fortnight open beside her as she held the phone to her ear.

"Should he do that?" Annelise said, on the other end of the line. "I mean, surely there's some sort of protocol for flirting with people on the job. You could probably get him sacked if you wanted to."

"Why would I want to do that? He was nice. He is nice. We get on really well."

Fleur was starting to regret mentioning Jack to Annelise, but she'd wanted to tell someone. For the last five days, she'd been texting him more regularly than any man since Robert, and it was fun. Their messages had been light and easy, just short texts, like him telling her to take her keys with her when she went for a run or wishing her a good day in the morning. And she'd replied with similar things. They chatted about the television shows they enjoyed and what music they listened to, but so far, no one had again brought up the topic of going for a drink.

"I think he could be waiting for me to make the first move," she suggested.

"Well, I don't think I like the guy. I think it's creepy that he'd give you his number while he was at work. But it's up to you. Which reminds me, you still haven't confirmed the date for your party yet."

In all fairness, they had been talking for a full five minutes, which was possibly the longest Annelise had gone without bringing up her birthday. All the same, Fleur's jaw locked.

"You don't want to have to deal with a party. You keep saying you're too busy with the children to have any time for yourself. The last thing you need is to use your time planning an event that I don't want."

"That you're pretending you don't want."

"I really don't want it!"

Pulling the phone away from her mouth, Fleur emitted a silent scream while casting a glance at the clock on the wall. In less than an hour, she was meeting the girls for a drink, and she really wanted to finish the book before then. It was almost a full week until their next meeting, but she'd been hooked from the first chapter. It was just the relaxing tonic she'd needed after all the tension of the thriller from the previous week. And she was so close to the end. The happy ever after was just within her reach, assuming it didn't take some horrendously unexpected turn.

"I need to get going," she said, cutting in before her sister could start telling her about one of the amazing parties she had been to that week or a guy at her tennis club who was recently divorced and would be just Fleur's type. Whatever that meant. "I'm meeting up with some of the girls for drinks. I'll ring you over the weekend?"

"Drinks? Girls? That sounds sociable. You know you could invite your new book-club buddies to your party?"

"Goodbye, Annelise."

With the phone hung up, Fleur let out a long groan. As much as she loved their chats, every conversation left her frustrated. If it wasn't a party, it was dating or freezing her eggs. At no point had Annelise thought Fleur might just be happy as she was.

Trying to view her sister's interfering as a sign of love, she put down the phone and picked up the book. The last chapter turned out everything that she'd hoped it would be. A full happy ever after that even brought a slight tear to her eye. As she closed the cover, she sat back in her seat and held it to her chest. Maybe it was the emoji that Jack had sent her only two pages from the end, but she knew it had been a long time since a book had struck her heart the way this one had. It was the type of story that made it impossible not to believe in true love. Of course, she knew that it was fiction. And she wasn't like the heroine in the book, expecting to have her life turned around by a grumpy but soft-hearted fisherman, but it wasn't about that. It was about the feelings. The connections they formed. Whoever had written this knew how to harness the exact emotion of true love. That itself was enough to prove its existence, wasn't it?

Once again, against her will, her mind wandered to Henry. She couldn't even imagine what fictional character could crack that hard exterior. No doubt he would be even more cynical than her sister when it came to Jack. Not that his opinion mattered. Not in the slightest.

As if he knew she was thinking about him, her phone buzzed, and Jack's name appeared on the screen. *Have a fun time out X*, it read. It was hardly a spectacularly romantic declaration, but it was the little things that counted. A smile blossomed on her face.

I will, xx she typed back, only to stare at the message. A second later she deleted the second kiss before pressing send. After all, she didn't want to look too keen.

CHAPTER 13

They were meeting at the Oak House, a restaurant-come-bar next to the church at the top of town. From early morning until noon, it was packed with customers grabbing a cooked breakfast before the lunch crowd came in. Then, at somewhere around five o'clock, people started swapping their cups of tea and diet cokes for beer on tap and sparkling wine.

Jules was the one responsible for arranging the impromptu get together and was already sitting with Maria when Fleur arrived.

"My lodger said she didn't mind babysitting, so I didn't need to be asked twice," Jules said, as Fleur took a seat. "We ordered a bottle of white and a bottle of red. Gemma only drinks white, and we remembered you prefer red. Maria and I are easy. I'm sure it will all get drunk, either way."

"Thank you," Fleur said, surprised. It was endearing that they'd remembered what she liked after only one meeting. After taking off her coat and hanging it on the back of her chair, she took the glass offered to her. "Gemma's joining us too, then?"

"She'll be here any minute. Just had to close the café first," Jules replied. "So, how have you found the move?"

Before Fleur could respond, the door flew open, and Gemma swept in.

"Okay, I need a drink," she said, taking a glass and filling it with wine before anyone could even offer it.

"Bad day?" Maria asked.

It took Gemma several gulps before she responded. "Not really. Well, it would have been better if Sophie hadn't been in tears most of the time."

"Sophie as in Book Club Sophie?" Fleur asked. "Is she okay?"

"Oh, trust me; you don't want to know. It's that damn fella of hers. Honestly, how I've not strangled him by now is a miracle."

By the looks on the other girls' faces, they were all in agreement.

"So, have they broken up?" Fleur asked, assuming that would be the cause of all the upset.

"Well, this morning they had, but by the time we shut, he was picking her up and taking her for a *romantic dinner*. Honestly, I can't talk about it anymore. I really can't. Let's change the subject. What were you guys discussing?"

A brief pause followed. Fleur didn't want to steer the conversation back around to her. Thankfully, Jules responded quick enough.

"We were just asking Fleur how she's found the move," she said.

"Really? Has it been okay? I found it took a bit of getting used to, but I can't imagine living anywhere else now."

"I thought you always lived here," Fleur said, "although I

don't know why I imagined that. I guess it was with you owning the café and everything, I thought it might even be a family business."

"Oh, I don't own the café. I just run it." Gemma was already topping up her glass, despite it still being half full. "I fell into it by accident. A friend of my mum's was the chef there. That's how I heard the job was going. But to be honest, it does feel like I've always been here."

"And what about you?" Fleur turned to the other two. "Have either of you lived anywhere else?"

"We're both from Maldon," Jules said. "Although Maria disappeared in our late teens and left me."

"Where did you go?" Fleur asked, keen to learn as much as possible about her new friends. Although it seemed Maria didn't want to give much away.

"Oh, just here and there."

Her response elicited withering looks from both her friends.

"She went on tour. She was dating a rock star." Jules offered Fleur a sly grin as she spoke. "He's *the one who got away*."

"He's not. It was a different life back then. One where I didn't need this to walk," Maria said, lifting her stick.

"One thing you need to know about Maria is that she's obscenely talented," Gemma said, jumping on the bandwagon. "Singing, acting. She could have been famous. Easily as famous as Dan."

"Dan?" Fleur questioned.

"Dan Fauci. The rock-star ex."

Fleur's jaw dropped. She would have never considered herself up to date with modern music, but even she knew that name. "Dan Fauci, from the Neptune's Moons?"

"It was a very long time ago." Maria's tone clearly implied she didn't want to talk about it further. And Fleur got it. Who wanted to talk about their ex, even if they were a multi-platinum-selling artiste who travelled the world playing on stage to millions?

"So, what do you do now? You're a music teacher, aren't you? Did I get that right?"

"She's a rock star is what she is."

"Please, we don't need to talk about me. Let's hear about Fleur. How come you made the move to Maldon? Do you have family around here?"

She should have expected the questions. There had been a few at the Club before they'd started chatting about the book, but she'd evaded most of them. The thing was, she still wasn't comfortable talking about how she'd packed up her old life, her only aim being to get distance between her and Robert. She didn't want to talk about how she had invested so many years in a relationship only to find out they wanted different things or how she had given up what most people would consider an amazing job because the stress had got to her. She didn't even want to talk about Jack, because it was too new and saying anything felt like it would be jinxing it. So instead, she topped up her drink and looked back at Maria.

"So, when am I going to hear you sing?" she asked.

THOUGH FLEUR DIDN'T GET to hear Maria sing, the night was the most fun she could remember having in ages. A lot of talk revolved around books and how irate some of them had become over certain ones.

"Never insult Neil Gaiman in front of Graham," Jules warned her.

"Why would anyone ever insult Neil Gaiman?" she replied.

She'd only read one of his books but had loved it. As such, she made a mental note to put another on her list.

"I don't know. But don't. And never say that graphic novels aren't proper novels to him either. He's writing one."

"He is?" *Wow*, Fleur thought. Graham was one of the people she hadn't spent that much time talking to, but she'd made some unsubstantiated assumptions, like he worked in I.T. or something similar. She hadn't pegged him as an artist, that was for sure.

"He's also completely in love with Sophie," Gemma added. At this, Fleur's attention piqued. "Yup, really. And they'd be perfect together. Or at least substantially better than the idiots she normally dates."

"But she's not interested in him?"

"I don't think she even notices him if I'm honest. Oh, to be young."

Fleur and the others laughed at this.

"You're not exactly old, Gemma."

"I'm twenty-nine," she said, indignantly.

Fleur nearly choked on her wine. "Twenty-nine is not old. You can't possibly believe that. I'm going to be forty in two months."

"Forty!" The girls around the table clapped their hands excitedly. "Does that mean a party is on the cards?"

"No, it doesn't. Definitely not. I do not want a party. But something like this would be nice."

Jules lifted her glass in a toast. "Then that's what we shall do," she said.

It wasn't long after that when they called it a night. Gemma still had to work on Saturday, as did Maria, who was running a children's theatre camp at one of the primary schools.

"So, we'll do this again soon, right?" Jules said, hugging Fleur tightly before they left.

"Absolutely."

Back at her flat, she mused over how lovely the night had been and how easily the conversation had flowed. So easily, in fact, that she hadn't even looked at her phone. Collapsing onto her sofa, she tapped on the screen to see two messages. One was from Annelise and contained a link to a venue she thought could work well for the party that wasn't going to happen. The other was from Jack. As usual, it was short and sweet. *Hope you had a good night xx*, it read. With the warmth of the wine still flowing through her, she stared at the message and the *two* kisses that now marked the end.

Yes, moving to Maldon really was looking like a great decision.

CHAPTER 14

$\mathcal{H}$enry checked his watch, only to do a double take. Where had the last hour disappeared to? He tapped his mouse, then viewed the clock in the top corner of his screen, to ensure it wasn't somehow on the blink.

Now that he realised what the time was, it probably shouldn't have come as a surprise that almost every other light in the office was off. The only other people still there were two senior partners, working on a case together, although he suspected that by now they'd already cracked open the scotch and were winding down. He didn't have that privilege yet. No, it would be a few more years before he could pick and choose the way they did.

Stretching, he let out a long yawn and clicked his neck from side to side, trying to ease the cramp that had formed from hours of sitting in the same position. Just like every other week, this one had been jam-packed with back-to-back meetings. And he wasn't done yet. Half a dozen items remained unchecked on his to-do list, and he still needed to get all his documentation ready for his first meeting on

Monday morning. At least it was Thursday, he thought, longing for a weekend to catch up with other things and rest, only to recall that he had meetings arranged for the Sunday, too. Some days, he struggled to remember why he'd believed becoming a lawyer would be a good idea.

Reaching into his pocket, he glanced at his phone, only to see no notifications on his home screen. The sense of relief relaxed him just a fraction. He liked days with no notifications. Then he could focus on the chaos at work without having to stress about anything else. Happy that he could carry on working for another couple of hours before heading home, he laid his phone on his desk, only for it to start ringing the instant he turned back to work.

"Auntie Eunice, is everything okay?"

It was a hard-wired reflex that, every time she rang, his pulse rocketed, and he was already on his feet before she spoke.

"Well, I don't know. You tell me," she replied. "I thought you were going to come over for a cup of tea and a chat before you dropped me at the Club. Assuming you don't want to come with me?"

"Book Club?"

There was no point in pretending he hadn't forgotten. She knew him too well for that. How the hell had that come around so quickly? But a quick check of his calendar confirmed she was right. It was that time again.

"Sorry, I'll be there in a minute," he said, closing his laptop and gathering up the various piles of paper around him.

"You don't have to rush. I don't mind walking," she said.

"No. No, you don't need to do that. I'll be there. Just give me ten minutes."

"As long as you're sure?"

"I'm sure."

He hung up before she had even wished him goodbye.

Ten minutes turned into fifteen after he'd triple checked all the documents he needed to take home were in his briefcase and then said goodbye to the partners — who were, as expected, sitting on the sofa in the corner office, drinking. By the time he was outside Eunice's house, she was standing there with her coat on.

"I was starting to get worried," she said.

He jumped out of the car, rushed over and kissed her swiftly on the cheek before offering her his arm to guide her to the vehicle.

"I'm so sorry. And why are you waiting outside? Come on. Whose house are we going to today?" He opened the car door and helped her up.

"It's Jules'. On Cross Road."

He nodded. Taking his aunt to Book Club meetings had been instrumental in him learning his way around Maldon, and though he didn't know any of the members very well, he now knew where they all lived.

"I'm really so sorry I'm late," he said again, as they drove off. "I got held up."

"Burning the candle at both ends," she replied. "You need to look after yourself. Self-care. That's what they call it nowadays. It's in all the magazines."

It took a great deal of restraint for him not to laugh at this comment. He could just imagine telling his boss he hadn't read through all the case notes before his meeting because he needed a scented bubble bath as part of his self-care routine.

"So, tell me," she said. "How did your date go?"

This was almost enough of a surprise for him to slam on the brakes.

"Date?" He turned to his aunt in confusion. "What date?"

"The one you promised me you were going on after our

last meeting, remember? You told me you would make an effort and put yourself out there. Now, was it someone at work, or did you swipe right on one of those app things?"

"I ... I ..."

She was staring straight at him, unblinking, like one of those strange lizards with extra eyelids. He always crumbled under this gaze, and she knew it. Still, he tried to defend himself.

"It's been a really busy fortnight," he blurted out, annoyed at himself for sounding like some weak-willed teenager.

"It always is busy, according to you," she replied.

"That's because I'm a junior partner. I don't conjure up this work, you know." He spoke with a fraction of annoyance.

"Oh, I don't doubt it. You just make up the story that you're going to try and meet someone to keep your busybody aunt happy."

He drew in a long breath and his back teeth ground together as he considered his next words.

"Honestly Auntie Eunice, is it that difficult for you to believe I'm happy on my own? That I like my life as it is?"

"Very. You know, when you were small, you used to laugh all the time. Such a practical joker. Couldn't keep still for all the mischief you would get up to. You used to have me and your uncle in stitches. I sometimes wonder what happened to that boy."

"I'm sorry I'm not so amusing anymore," he said, with a little more petulance than he'd intended. "I think you'll find it's called growing up."

"Is it? Because *I* still laugh. And even with what happened to him, your uncle still laughed every day until his death. Sometimes I wonder if you've forgotten how to. You know, muscle memory is a real thing. They say that in the magazines, too."

"Well, I don't think muscle memory applies to laughter," he said, grateful for the lack of traffic. Another minute was all he was going to have to endure being lectured at. Not that he expected her to forget during the meeting, but she might have other things she wanted to talk to him about when he collected her.

"You should come and join us tonight," she said, still not giving up. "It would be nice for Graham to have another young man there. It's always a giggle *and* you can ask Fleur out for a drink?"

There came the kicker he was waiting for. Sucking in a deep breath, he gripped the steering wheel so fiercely, his knuckles turned white as he forced himself to count to ten. She meant well, and he adored her, he reminded himself. And it was true. He did love his aunt deeply. Except when she tried to set him up like this.

"I'm sorry; you mean well. But that woman is simply not my type."

"I find it hard to believe you know that. You've barely had a full conversation with her. Trust me; you'll see. Have a proper chat tonight. I know you two will get on like a house on fire."

Yes, Henry thought as he parked. They might. But the type of fire where the house was left in ashes at the end.

CHAPTER 15

They had been delayed getting started. Both Eunice and Sophie had arrived late, and then Jules couldn't find her copy of the book, which she really needed, as she'd filled it with tiny post-it notes covered in scribbles. Then the pizza had been delivered earlier than expected. So, unlike what normally happened, they were all tucking into their food, having only just started their discussions.

"I loved the scene by the jetty," Fleur said, after a scalding hot mouthful. "I was screaming at the book, begging him to wait. I think he should have waited for her."

"Of course, he couldn't. It wasn't going to work that way. And anyway, the ending wouldn't have been as good. And it was *so* good. The way he came to the party for her. And the way she wanted him to be there more than anyone. That's just how it should have been."

Jules' house was substantially smaller and less grand than Dee's, but it wasn't without its charm. The low ceilings were braced with dark, wooden beams, and the sofas, while well worn, were the comfiest she had ever sat on.

So far, Jack had texted her twice during the evening. Just silly memes. One of a woman surrounded by books. Another a cute digital image of a bookworm. It was sweet. A little reminder that he was thinking of her, even though they still hadn't met up yet. He had taken over a day to respond to her message, asking if he wanted to go for a drink, at which point she'd panicked she'd pushed things along too quickly. But he'd texted back at the beginning of the week, saying that he was pulling double shifts for the next fortnight but after that, definitely.

"So, who is choosing the next one?" Sophie asked, at the exact moment Fleur's phone buzzed in her pocket. As subtly as she could, she reached down and slipped it out, hoping to send off a quick message.

"Everything okay? You seem distracted?"

It took a moment for her to realise someone was speaking to her. She looked up and saw Gemma staring at her.

"Is everything all right? You've been checking your phone a lot this evening?"

"Sorry. Yes ... um ... it's all fine."

"You're messaging a guy!" Sophie said.

"I ... I ..." Fleur stuttered, taken aback by everyone now looking at her. She had no idea how Sophie had come to that conclusion, and she considered denying it, but they were all watching her expectantly, and the last thing she wanted was to start lying only two weeks into their friendship.

"Okay, so I know the Book Club rules and everything. But we haven't actually met up yet."

"Eek!" The shrieks went up around her. Considering they were a group that had sworn off relationships, they seemed more than a little excited by the news.

"Well, tell us everything."

"When did you meet?"

"How many times have you seen him?"

"What does he do?"

Questions flew at her from every direction, and she felt somewhat guilty for not having more to tell them. Still, they seemed to get plenty of amusement from the story of her locking herself out of her flat and him turning up to check if she was a burglar.

"Wait," Gemma said, lifting her hands to halt the conversation. "You were already chatting to him when we went for drinks? And you didn't say anything?"

"There really wasn't that much to tell you, I promise. It's just at the messaging stage. I'll report back after our first date," she said, desperate to turn things away from her and Jack. "Anyway, I want to talk about the sister. I'm pretty sure the next book in the series is about her."

"It is?"

"That's what I read at the back."

With the conversation on course again, Fleur breathed a small sigh of relief before joining in. She would message Jack back at the end of the night.

Before the evening drew to a close, they decided on the next book — a dystopian, alternative future about people used as organ donors, chosen by Graham. It wasn't the type of thing Fleur would have picked herself, but it was hard not to get excited after hearing him enthuse about it. After typing the title into her phone, she stood up and prepared to say her farewells, only to find Eunice standing directly in front of her.

"Fleur dear, Henry's picking us up again. Have you got your bag and things?"

"Oh, I'm fine Eunice," she replied, as surprised by the offer as she was by her sudden appearance. She couldn't think anyone in their right mind would want to sit in a car with her and Henry again. "I don't mind walking."

"Don't be silly. I told him he'd be taking you home again tonight. He's looking forward to it."

Somehow, she didn't think this was true. She couldn't imagine him looking forward to anything other than buying extortionately priced cars. Or possibly checking his perfect reflection in the mirror. She was about to refuse again and say how unnecessary it was, when Eunice looped her arm through hers and began to lead her out of the living room. By the time they reached the front door, it was already open, and Henry was standing outside.

Despite the lateness of the evening, he appeared to have come straight from work. He was dressed in a pale-blue shirt with a loosened tie.

"Henry, perfect timing. I told Fleur you were going to take her home again."

"Yes. Apparently, I've become a private taxi service," he said, looking straight at Fleur as he spoke.

She clenched her hands by her sides, wondering how it was possible that someone could infuriate her so much with a single sentence.

"It's fine. I don't need a lift. I'm very happy to walk."

"Nonsense," Eunice said, surprisingly sharply.

"It's fine," he said, although his voice grated. "It's not too out of the way."

It took every inch of restraint for Fleur not to bite back. How anyone could make an offer sound so utterly insincere was beyond her.

"Fantastic," Eunice said, slipping her arm out of Fleur's and heading to the car. "You go in the front again, dear, I'll go in the back."

Somehow, this felt even more embarrassing than the previous journey together, and this multiplied the moment the engine started, and Eunice spoke again.

"So, Fleur's only been here a few weeks, and she's already got herself a fella," she announced, proudly.

Fleur's jaw dropped open. Of all the things that she could think of to start a conversation, why on earth would she have chosen that?

"Congratulations, Fleur," Henry replied, dryly.

"I haven't exactly …" Fleur stuttered, wishing she had the skill needed to jump out of a moving car. To make matters worse, Eunice hadn't finished.

"Perhaps if you'd put in a little more effort, Henry, and put yourself out there, you'd be able to find someone, too."

"I don't want to find anyone," he replied through a locked jaw. A vein twitched on his temple. "I am perfectly happy as I am."

"Tosh! I don't believe that for a second. It's much better having someone there to talk to, isn't it, Fleur? You tell him."

On the plus side, Fleur was one hundred percent certain Henry was feeling as horrendously embarrassed as she was. But that didn't stop Eunice from looking at her expectantly, and she knew she had to say something.

"I think everyone would like to have somebody to talk to in the evenings," she said, trying to be as diplomatic as possible.

"Fleur's new fella is a policeman," Eunice continued. "He rescued her when she was locked out of her home."

"He didn't rescue me," Fleur said, hating the fact that she now sounded like some damsel in distress. "I rescued myself. He came to see if I'd been breaking and entering."

"Sorry … what?" For the first time ever, it almost looked like Henry was going to smile, and as he turned to look at Fleur, there was a definite glimmer in his eyes.

"You were accused of breaking and entering?"

"I was *not* accused of breaking and entering," she said, tension building across her shoulders. "I locked myself out. And someone, obviously being a good neighbour, informed the police that they had seen me entering my house through an upstairs window."

"And this policeman? He came to your door and then just asked you out?" Henry questioned.

It had been bad enough talking to Annelise about the way she and Jack had met, but this was excruciating. The way he was looking at her, as if he thought she was insane, made her want to sink into the heated leather upholstery and disappear.

"Well, that's a red flag if ever I heard one. You can't possibly be thinking of meeting up with this guy. *Have* you met up with him?"

"I don't think that's any of your business," she said, curtly.

"They've just been messaging on the phone for now," Eunice said, from the back. As much as Fleur had initially loved the old woman, she felt the soft spot she'd had for her rapidly evaporating. She was under no illusion that this busy-bodiness was all to do with Henry and not her, but that didn't make it any the less irritating.

"Well, call me cynical," Henry said, his focus back on the road, "but this has got ghosting written all over it."

"Ghosting?" Eunice said.

"It's when you're dating somebody and they suddenly stop contacting you," Fleur explained. "You know, like they've suddenly turned into a ghost. But you're right, Henry. I do call you cynical. We've been chatting for nearly two weeks now."

"Wow, nearly two whole weeks? Well, I'm sure you'll prove me wrong, and I look forward to hearing updates after the next Book Club get together. Assuming you'll want to scrounge a lift back home then, as well. This is the right one, isn't it?" He gestured out of the window, where they were indeed on North Road outside Fleur's flat.

Flicking off her belt, she twisted around to face the back.

"It was lovely to see you again, Eunice," she said, then opened the car door and stepped out. She didn't even bother saying goodbye to Henry.

CHAPTER 16

*H*enry could feel his aunt's eyes boring into the back of his skull, although what she had to be mad about, he had no idea. She was the one who'd got them into this situation, despite the fact he'd emphatically told her, countless times, that it wasn't what he wanted. The rest of the journey passed in stony silence. He could tell she was expecting him to apologise, but for what? Telling Fleur the truth about this man she was apparently dating? No. That had disaster written all over it.

He parked up outside Eunice's house and unbuckled his belt, but before he could get around to the back door, she was already letting herself out.

"Here, let me help you," he said, offering her his arm, which she promptly ignored. Only when she had both feet firmly on the ground did she turn and look at him.

"Did you really have to be that rude?" she asked.

For a woman who was barely five feet two, she could make herself look extremely intimidatingly. But he wasn't having it. Not when he still had piles of work left to get back to.

"Me? Rude? To start with, I had no desire to give that woman another lift and nor did she need it. Secondly, there wasn't a thing I said that wasn't true. And you know it."

She let out a deep sigh. "It's not what you say, Henry dear, it's how you say it. And I know you understand what I mean. Surely, you'd like someone to talk to in the evenings, too?"

He moved to the front door and unlocked it with his own key. It was bad enough that he was arguing with his elderly aunt. The last thing he wanted was to do it in public. Holding the door open, he waited for her to step inside and closed the door behind them. Several deep breaths later, as she removed her coat, he went up to her and took her hands.

"Look, I know you mean well. I do. But please don't keep pushing things like this. If I am going to meet someone — which I have no desire to— then it will happen organically. Not by you trying to force me towards someone who clearly thinks the same about me as I do them. You understand that?"

He looked her straight in the eyes, noting the way she pouted.

"I will consider keeping my nose out," she said, eventually.

He released a deep internal sigh. That was probably as good as it was going to get. Still holding her gaze, he offered her one of his most endearing smiles, the type he'd used since he was four years old and wanted to get his own way. It had worked on her then, as it had during his teen years and just as it was going to work now. For added affect, he widened his eyes and allowed his bottom lip to stick out just a fraction.

"Am I forgiven for being rude?"

Her mouth twitched, the smile she didn't want to release playing at the corner of her lips. Finally, it broke into the warm twinkle he loved.

"You will be the death of me; you know that?"

"Really?" he replied, following her into the kitchen. "I thought it would be your love of cake and wine."

Ten minutes later, and he was back at home, scanning through paper after paper. As he reached for his glass of red wine, he couldn't help but let out a cynical laugh. *Someone to talk to at night? Really?* he said to himself. As if he'd ever have the time for that.

CHAPTER 17

*F*leur was pacing her living room floor. Scrounge a lift? Henry had actually said that to her when Eunice had been the one who'd insisted she come with them. And she still hadn't forgotten the way he'd spoken to his aunt after the previous Book Club meeting, either. The way he'd commented on how many glasses of wine she might have had. She'd wanted to punch him right there and then. The arrogance of the man. She'd heard of controlling spouses before, but controlling great-nephews? Maybe he was one of those evil pieces of work you read about in magazines who kept their old relatives close so they could siphon off their wealth without them noticing. She bet a lawyer would know exactly how to do that without getting caught.

Crossing into the kitchen, she began to fill the kettle, only to change her mind and fetch a wineglass from the cupboard, instead. She deserved one after that journey.

With her drink poured, she flopped onto the sofa and flicked on the television, though her mind had difficulty switching off from Henry and his blatant pomposity. Not to mention the comments he'd made about Jack ghosting her. How had that been necessary? Maybe women had ghosted him when they'd realised what an arrogant, conceited know-it-all he was. It would certainly be preferable to ghost him than to listen to his insufferable rantings. But that wasn't the case with her and Jack. And she was going to prove it. When she saw Henry again, she would tell him exactly how well things were going between them. She could even ask Jack to walk her to the Book Club next time, just to prove a point. With a new sense of motivation, she picked up her phone and opened her messages to Jack.

Are you free for a drink tonight? Or tomorrow?

Immediately, a message pinged back.

I wish. Later in the week?

Later in the week would be great, she wrote, finishing with a smiley face emoji.

Her chest fluttered as the reply came: a heart emoji.

Yes, she thought with smug satisfaction. She would show Henry exactly what kind of relationship they had. With that, she sat back in her seat and took a long draw of her wine. This week was going to be a good one.

JUST AS SHE'D HOPED, the following week went well, work wise at least. Whether it was her overriding good mood, or simply the fact that she had now been in her current position for several months, she sped through all the tasks she'd been set, leaving her plenty of free time to go for runs or else sit and enjoy a book at the Waterfront Café.

"So, any more gossip with you and the policeman?" Gemma said, when Fleur popped in for a slice of lemon-drizzle cake on Thursday afternoon.

"Not yet," she said. The optimism she'd been feeling at the beginning of the week had dimmed somewhat. "He's been crazily busy with work."

"I can imagine, with his job and everything."

She nodded, her smile tighter than she would have liked. Whilst Jack had been quick to agree to a drink, pinning him down for a date proved substantially harder. It was the shift work, he explained in one of his messages. And sometimes he worked days, sometimes he worked nights. They were also short staffed.

I'm happy to meet for lunch or brunch, she'd messaged once, trying to make things as easy as possible for him. After all, there was plenty of flexibility with her job. She could happily take a morning off or an extended lunch break if she needed to.

We'll see, Jack replied. He'd sent that message on Tuesday, and she still hadn't heard anything else from him. Not even a casual *Morning* or *Goodnight* text.

Staring at the cake in front of her, she couldn't help but remember what Henry had said in the car: *That's got ghosting written all over it.* The memory was enough for her chest to tighten. It would be bad enough if Jack had been stringing her along for nearly three weeks, but Henry being right would make the whole matter a thousand times worse.

"He'll get back to me," she said as she picked up her fork and severed a corner of the cake. "He'll definitely get back to me."

By Friday night, she wasn't feeling so confident, and on Saturday, when three of her messages had been left unread, she was feeling more and more like she might have to swallow her pride. There were only so many times she could contact him without some form of response.

As much as she didn't want to feel dejected, it was hard not to. She had let her mind wander, imagining a future where she wasn't constantly cooking meals for one or taking strolls by the water on her own. But it was better this way, she tried to convince herself. After all, a couple of weeks was nothing in the scheme of things, and at least she'd got to practise her flirting skills, although apparently not very successfully.

After spending a lazy Saturday ironing while catching up on television shows, she had planned to head out on Sunday, though she wasn't exactly sure where. The buses from Maldon went to a variety of places, including Colchester which was home to an eleventh-century castle.

She considered asking her Book Club Friends if anyone fancied going over and grabbing some dinner there, but she wasn't planning on doing that until the afternoon, which was why at ten thirty when her doorbell rang, she was still dressed in her pyjamas. Rather than the short ring that the delivery drivers normally used, this one was different. Someone was holding down the button.

"Okay, okay," she said, only to stop in the hallway. Did delivery men work on Sunday she thought before trying to recall if she'd actually ordered anything. A quick trawl through her mind left her none the wiser. There was nothing she could think of, and neither could she imagine who would come to her door on a Sunday morning. That was when her pulse rocketed. Jack. He knew her address. After all, it was how they'd met. And it would make sense that he hadn't replied to any of her messages if he was planning on surprising her.

Her pulse kicked up another notch as she tried to remember whether she had cleaned her teeth that morning.

"One second!" she yelled, despite knowing she couldn't be heard from upstairs.

Remembering that she had brushed them before her first

coffee of the day, she ran a comb through her hair and had a quick look in the mirror. It certainly wasn't the appearance she would have gone for had this been a planned date. But then, considering he'd wanted her number after she'd just been for a 5K run and climbed in through a window, he obviously wasn't too fussed about a manicured look.

With her heart drumming, she went to her door screen. When she saw the image of the person staring at the camera, her stomach plummeted.

"Annelise?" she said, pressing her finger on the intercom button. "What are you doing here?"

"Currently dying from lack of caffeine. Now, are you going to let me in or not?"

CHAPTER 18

*I*f Fleur had been worried about what Jack might think of her not-yet-dressed, zero-makeup look, it was nothing compared to how she felt about Annelise seeing her in this state.

Even as teenagers, her sister had been flawless in her appearance. She had been the girl who could rock any look, from grungy ripped jeans to black tie and everything in between. Her wedding photos had featured in two national magazines, and she and her husband, Jude, looked more like models than actual models did. She didn't think that it was a coincidence that none of the photos she was in were used in either spread.

"This place is so quaint," Annelise said, as she plumped up several cushions before taking a seat on the sofa. The fact she'd said nothing at all about Fleur's appearance didn't mean she wasn't thinking about it. Fleur knew her sister better than that. "The whole town is quaint. Although I can't believe there isn't a train station here. You know I had to get the bus from Chelmsford."

"You didn't have to get a bus. You didn't have to come and see me. Not that I'm not happy to see you or anything, but is there a reason you're here?" She handed Annelise a cup of black coffee, no sugar, just the way she liked it.

"I did have to come," she replied, folding her feet under her. "You weren't exactly going to invite me, were you? And I've been dropping enough hints. So, I thought, screw it. I want to spend some time with my baby sister. Even if she doesn't want me there."

"Of course, I want you here," Fleur said, feeling rather guilty for her less-than-enthusiastic response. "But what about the children? It's the weekend. Surely you should be spending time with them."

Annelise wrinkled her nose. That tiny action was all Fleur needed to know there was more behind her unexpected visit than she had first let on.

"Jude's mother is over for the weekend. I thought it would be nice to give them a bit of space. You know how crowded the house can be when everyone is there."

"You mean you wanted to get away from her."

"Perhaps," she grinned.

At times like this, when her sister's eyes twinkled, Fleur would see the girl she had grown up with. Her best friend. They had been so close when they were younger and even in their teens and twenties. It was only the last few years, when things had all come to a head with Robert, that the pair had seen so much less of one another, and it wasn't as if Fleur could blame her. Annelise had tried her best. She'd invited her on family holidays and even offered to build a granny flat in the garden for her. But Fleur didn't want to be reminded of what it was like to have a picture-perfect life when hers had crumbled around her.

Placing her mug on the table, Annelise's expression turned

serious. "Now, regardless of the reason I came, since you've got me here, it seems like a perfect opportunity to discuss your party."

Fleur let out an involuntary groan. "There is no party."

"Because you haven't got around to arranging it."

"Because I don't want one."

The problem with them fighting like this was that neither of them would ever back down. It was different from arguments generally, when Fleur would usually concede just for the sake of a quiet life, or because she didn't want to offend the person she was disagreeing with. But when it came to her sister, the same rules didn't apply.

"Of course, you want a party," she insisted. "Everyone likes a party. You just have to decide on what sort you want. It doesn't need to be anything raucous or fancy. We could go out for a meal in a group. Or to a cocktail bar? We could do a cocktail-making class. And there are some great places in Covent Garden that do wine-tasting bashes."

"Really? And how much would they charge?" Fleur asked, infuriated that her sister wasn't letting her get a word in edgeways. Not to mention how she seemed oblivious to the financial situation most people were in.

"Don't worry, Jude and I could cover that."

"I don't need you to cover anything. I don't want a party. I thought that maybe I might just go for a meal with some of the Book Club girls. You could come too." She hoped this suggestion would be enough to placate her sister; she was wrong.

"You can go for a meal any day. Or on any other birthday, for that matter. But not this one. This one's special. A chance to show the world that you're really living your life again, just like other people."

She was about to say that she was living her life and that

she was rather enjoying it now, when something made her stop. The way she'd said *other people* wasn't quite natural. And now she was looking at Fleur strangely, as if she was worried something might just tip her over the edge and send her to that dark place she'd fallen into during the divorce.

"Annelise, what is it you're not telling me? Why *are* you here?"

"I told you. Jude's mum is over for the weekend. And I wanted to get your party organised."

Had it been anyone else speaking, Fleur would have probably believed them, but this was her sister, and she knew when she was lying as clearly as if she were doing it herself.

"Annelise …"

This time, her sister didn't reply. Rather, she took in a long, deep breath and pressed her lips together as if she was nervous. But that didn't make sense. She didn't get nervous. About anything.

"Is this about Mum?" Fleur asked, a bubble of fear growing within her.

Fleur and her mother never had a particularly tight relationship, but it had got worse after the divorce. Now, she avoided speaking to her unless absolutely necessary, for the sole reason that they couldn't get through a single conversation without her mother mentioning Robert and what a wonderful man he was and how it was a shame she had messed it all up. But if there was something wrong with her, she would have said, wouldn't she?

"Annelise?"

"No, it's not. Mum's fine. She's on holiday, actually. The Dominican."

"Oh," Fleur said, only slightly put out that she didn't already know this.

"It's about Robert."

The bubbling fear was replaced by a hollowness. A deep-rooted numbness which she only slightly preferred to the gut-wrenching heartbreak she'd previously felt when her ex-husband's name was mentioned. "Oh." She tried to keep her voice light but knew she'd failed hopelessly. It didn't seem right that one man, out of the billions on the planet, could have such an effect on her. And yet he did. He always had. "What about Robert?"

Annelise responded with a deep intake of breath. The look of sadness in her eyes was undeniable, and Fleur desperately wanted it to stop. She didn't need her sister's pity. She was doing well now. She was okay without Robert. Building her life again.

"I saw him the other weekend. We were at Paloma's. It's a new restaurant. It's got great reviews, but to be honest, I wasn't impressed. We went there for brunch, and they put bacon in their shakshuka. Who does that? Jude thought his meal was nice, but I can't imagine us going back any time soon. Not to a place that puts bacon in shakshuka."

"Robert, Annelise. You were telling me about, Robert."

"Sorry." A sheepish look flickered on her face, as though she'd hoped by mentioning brunch, Fleur would forget what they were talking about. "Yes Robert. He was there … with his wife."

"His wife?" Fleur took a second to comprehend what Annelise was saying. She was Robert's wife. Or at least she had been. "He's remarried?"

Annalise nodded. It was Fleur's turn to take a deep breath, but it didn't feel like she could get enough air into her lungs. Robert had remarried. Of course, it was to be expected that he'd move on. Wasn't that what she was hoping to do with Jack? But there was moving on as in dating again and moving on that involved making a legally binding vow in front of your friends and family, saying you wanted to be with this person forever.

"There's something else," Annelise said. She'd turned pale now, as if what she had just told Fleur wasn't bad enough. But what could be worse than that? What could be worse than hearing you had been forgotten so easily? Then, before her sister even opened her mouth, she knew exactly what it was.

"They've had a baby."

CHAPTER 19

*R*obert had a baby. It didn't make sense. No matter how many times Fleur rolled the thought over and over in her mind, it didn't compute. Robert had a baby. But Robert hadn't wanted children. Wasn't that the entire reason their marriage broke down in the first place? Because he had never been able to commit to having a family.

"So it wasn't that he didn't want children," she said, when she finally found her voice again. "He just didn't want to have them with me."

"Oh Fleury, I don't think that's true," Annelise said, going in for a hug, but Fleur had her hands out, blocking her sister.

"No, it is true. It's completely true. They can only have been together a couple of years at most. Even if they got together the day we split up, that would be, what, three years? Less than half the time we were together." She shook her head, hoping to clear the tears that were burning behind her eyes. "I wasted so much of my life, Annie. I wasted so much time holding on, thinking that he'd be ready soon. But it was me. I was the problem all along."

Pain was now occupying the places numbness had previously been. That feeling of never being good enough. Of always being second best, if not worse. The inadequacy that she'd felt for so many years in her marriage, and even more so after the breakup, was back again.

It was no surprise that Jack had ghosted her, she thought as she swallowed back several deep breaths. He probably saw how difficult she would make things. How much reassurance she'd require. After all, she never felt pretty enough. Or smart enough. Or just simply *enough*. Tears were welling in her eyes, and she was sure that, at any moment, she was going to dissolve into a puddle on the floor. Shifting her gaze upwards, she forced them down. She wasn't going to do it. She wasn't going to cry over him again. Yet she could already feel the thickening in her throat. And the heat burning at the base of her skull. Then, a millisecond before the sobbing began, Annelise was on her feet.

"No, you're not doing it," she said, grabbing Fleur's hands. "You're not shedding another tear over that man. He's not worth it. We are going out and we are drinking Champagne and we are celebrating how wonderful you are and how cute this little town you live in is."

Fleur sniffed. "I know you're trying to cheer me up, but I'm not in the mood for Champagne. And even if I was, I don't think my budget can really stretch to it."

"Well, mine absolutely can, and besides, this isn't all about you, you know. I have a day away from the children with my little sister and I plan on fully enjoying it. Now, get yourself in the shower. I want you to be ready to go in half an hour."

Fleur had to give it to her sister, by the time she'd dressed — in an outfit that finally met her approval — slicked on a quick smudge of mascara and spritzed herself with perfume, she felt a fraction better.

It was the mind-boggling hypocrisy that was the worst thing. Robert must have told her at least a hundred times that he had no interest in children. And not just the idea of theirs, but anybody's. He'd wanted nothing to do with Annelise's two, despite them being his niece and nephew. He hadn't even wanted to hold them for a photo when they were first born. God, how Fleur had to nag him to do that. She'd thought he was scared, that was all. And it wasn't only her sister's children. He had several young cousins too, which he had no time for, and he was always the person in the restaurant to ask for a table away from one with a young family on it. A habit she'd hated. She used to love making faces and playing peekaboo with random children, offering them a little distraction while their parents ate their meal. That was what got to her. What was so special about this new woman that she could make him do a complete U-turn?

"Okay, so tell me, where are we heading?" Annelise said as they stepped out onto the road. Despite arriving dressed flawlessly, she too had changed her outfit and her skinny jeans were now paired with a white top and red heels that Fleur would have pinched had they been her size.

"I don't know. I haven't been out much here. There's a café on the waterfront that's nice. Gemma from my Book Club runs it."

"Does it sell Champagne?"

"Probably not," she conceded.

"Then we're not going there."

"Fine." She thought about it. There was the Oak House she'd gone to with Gemma and the other girls, but it would be nice to try somewhere new with Annelise. "There's a restaurant at the top of the town. It does drinks. And it's got tables outside, too. We can make the most of the nice weather."

"That sounds like a plan."

It took longer to reach the place than it normally did, as Annelise stopped every couple of minutes to peer into shop windows.

"What's down there?" she asked, when they reached a little alley.

"Um, a zero-waste shop and another café," Fleur said, hoping she'd recalled it properly.

"I like this place. I really do. Oh, hold on, is that a toyshop? I promised Paxton and Margot I'd buy them something. We'll need to stop there on the way back."

By the time they finally reached the restaurant, Fleur was looking forward to her food even more than normal, given that her sister's unexpected arrival had come before she'd had time for breakfast.

"Can we take that one?" Fleur asked a waitress, pointing to a table set beneath a decorated pagoda in the outside courtyard.

"I'm afraid that it's booked."

"At what time?" Annelise said. "We won't be long. And we can move if they come before we're finished."

The waitress pursed her lips as she checked the time.

"They're due here at two."

"Two? It's not even midday. That's loads of time," Annelise said, slipping into one of the chairs.

Fleur fell silent as she took a seat opposite her sister. She had been like her once. Refusing to take no for an answer. Paying extra to get what she wanted. But where had that got her? Not where she wanted to be, that much was clear.

"Can I fetch you any drinks?" the waitress asked, returning with menus.

"A bottle of Champagne," Annelise answered, without hesitation.

The waitress wavered. "We have Prosecco. Is that okay?"

"No Champagne at all?"

"Prosecco is fine," Fleur cut in.

"Super." The waitress smiled gratefully at her. "And is that with two glasses?"

Fleur was about to reply that yes, they needed two glasses for their bottle of bubbles when, beyond the waitress, she saw a familiar figure standing on the opposite side of the street. The old woman was impeccably dressed in a racing-green coat and was looking from side to side, as if she was waiting for someone.

"Eunice?" Fleur called.

Across the road, Eunice turned her head.

A smile spreading across her face as she ambled over to them. "Fleur," she said, "How nice to see you."

"We're just about to have a drink and some food. Would you like to join us? Unless you have plans, that is? Are you waiting for someone?"

"Theoretically, yes. Henry. He's meant to be meeting me." She frowned as she glanced down at her phone.

"You could join us until he comes?" Fleur suggested. The last thing she wanted was to spend any of her weekend with Henry, but at the same time, it would be nice to chat to Eunice outside the confines of his car. Particularly given how coercive she suspected he was.

After one more check of her phone, Eunice looked up and smiled. "You know what? That would be lovely."

"In that case," Fleur said to the waitress, "make that three glasses."

CHAPTER 20

*T*here was a small chance their constant giggling was due to the fact that they had drunk a whole bottle of Prosecco on nearly empty stomachs, but even with the prospect of a hangover looming over her, Fleur didn't care. After the news about Robert, she'd expected the day to be horrendous. She'd even felt herself slipping back into that state where her mind refused to function because it was so utterly overcome with grief. But there she was, out in Maldon, having fun. And one thing was for certain: inviting Eunice to join them had been an excellent idea. And they weren't even talking about books. The elderly lady was undoubtedly one of the most well-travelled, interesting women she had met in a long time. It was amazing to hear just what an eventful life she had lived.

"Campervans back then weren't like they are now," Eunice said, as she told them about her travels around Australia in the seventies. "No toilet or heaters or anything like that. Just a mattress, that's all we had. People thought we were hippies. I suppose we were, but we had a lot of fun. Oh yes, waking up on a beach or stargazing and seeing the entire Milky Way stretched out above you … you don't forget days like those in a hurry."

Fleur could see it. Young Eunice, flower braids in her hair, as she danced in a flowing dress. A million miles from her stuck up, dispassionate nephew.

"When was the last time you went away?" Fleur asked, desperate to hear more about her adventures. If ever she'd needed inspiration on how to live her life, it was sitting in front of her right there.

Unlike many of the questions, which she'd answered without hesitation, Eunice frowned and tilted her head to the side, considering her reply.

"Uhm … last year, actually. I went to Spain. Six weeks. I rented a little flat in an apartment block by the sea. Just peace and quiet by myself. Not much of an exploit, really."

"You went to Spain for six weeks on your own?" Fleur said, flabbergasted. She had never done anything like that herself, and to imagine someone double her age doing it made her feel more than a little inadequate. But the old lady waved a hand in the air as if it were nothing.

"I'll be honest. I read a lot. And it was winter, so I didn't get the tan you'd expect."

"It still sounds amazing. Do you have any photos?"

"Photos?" She frowned again, more deeply this time, and then shook her head. "No, I know what you young people are like with your phones, but my generation isn't like that. I was there to breathe in the sea air. See it properly, you know. Not just through the lens of a camera."

Yes, she really was an inspiration, and the fact Eunice had referred to her as a *young person* was something else Fleur was revelling in.

"Eunice, have the last bit of cake," Annelise said, pushing the plate towards her.

"I really shouldn't."

"Go on. Although we're nearly out of Prosecco. I should get us another bottle."

"No," Fleur said, raising her hands. "I have work tomorrow. There's no way I can drink anymore. And I'm going to London, to the office, on Thursday. The last thing I want is a bad review because I've been so hung over."

"Just a glass?" Annelise tried instead. "I'm buying."

"I don't think I should," Fleur replied, but her sister was already on her feet, heading indoors to order them more drinks. Leaving Fleur and Eunice alone for the first time.

"She's a lot of fun," Eunice said.

"Yes. She is. She's a good sister, too, coming down to check on me." A sinking feeling of melancholy that she'd managed to avoid all morning attempted a return. Refusing to let it settle, she pushed back her shoulders and looked at Eunice.

"I thought you were meant to be meeting Henry. Wasn't that why you were here?"

"Oh, I know. He's probably got caught up in work."

"On a Sunday?"

Eunice raised an eyebrow ironically. "Why do you think I arranged to meet him? It's because otherwise he won't leave the office."

"But on a Sunday?"

"An important meeting, apparently."

"It sounds like your nephew needs to get a life."

Annelise was back, holding another bottle of Prosecco. "It was practically the same price as two glasses," she said, topping them up, although before she could reach hers, Eunice had placed a hand over the top.

"I don't think I should. It's hardly very sensible getting drunk at my age."

Fleur was about to comment that if she didn't drink her fair share then her hangover was going to be even worse, and it would hardly be sensible for her to work like that when she was nearly forty, but before she could get a word out, she was stopped by Eunice's phone beeping in her bag.

"Do you want to get that?" Annelise said, the bottle still hovering in her hand. "It sounds angry."

Fleur couldn't help but laugh. It was true. The phone really did sound irate, but Eunice ignored it.

"It's just the battery playing up," she said. "It's fine."

With Eunice's hand no longer covering her glass, Annelise saw her opportunity and poured in more Prosecco. "Just a half," she promised her. "For now, at least. So, you were talking about your nephew. That he's a workaholic?"

With the phone still beeping away, Eunice took a delicate sip of her drink. "He wasn't always that way, but I think it keeps his mind off things. He would never admit it, but I do think he gets lonely."

Several thoughts ran through Fleur's mind, most themed on how it wasn't a surprise that he was alone, given how he spoke to people. She couldn't imagine anyone wanting to spend more than five minutes in his company without throttling him.

"I should give him a call, actually," Eunice said, suddenly standing. "Check he's on his way."

Fleur hurriedly got to her feet, too, to help Eunice move her chair back.

"She's awesome," Annelise said, leaning across the table to speak to Fleur once Eunice had moved away for some privacy. "I want to be like that when I'm her age."

Fleur laughed. "Though without the miserable great-nephew."

"You know she was saying he's lonely. Perhaps you two could get together. Have you met him? Is he attractive?"

"Oh, he's attractive all right. Very attractive. And arrogant. And self-righteous. And condescending and rude and—" Fleur stopped abruptly as Eunice appeared back at their table.

"Well, I've left him a message," she said, sitting down. "Again. Now, what were you talking about? Someone unpleasant, by the sound of it."

A deep burning sensation flooded Fleur's cheeks, and she was certain she was going to go so red that Eunice would read exactly what it meant, but before she could offer a fumbling excuse, Annelise was talking.

"Fleur's ex, Robert. Horrible piece of work. I tried to warn her before they got married, but she wouldn't listen to me."

"He wasn't that bad," Fleur said, feeling both relief at Annelise's flawless cover and the need to defend what had been her most substantial and important relationship. "He had his good points."

"Very few."

"Mum loved him."

"That really doesn't say a lot."

"It sounds like you're better off without him, Fleur," Eunice said, promptly putting an end to the women's bickering.

She wasn't sure how to reply to this. In so many ways, she did feel better off without Robert. She hadn't realised how tiring it had been, constantly living up to someone else's expectations and never managing to meet them. But that didn't change the fact that her life felt a little emptier now there wasn't someone to share it with. Thankfully, before she had time to think of a suitable reply, Annelise was already raising her drink.

"I couldn't agree more. Let's drink to that. Fleur being better off without him."

And the three women clinked their glasses together.

"What a fabulous morning," Eunice said, taking another tiny sip. "Quite unexpected and wonderful."

"I have to agree," Fleur said, taking a far more substantial swig of her drink. She didn't know if it was possible, but this bottle tasted even better than the first and her glass soon needed topping up yet again, although Annelise promptly decided they needed something else to accompany it and ordered another slice of chocolate cake for them to share.

Fleur was about to take her first forkful, when a voice from the footpath caught her attention.

"Auntie Eunice?"

Henry was standing on the pavement behind them. Dressed in his work clothes, he looked completely out of place amongst the casual, coffee-shop clients there for a relaxed Sunday brunch.

"What are you doing?" he said, staring at his aunt. "Are you drinking? At midday?"

"I've just had a couple of glasses, Henry. I'm quite all right."

Anger surged through Fleur. It was bad enough that he spoke to Eunice like this in the semi-privacy of his car, but to do it in front of everyone in the courtyard was just not on.

"You can't behave like this," he carried on. "It's irresponsible. You know your phone is beeping, don't you?"

"Henry, I'm fine."

"I'm taking you home. Now. Get your things."

The anger Fleur had tried to control rose again, and this time she didn't try to stop it. Before she could think twice, she was on her feet.

"Why don't you leave her alone? She's a grown woman."

"Excuse me?" For the first time since addressing his aunt,

Henry had turned to see who she was with. At the sight of Fleur, his eyes blackened. "You! I should have known it would be one of your lot encouraging behaviour like this."

Before Fleur could take another breath, Annelise was on her feet too, ready to defend her baby sister. "What the hell was that supposed to mean?" she said, squaring up to him with her hands on her hips.

"It's fine, Annelise." Fleur rested a hand on her shoulder and lowered her back onto her seat. "I've got this." Turning back to face Henry, she also put her hands on her hips. "What the hell was that supposed to mean?" she echoed.

His jaw clicked from side to side as a small vein throbbed in his temple.

"You don't think about consequences, do you?" he continued, looking at Eunice. "You just turn up here, acting like you're twenty-two, getting drunk on a Sunday lunchtime."

"The only consequences here are that people are having fun, something I don't think you'd know anything about," Fleur blurted.

"That's it. We're going." Henry turned and strode towards the pathway. "Auntie Eunice? You need to come with me. Now."

Fleur was aghast. She was almost in tears, in fact. Not for herself, though. She didn't give a damn about Henry speaking to her like that. It was Eunice she was so upset for.

"You don't have to go," she said, taking the old woman's hands. Eunice had paled. All the colour had drained from her face. Fleur's heart ached at the sight. "You can stay with me. We can sort something out."

"That's very sweet of you to offer, dear," she said. "But I'm just fine. Please, don't get angry. It's complicated. Henry means well."

"He can't speak to you like that."

"Thank you for a lovely morning," she said, with a sad glimmer in her eyes. She leant forwards and gave Fleur a quick squeeze. "I'll see you at the Club."

"You don't have to go. I can walk you home," Fleur tried again, her heart pounding as she desperately wished she could do more.

"I'll see you at the Club," Eunice repeated, before turning around and walking towards her nephew. A minute later, she was gone.

CHAPTER 21

"Thank you for meeting me today," Henry said to the two men sitting opposite him. "I know it's difficult when we all have so many commitments and no one enjoys using their Sunday mornings like this, but I know we'll all be grateful when everything is sorted."

"You're grateful because you two get to bill us for double time," one of the men said. He was dressed like so many that Henry had to deal with in his line of work. Tan chinos and a pink shirt with both sleeves rolled up so that his fancy watch was on display. If Henry had to guess, there would probably be an eighty-grand SUV or sports car parked outside. Not that he could really comment about owning an extravagant vehicle. But for him, it had been a necessary investment. People wouldn't hire him if he drove around in a ten-year-old hatchback. And given how quickly he'd needed to build up his client list when he'd moved to Maldon, anything that helped get the ball rolling was worth paying for. And so, he had bitten the bullet and bought the big car.

"And while we're talking about money, I don't see why I

should have to pay her anything," the man continued. "She'll just spend it on fake tans and holidays." He directed the comment to the woman sitting beside Henry, who was nonchalantly assessing the state of her nails.

"That's called self-care, Hubert," she said dryly. "Something you would know nothing about."

"It's called burning through my hard-earned money. That's what it is."

After sharing a sideways glance with the other lawyer, Henry fought the urge to put his head in his hands and groan. He'd encountered so many people like this, who said they wanted to do things amicably and fairly, only to relish the chance of dragging their partner through the courts at the first opportunity. He would bet his ugly, enormous car outside that was the way this one was going to go. Both sides would reject every offer placed on the table out of sheer stubbornness. On the plus side, it meant more minutes billed. Every cloud had a silver lining.

"We have drafted what we believe is an acceptable agreement," he said, into a pause in the bickering. "My client believes that these conditions are fair and reasonable, given everything she endured during the relationship."

"Endured? What the hell did she have to endure?" the man said.

Henry ignored this comment and slid a cream-coloured folder across the table towards the other lawyer. "If you would like to take a look."

The two men had just begun whispering to each other about the document when Henry's phone beeped loudly.

"Really?" His client finally looked up from her nails to glare at him. "The money I'm paying you, the least you could do is switch your phone off."

Had it been early in his career, he would have probably

offered his most heartfelt apology and begged for pardon, but he had been doing this long enough that comments like that were like water off a duck's back. He would get her far more than she deserved. He always did. Given his success rate, his fees were more than reasonable, and she had known this before she'd retained him. As such, he didn't bother to grace the comment with a response.

However easily he could deal with rude or entitled clients, that noise on his phone was an entirely different matter. Every time he heard it, anxiety gripped his body and hijacked his thoughts. There was no way he could carry on with this meeting until he'd checked what it wanted to tell him. One of the best and worst things about having the app was that it couldn't be turned off. Unlike an alarm clock or a general messaging tone, there was no way of silencing the sound. And that was a good thing, for as anxious as it made him, it was a lot better than not having it. Only when he had to appear in court did he have no choice but to turn it off.

There was no denying, though, that it had a habit of beeping at the most inopportune times. Thankfully, his colleagues knew the situation with his aunt and were perfectly understanding. Most clients were too, and he'd even had a situation when one knew he had the app, just by hearing it, as they had a relative with the same condition. But there were some occasions, like today, when he didn't want to divulge personal information about his family. Thankfully, for now at least, these clients should be fairly amenable, considering he was fitting them in to move things along.

As Henry forced a smile and turned to his client, his phone beeped again. The smile tightened. A second alert, so soon after the first, wasn't a good sign.

"I'm sorry, if you'll excuse me just a moment," he said,

standing up and pushing his chair back. "My wife is expecting. Due any day now. You don't mind, do you?"

He lifted his phone and headed outside to the corridor, suppressing the smile which teetered on his lips. That line always worked. And apart from one or two, who required his services far more often than the national average would have predicted, his clients were never with him long enough to know that this mysterious, permanently pregnant woman was a complete figment of his imagination. He hit dial.

"Now, don't start fussing." She had answered and was talking before he'd had a chance to draw breath. "I've already sorted it. I fancied a cooked breakfast, and the bacon took longer than usual, that's all. But it's all dished up in front of me, and I've even got a sneaky hash brown. I can send you a photo if you want?"

He grunted, frustrated that his aunt hadn't let him get a word in.

"Now, I'm glad you called, actually. You haven't forgotten you're meeting me in town at lunchtime, have you? We need to go present shopping for that little cousin of yours and you're so much better at picking out gifts than I am."

Having been fully prepared to lay into his aunt, he was now the one struggling to work out what to say. He glanced through the glass doors to the office, where his client's husband was currently throwing his hands up in the air, seemingly less than happy at the deal Henry had laid out.

"Okay, that should be fine," he said.

"What do you mean, should be? Where are you? Please don't tell me you're at the office on a Sunday."

At this, he felt guilt more suited to a teenage boy than an adult, but there was something about Eunice that made him respond like he was thirteen all over again.

"It's just one meeting," he said.

The silence that followed said everything. Anyone who didn't know her would think the line had gone dead, but he knew well enough that she was still there. Waiting. No one did it like Aunt Eunice.

"You know you can't carry on like this," she said, eventually.

There was no reply he could give that would appease her. He glanced back through to the office. Catching his eye, the other lawyer tapped his watch.

"It's just a quick meeting, that's all, but I need to get back to it. Just promise me you're okay?"

With a quick look at his phone, he noted the number on the screen slowly going up. At least she had been telling the truth.

"I want you to promise you're going to come and meet me for a walk, to make sure you're not going to be there all day."

"Okay, a walk. Fine. I'll come to your house."

The other lawyer was tapping his watch even harder now, and both clients were on their feet, shouting at each other across the table. If he wasn't back in there soon, it could end in fisticuffs, and he didn't want to have to explain that to his superiors.

"How about we meet in town? By the Continental?" His aunt was still talking.

"Yes, yes, by the Continental. Speak soon. Love you," he said, then hung up, just as a glass went flying across the room.

CHAPTER 22

*A*s Henry had predicted, a settlement was not reached. Rather than finding an amicable solution, as both parties had initially insisted they wanted, it had descended into insult throwing and baseless threats. By the time everyone had left the building, he was exhausted. Sometimes it felt more like he was trying to control sugar-high toddlers, or hormone-riddled teenagers, than actual full-grown, professional adults. Not that it surprised him. From an early age, older people had said some pretty callous things to him. That was the life he'd grown up with.

On the plus side, the sudden descent into chaos had brought the meeting to a close far earlier than he'd expected, which meant he could meet Eunice at the arranged time.

"I think it would be best if we reconvene when we've all had time to calm down," the husband's lawyer had said.

Henry knew how his client would react to that suggestion.

"Like hell we'll reconvene." She picked up the folder and hurled it at her ex. "I'll see you in court."

After that, he'd led her out of the building, insisting that her husband and his lawyer waited until she'd gone before they left. The last thing he wanted was for his client to do something stupid like keying the ex's car before they even got to court. He'd watched until she'd driven away in her Porsche 911, and only when he was certain she'd gone did the others leave.

With the office finally empty, Henry allowed himself a sigh of relief and began to relax. Unfortunately, it didn't last long. All the yelling that had been going on had drowned out the sound of his phone beeping again, which was a rare occurrence. He'd once been in a theatre with a full eighty-piece orchestra playing, and he had still heard that unmistakable noise coming from his pocket, much to his companion's disgust. That was the last time he'd gone on a date. She'd seemed lovely to start with, and this hadn't been their first time out together. But the fact she had made a scene about him leaving her there, even though he'd explained the problem and given her the money for a taxi, proved to him that it wasn't going to be possible to make a relationship work in his current situation.

"Don't make me ring you, Eunice," he said aloud, his eyes still transfixed by the number. As much as she thought otherwise, he didn't like constantly checking up on her. He had much preferred the role of fun-loving nephew to the one where he nagged her all the time, but sometimes she didn't leave him with any choice.

Biting down on his lip, he forced himself not to overreact. He had done that this morning when she clearly had everything under control. He shut his laptop and put it away in his bag. The office was only a five-minute walk from the Continental Café. If she hadn't sorted herself out by then, he would be able to nag her in person.

Despite the office being so close, Henry rarely went into

Maldon centre, unless it was to grab some food from Marks and Spencer. While the store wasn't particularly large, it had more than enough choice to meet all his requirements, from ready meals he could leave simmering in the oven while he worked late, to sandwiches he could eat at his desk during the week. In fact, the only time he ever went into any of the other shops or cafés was when he was with Eunice.

When he crossed the road at the traffic lights by Moot Hall, his phone was still beeping. As much as he fussed, nine-times out of ten, like that morning, Eunice was already sorting out the issue before it could develop into anything serious, but this had been going for a good fifteen minutes. The thought caused his chest to tighten. He should have rung her, he thought as he picked up his pace to a jog. He slid open his phone, only then seeing that he had a missed call. His stomach lurched. How the hell had that happened? Standing outside the café, he hit dial and pressed it to his ear, when a voice cut through the sounds of the street.

"What a fabulous morning. Quite unexpected, but wonderful all the same."

He could have been in a hall among a thousand people, but he still would have recognised that one. Dropping his phone to his side, he walked forwards, blinking at the sight. His aunt was sitting there, with a glass in her hand, like nothing was at all wrong.

"Auntie Eunice? What are you doing? Are you drinking? At midday?" For a split second, he thought that perhaps it was just water in her Champagne flute, but as soon as she spoke, that hope evaporated.

"I've just had a couple of glasses, Henry. I'm quite all right."

The phone kept beeping in his pocket, and with it came visions of a year ago. Memories he never wanted to relive.

"You can't behave like this. It's irresponsible. You know

your phone is beeping, don't you?" He heard the quiver in his voice, but there was nothing he could do to control it. And worst of all was how relaxed Eunice was about the whole thing.

"Henry, I'm fine."

"I'm taking you home. Now. Get your things."

As he stepped forwards to help her out of her chair, another voice spoke up from the table.

"Why don't you leave her alone? She's a grown woman."

"Excuse me?" The truth was, Henry hadn't noticed Fleur or the other woman sitting there at the table. He'd seen his aunt was with people — he wasn't blind — but he'd been so fixated on her, on getting her home and out of this situation, that he hadn't looked any further than that. But now she was on her feet, staring at him, and for some reason, the sight of the ridiculously romantic woman, with her overly colourful clothes and deluded ideas about relationships, caused his blood to boil. Perhaps it was anger he really wanted to direct at his aunt but knew he never would. Or it could have been that, after a morning listening to a couple who were previously *so in love* hurl insults at each other, his temper finally snapped.

"You! I should have known it would be one of your lot encouraging behaviour like this," he said.

In a split second, it wasn't just Fleur on her feet, but the other woman next to her, too, and she was glowering up at him.

"What the hell was that supposed to mean?" she said.

"It's fine, Annelise," the Fleur woman said. "I've got this. What the hell was that supposed to mean?" she said, turning on him.

Now there were two angry women yelling at him, like he'd done something wrong, as opposed to being the one who was trying to stop the situation descending into a complete nightmare.

He clicked his jaw from side to side, trying to control his anger, only to find it wasn't possible.

"You don't think about consequences, do you?" He wasn't even sure if he was talking to Fleur or his aunt, but they were words he had to get out. "You just turn up here, acting like you're twenty-two, getting drunk on a Sunday lunchtime."

"The only consequences here are that people are having fun, something I don't think you'd know anything about," Fleur snapped back at him.

His head was starting to spin. It didn't make any sense. How was he being turned into the villain of this drama? The two phones were now beeping in unison, and his hand started to tremble. But worse than that was the pallid hue of Eunice's complexion.

"That's it, we're going," he said and took several strides onto the pathway before turning back to face the table. "Auntie Eunice? You need to come with me. Now."

CHAPTER 23

*F*leur couldn't sit still.

"I shouldn't have let her go. I should have gone after her," she said, taking a seat on the sofa, only to change her mind a second later and stand up again.

After the scene at the café, she and Annelise hadn't felt in the mood for continuing their frivolities. She hadn't wanted to drink any more. The Prosecco tasted sickly and sweet, and her head had started to throb. After settling the bill, they decided to walk off some of the morning's indulgences.

They made their way down the High Street, not yet ready to head back to the flat, and opted for a leisurely stroll down to the promenade instead. Despite all the times Fleur had wanted to show Anneliese the sights in Maldon— particularly the ones she thought the children would enjoy — her words kept falling flat. Grey clouds had settled in the sky, making the water at low tide look murky and dark. Children were crying and even the ducks looked moody. So, after reaching the beach huts, they turned around for home, with the intention of fixing themselves coffees strong enough to ward off the hangovers otherwise certain to hit soon.

The moment she'd arrived back, Fleur's mind went to the one place she'd been avoiding. "Do you think I should call the police?" she said, desperately hoping her big sister would tell her what to do. "The way he demanded she go with him. That wasn't right, was it?" But much to her distress, Annelise didn't seem nearly as upset by what had happened as she was.

"It wasn't exactly pleasant, but I don't think you can call them just because somebody is a dickhead."

"He wasn't just that; he was controlling. And the worst thing is that she only has good things to say about him. She thinks he's marvellous. It's not right, and it makes my blood boil."

"At least you're not thinking about the fact that Robert's had a baby," Annelise said optimistically.

It was a case of wrong words at the wrong time. Feeling like the entire weight of the world had fallen onto her shoulders, Fleur dropped down onto the sofa again and buried her head in her hands. How could a day that was meant to be perfectly non-eventful and pleasant turn into such an unmitigated disaster? She stayed like that for a moment longer, only to lower her hands and spring back up from her seat.

"I'm going to get her alone at the next Book Club. See if I can get her to open up. Find out if there's a reason she lets him have so much control over her." She was talking to herself as much as Annelise. "Perhaps I should talk to Gemma, too. Or Dee. They've known her longer. They might know something about the situation. Maybe he's taking money from her."

"Maybe her family is her business. You heard all the things she's done. Campervanning around Australia. Backpacking in Nepal. She's not exactly a wallflower."

"Well, something's very wrong there, and I'm going to put a stop to it."

Fleur took a sip of her coffee, only to find that she'd spent so long pacing and ranting that it had gone cold. With a groan, she ambled over to the sink and poured it away before filling up the kettle with fresh water. At some point, she knew she should ask her sister how long she was intending to stay. Given that she hadn't mentioned train or bus times that day, it was safe to assume she was planning on spending the night, meaning she'd need to change the sheets. Annelise would be more than happy to share a bed with her, just providing it was clean. She recalled a time when Annelise had slept in a bed with baby vomit and other unidentifiable excretions around her. This was something she didn't bring up.

Opening her mouth, she was about to ask about her plans when the door buzzed. Only then did she note that she'd let the kettle fill well past the maximum line and turned off the tap.

"Are you expecting someone?" Annelise asked.

"No. I'm never expecting anyone," she said, only to recall her sister's arrival that morning and how positive she'd been that it was Jack standing outside her door. Her pulse kicked up a notch.

"Actually, I could be." She tipped some of the water out and placed the kettle back on the worktop before combing her fingers through her hair and heading into the living area. "How do I look?"

"You look like you. Good, you look good," Annelise said, with just a hint of confusion.

"Great. Great." Fleur's heart rate continued to rise, causing a nervous tingling to spread through her. The buzzer went again. Once, then twice. Was it her imagination or was a sense of excitement filtering through from it?

"Wish me luck," she said, as she headed through to the hall.

Whoever it was, couldn't be familiar with the idea of video doorbells. Either that or they didn't want to be seen. Currently, the only part of them visible was a mass of hair, entirely black and white on the colourless screen, and they were so close to the camera it was impossible to even tell if it was a man or woman. One thing was certain, though, it was far more hair than Jack had. The disappointment was only marginally less than it had been that morning. Fleur quashed it hurriedly and pressed the intercom button. The buzz on the outside speaker made her visitor jump.

"Hello," she said.

The person turned around in a circle before finally spotting the intercom camera and then staring directly into it.

Fleur's blood ran cold. "What are you doing here?" she said, making no attempt to hide her animosity.

The tiny image of Henry took a step back, his hands dug deep into his pockets. Despite his smart dress and height, she couldn't help but be reminded of a pouting toddler.

"I believe I owe you an explanation. And possibly an apology. Could I come up, please?"

Her teeth ground together. The way he spoke was enough to make her want to hit something. *And possibly an apology?* Was there no end to this man's arrogance?

"You don't owe *me* an apology. You owe your aunt one. A big one. Not to mention Grace at the pharmacy."

A hiss reverberated through the line as he took a deep breath.

"Please, if you could just let me explain. It will make sense; I promise. I just need to talk to you."

There was something in the way he said the word *need*. It was like when her sister had first mentioned living her life that morning. Fleur didn't know Henry very well at all, but she knew there was more to what he was saying. And that's when it clicked.

"Eunice sent you here, didn't she?"

He cleared his throat and looked awkward. Fleur was happy to know that however badly he might treat his aunt in public, the old woman still had the strength to send him out onto the street to put things right.

"Fine," she said after a suitable pause. "I'll hear you out. But only for her sake. Not for yours." And with that, she pressed the button and opened the downstairs door.

CHAPTER 24

*I*t took far longer for Henry to reach the top of the stairs and the door to Fleur's apartment than she expected. It was almost as if he was deliberately taking his time. Like he didn't want to face her.

When he finally arrived, his hands were out of his pocket, although the toddler-esque pout remained.

"Thank you. Thank you for hearing me out," he said as he stood in the doorway. "I owe you an explanation. Or at least, Eunice thinks I do."

Fleur raised her eyebrows. "I'll be honest, saying an elderly relative made you come here is a poor start to any apology."

"I will concede that is probably true." His lips twitched, though he paused before he spoke again. "May I come in?" he said, eventually.

Without a word, she turned her back on him and walked into the flat. A second later, the door clicked closed as he followed her inside.

In the living room, Annelise jumped to her feet. "Henry, isn't it?" she said. "Isn't this an unexpected surprise?"

Fleur had no doubt that this was tough enough for a man like him, but it was clear from his expression that he'd been expecting her to be there on her own. At the sight of her sister, that same vein protruded from his head.

"Sorry, I didn't catch your name earlier."

"Annelise. I'm Fleur's sister," she said, stretching out her hand. "Can I get you a coffee?"

"He doesn't need a coffee," Fleur cut in before he could reply. "He needs to say what he's come here for and then he can leave. You know, you're lucky I didn't contact someone after the way you treated you aunt in public. I could have rung the police."

"No, you couldn't," he replied. "Or if you had, they would have taken my side in the matter. Because whatever you think of me, I was trying to help her. To look after her."

"By stopping her from enjoying herself?"

"Do you ever let anyone else speak? I'm trying to explain to you, and you are refusing to listen."

The sudden rise in volume caught Fleur by surprise, though given how he spoke to Eunice, she wasn't sure why. She was glaring at him now, the very sight of his perfectly symmetrical face infuriating her.

"I'm going to put the kettle on, anyway" Annelise said. "Why don't you two sit down?"

"We're fine standing."

"We're fine standing."

They said in unison, only to turn to each other with the same look of surprise.

"Freaky," Annelise said, once again attempting to ease the tension. "Well, you guys stay standing then. I'm going to make us all a coffee. Possibly an Irish one."

With Annelise gone, the room felt uncomfortably quiet. So quiet, Fleur could hear her breath as it hissed in and out of her throat and her heartbeat as it drummed against her ear. She cursed how ridiculous this was. Who the hell was this man to make her feel this awkward in her own home? The sooner he was out of there, the better. And she would not be getting any lifts back from Book Club with him again, whether Eunice liked it or not.

"So, you have something to say to me?" she said. The sooner she got him talking, the sooner she could get him out of there.

"Yes, actually." His hands were back in his pockets. "Do you mind if I do sit down? I'm going to sit down. I hope that's okay?"

For the first time since they'd met, he was showing some basic manners, although it wasn't that which left Fleur so confused as much as his nervousness.

"Auntie Eunice asked me to come here and apologise, but the thing is, she also didn't want you to know the truth about why I got so upset. This has put me in a rather difficult position, because if I don't tell you the truth, you won't understand why I got so angry and thus why I reacted the way I did."

"You shouted at an old woman," Fleur said. "In no situation was that needed."

"Perhaps not, but ..." he paused. A greyness shadowed his eyes. He looked exhausted. He probably was if he spent all his Sundays at work. Still, it was hard to feel any sympathy for him.

"Auntie Eunice has diabetes. Type one."

"Diabetes?"

"Yes. But you can't tell the rest of her friends this, please. She prides herself on her independence. I'm sure she's told you her stories of trekking and backpacking around the world. She's embarrassed that this makes her look less capable. She doesn't want people treating her any differently because of it."

"Embarrassed?" Fleur said. "That's crazy. Why would she be embarrassed?"

"I have no idea. Trust me, I am fully aware of how ridiculous her behaviour is. But I think part of it is an age thing. The older she gets, the funnier she's become about it. She would rather sit there and eat enough chocolate cake to send her blood sugars through the roof, than admit to someone she needs to go and inject herself. I wish I could say her thinking is logical, but it's not."

He pressed his lips together and looked down. It was only then that Fleur realised she was still standing. Quietly, so as not to disturb his train of thought, she took a seat on the chair opposite him.

"My great-uncle got early-onset Alzheimer's," he continued. "I'm not sure if she told you that or not? Probably not. She doesn't like to talk about it."

"No, I didn't know. I'm so sorry."

"It was hard on her, of course it was, but it was more than that. She had to watch the man she loved, who had lived such an incredible life himself, become entirely dependent on other people. I think that was when she became so fearful of doing the same. Of being a burden, not that she could ever be that. She sees needing help as a sign of weakness. But the thing is, she does need help. Not lots, but sometimes. She forgets things. And it's been getting worse. That's the reason I moved back here. To keep an eye on her. There was an incident, you see. She forgot she'd already injected herself and gave herself too much insulin. Her blood sugar went dangerously low. It's a problem if it goes too high or too low. And to be fair, she's normally very good. She's been dealing with it all her life.

Long before a phone could monitor your levels. But I worry. A lot."

Things were suddenly starting to make sense. If too much sugar could be so damaging for Eunice, then seeing her with a plateful of chocolate cake and drinking fizzy, sugar-filled wine, was likely to have made him a nervous wreck.

"Was she okay today?" she asked, guilt cascading through her. "She must have had too much sugar. Were her glucose levels too high?"

"They were. We sorted them out when we got back home. But if I hadn't come and found her …" He shook his head. "The thing is, I never know for sure. I don't know if she's all right and I'm worrying too much or whether I should be more concerned than I am. You've met her; she seems fine. But if she has another accident like before, then … I just couldn't bear the thought of that happening because I wasn't on top of things. "

As Fleur looked at Henry, sitting on her sofa with his head in his hands, the guilt she'd felt only a moment before was replaced with something else. Sympathy. Deep-rooted sympathy. No wonder he always checked what his aunt had eaten and drunk.

"That day in the pharmacy," she said, "when you got angry with the woman for not having your medication, that was for Eunice, wasn't it?"

He nodded. "She needed a needle for her insulin pen. She'd moved the bag with them in and couldn't remember where she'd put it. It should have been in the pouch with the rest of the gear, but it wasn't. And I should have checked on it. I should have made sure we had the spares handy."

"But you got them? She was all right?"

"She was, but it's tough. I feel like one slip up is all it might take."

He lifted his gaze and his eyes met hers. She'd always considered herself a great judge of character and not purely on first impressions. Although, in her defence, Henry had been less than amicable on more than one occasion. Besides, this slightly redeeming feature of being a doting nephew didn't erase how rude he'd been about the Book Club and romance books. Nor how he had poo-pooed her relationship with Jack — even if he had been right about it. Still, as her heart throbbed with a low ache, part of her wanted to reach out and take his hand.

"I didn't know how you wanted your coffee, Henry. Milk? Sugar?"

It was as if Annelise's voice had broken a spell. Within a second, he was on his feet, brushing out invisible creases from his trousers. And Fleur was standing too, suddenly aware of how far away she now felt from him. With what was almost a smile, he turned to Annelise.

"Thank you, but I should go. I've already taken up enough of your time." And with that, he turned back to Fleur and held her gaze.

"I'm trusting that you will be discreet about what I've told you?"

"Of course," she said. "Of course, I will."

"Thank you."

Then, without another word, he turned on his heel and left.

CHAPTER 25

*T*he following week was a disjointed one. Annelise stayed until Monday afternoon, insisting Fleur take her out for lunch before she got the bus. Lunch for Annelise, however, started at eleven and ended at three, meaning that Fleur lost the best part of a day's work. Not that she minded. Catching up with her sister had made her realise she needed to start making more of an effort to get back to London and see the family now and then. It did mean, however, that she'd only had one full day of work before she headed up there on Wednesday for the fortnightly team "Anchor Meeting".

Surprisingly, she'd been far more okay with the whole Robert thing than she'd expected. It had occupied her thoughts for a fair amount of time — probably about eighty percent of her waking hours, with the rest being filled with thoughts of Eunice and Henry — but she hadn't collapsed into a complete sobbing mess the way she would have once done. She'd even managed to hold back the tears when their first wedding-dance song came on the in-store radio when she was buying her groceries. Moving on was part of life, and she was okay with that, she told herself every time thoughts of him infiltrated her day. And she was telling herself that again as she checked her reflection in the mirror that morning having picked out a pair of green heels with purple bows to wear.

Gone were the days of Fleur enjoying heading to London for work. When she'd been young and fresh out of university, she'd loved it. She had loved standing on the tube in her heels with her pricey bag slung over her shoulder, feeling like she had really made it. She wasn't a student anymore. She was living and working in the big smoke. A city girl. She had revelled in it, in fact, but now she felt like a fish out of water.

As much as she hated to agree with Annelise, she couldn't dispute that Maldon not having a train station was a pain. The bus went from the top of town at an ungodly hour, and the train was always crammed full of commuters by the time it arrived at Chelmsford. She could never find a seat, and even when she did, people had no awareness of how much room they were taking up, spreading their legs into her space or else slinging their bags over their shoulders without checking who or what was behind them. Still, she didn't have to go in that often, and it was nice to catch up with real people, rather than talking to buffering images on a screen.

The morning in London was spent much the same way as in Maldon: long sections of time glued to her computer with occasional breaks at the coffee machine. The afternoon was all about the meeting, led by her line manager, Paul.

"Okay guys, I've seen some great numbers this month. Seriously good. Great work on that new account, Jeff. And Dan, really impressed with the ROI on your latest add spend."

He was a man who needed to give praise regularly and evenly. By the time meetings were over, everyone would have received at least three compliments, regardless of whether they deserved them or not. While she knew it irritated some people, she liked it. After all, it didn't do any harm to big people up now and then.

Sitting at the far end of the conference table, she was doodling away on her notepad, her thoughts constantly wandering to Henry and Eunice. It must be so hard, she kept thinking, to watch someone you love deteriorate in front of you. And why on earth did Eunice feel the need to keep something like that hidden? Surely, having people around her who knew about her diabetes would be a good thing. It certainly would have made Fleur think twice before filling up her glass with Prosecco.

"So, we'll wrap things up there and catch up again at the end of next month. Unless anyone's got AOB?"

Fleur's attention returned to the meeting at the acronym. Any Other Business meant they were near the end and given how everyone in the room, other than Paul, worked at home, there was almost zero chance of them wanting to prolong it. As such, she readied herself to leave.

"Great. Then I'll see you all next week. Fleur, if you could just hang on for a minute?"

She paused in an awkward, half-standing pose. "Me?" she said, despite there not being any other Fleurs on the team.

"I won't keep you long."

While the rest of her colleagues filtered out of the room, she remained standing behind her chair, tapping her feet nervously. It wasn't that she thought it would be anything bad. She could do her job, and probably Paul's too, with her eyes shut, but the longer she had to hang around, the later she'd be getting to the tube and then the station at the other end. She'd been hoping to get a seat so she could finish the book the girls had chosen for the next meeting.

"Fleur, why don't you close the door and take a seat?"

She withheld a groan; you didn't need to take a seat for a quick meeting.

Moving from his place at the head of the table, Paul pulled out a chair next to her and turned it around so he could look straight at her.

"Fleur, a new job has come up in marketing. A good position in middle management. I know from your resumé it's what you did before. And I think you'd be perfect for it."

"Thank you," she said, shifting uneasily. "But I like what I'm doing."

"Please, hear me out."

A spark of irritation lit within her. If she were some young, up-and-coming, new graduate, then she would have given whatever he was going to say consideration. But she was nearly forty. She could already predict what was coming next.

"As much as I enjoy having you in my department, you must be aware that you're wasting your talents in your current position."

She smiled, trying not to show how irritated she was, having her time wasted like this.

"I don't want to come across as rude or ungrateful. But I like my life now. I have balance and I enjoy working from home. I like the flexibility."

"I thought you'd say that, but you could do this job remotely, too. And pick your hours, the same as now. It doesn't even have to be a full-time position. I've spoken to the Head of Marketing, and she's happy to discuss all of that with you."

"Thank you. I will think about it."

She moved to stand but had barely pushed back her chair when Paul spoke again.

"I don't get it," he said. "I really don't. You work so hard at a job that doesn't even fulfil you. With your skill set, what I'm suggesting would be less work for nearly double the money. And you don't even want to consider it?"

"I said I'd think about it."

"You've said that to every promotion I've mentioned, and yet you've not handed in a single application."

She pressed her lips together. Calling people out wasn't something Paul normally did. Or at least not that she'd seen.

"If that's everything, I need to head back," she said, attempting to dismiss his last comment despite its sting. "You know, rush hour."

He nodded. "I know. You should get going. I'll send the details through to you, though. The deadline for applications is a week Tuesday."

"See you in a fortnight, Paul," she said, not looking at him as she left. She had a train to catch.

CHAPTER 26

a s Fleur headed out of the office, she couldn't help but think about what Paul had said and how he couldn't understand why someone wouldn't grab any opportunity to climb the career ladder. But he was young, she reminded herself. Younger than her, at least.

Back on the street, she pulled her phone out of her handbag, only to see an avalanche of messages filling the screen, all of which were from the same number. Annelise's.

"You have to be kidding," she muttered, reading the first one.

Somewhat naively, she'd hoped that, given all the drama of the weekend, her sister would have dropped the idea of a fortieth birthday bash, particularly as she hadn't mentioned it at all early in the week. Unfortunately, she was making up for it now.

I've got some locations for you to check out.

What do you think about Liverpool? It's a bit different, but I hear great things.

You want an adult only do, right?

If you can just give me a rough idea of numbers, then we can confirm the guest list for certain when we've got a venue, the last one read.

Numbers, Fleur thought with a groan. Had it been five years ago, when she and Robert were happily married, her fortieth birthday do would probably have been as big as a wedding. There would've been people from both his and her workplaces, all with their spouses. There would've been the friends they'd made through college and university, plus the random couples they'd met on their travels, like the one they'd shared a bus trip with around Rome. Five years ago, this would've been the bash to end all bashes. But now? Who was there she really wanted to celebrate with?

According to her social media, she had over two hundred friends, and a lot of them would send messages on her birthday. But they rarely met up anymore. And she couldn't entirely blame the divorce for that. If she was honest, she'd begun to isolate herself long before the papers were signed, retreating from friendships as an act of self-preservation more than anything else. There were only so many baby showers and christenings she could go to before it would wear her down completely. But now things were different. She'd found peace in her own company, and she really wasn't that lonely at all. Provided she didn't think about it for too long.

I'll let you know, she replied, only for a response to ping through before she could put her phone away.

I'll ring tomorrow.

Speak then. Love you.

Fleur was still thinking about her friendships and all those people she had once been so close to, as she boarded the tube. People come into your life for a reason, a season or a lifetime. That was what one of her work friends had told her once. And the saying had stuck with her, unlike the colleagues whose names she could no longer remember. She obviously didn't have as many lifetime friends as other people.

While she didn't get a seat on the tube, it was only three stops before she'd change for the overground to Chelmsford, and then it would be one bus home to Maldon. It was funny how quickly she'd come to think of Maldon as home. That little flat. The walks by the water. She really could envisage building her forever life there. If only she had someone to build it with.

As much as she wished otherwise, she knew she needed to accept that Jack had well and truly ghosted her. So, as she stood there on the tube, she did what she had to, deleting his number and messages from her phone, just so she couldn't call him out on such a cowardly move. Scrubbing him from her phone and life hadn't hurt that much, she noticed, as his digital footprint disappeared before her eyes. But it didn't erase that hollowness inside her.

As the tube reached her stop, she shimmied her way past some stubbornly sessile commuters and stepped onto the platform, only to note the overhead clock. "Time to get a move on," she muttered under her breath. The meeting with Paul had delayed her, but she could still catch the early train, provided she ran to the next platform. Unfortunately, her ability to do this was hindered by her choice of footwear.

"Damn heels," she said, as she tried to pick up the pace. Next time she came to London, she would put a pair of flat pumps in her bag, or else wear them the whole time. How was it that a couple of years ago she could race up and down steps in these things, and now even a jog had her terrified of falling flat on her face? After the platform came the first set of steps, heading downwards. She skimmed the handrail as she took them as quickly as possible, only to be surprised at how easily she managed it. As such, she quickened her pace further, while at the same time checking her phone and discovering she had only two minutes before the train left.

Two minutes to get to the next platform. She could do it, she told herself. She could do it. Her heart was pounding as the bottom of the staircase came into view. From there it was only a few metres up the next set of stairs and onto the platform. She was going to make it. She was determined. Feeling confident now, she took the last two steps in a leap. One which turned out to be just a fraction too short.

It was her right heel that didn't quite make it, as it caught on the edge of the final step. Her entire body lurched forwards as she reached out to grab the handrail beside her. But the angle was off, and her palms slipped against the cold metal. What happened next was inevitable. Her knees went down first, slamming against the concrete with a thud. The rest of her quickly followed.

"Oh my God, are you okay?"

"Wow, it's all right. Steady now."

"I've got you."

Several pairs of hands reached down to help her, though Fleur was too embarrassed to take them.

"I'm fine. I'm fine," she kept saying, desperately trying to hoist herself up, while blinking back the tears which burned her eyes. Her knees were throbbing, and her hands stung from the impact, but most of the pain came from pure humiliation. "Honestly, I'm fine. I really am," she repeated.

A small crowd had gathered, and she looked around, trying to smile, but her eyes stopped moving as she heard someone speak. Through all the hubbub and the rumbling of trains overhead, this male voice was so clear it could have just been the two of them in the entire space. Not that he was addressing her.

"We should go and find mummy," it said.

Fleur stared. His hair was shorter than it had been the last time she'd seen him, but somehow it made him look younger, perhaps because it reminded her of their early years together. He was wearing jeans and had, slung over his shoulder, a large and decidedly feminine bag, although that didn't hold her attention for long. Her gaze moved to the fabric carrier that was strapped across his chest. There, looking out at the world, was a baby.

Her hand flew to her mouth as her eyes filled with tears, and at that exact moment, he turned and looked straight at her.

"Robert," she said.

CHAPTER 27

*P*eople continued to look on with concern, worried that she might have banged her head or broken an ankle, but Fleur wasn't paying them any attention. She just stared at Robert. Robert and his baby.

"Are you okay?" his voice was tentative, as if he was afraid of speaking to her.

"I'm fine. Fine." She brushed down her skirt and forced herself up. "I have to go. My train. I need to get my train."

Her throat was dry, the pain of her knees now surpassed by the ache behind her ribs. All she wanted was for her legs to carry her as far away from this as possible, but her feet were frozen to the spot. Her eyes locked on the soft downy-covered head which was protruding from the top of the carrier.

"It's good to see you—"

"It's good to see you too, Robert," she replied, unable to take the pain of his formality. "Congratulations."

Ignoring the searing heat that gripped her body, she turned and hobbled up the stairs towards her platform.

"Fleur!" she heard him call out, his voice once again cutting through the noise of all the busy commuters.

She so wanted to turn around. To march back to him and ask why. Why hadn't she been enough for him? Why had he never envisaged having a family with her? What did this other woman have that she didn't? Bitter tears lodged in her throat. She nearly stumbled and had to grip the handrail tighter as she stepped up to the platform ... just in time to see her train leaving.

The next one wasn't due for another forty minutes. Time she would normally have spent happily reading a book. All she could think about, as she sat on the platform, was Robert and his child. He'd said they were going to find mummy and Fleur's head spun with images, envisioning their perfect family life. Perhaps they were going away for a long weekend somewhere romantic and child friendly with a spa and a crèche. Maybe Robert had brought the baby into the city to meet up with someone, like his sister. After all, they might have grown closer now that they both had children. Images of family barbecues and Christmases now arrived in her mind. The type of event she'd imagined herself being part of for so long, that she had assumed she would be part of. But now that was never going to happen for her.

By the time the train arrived, dark clouds were threatening rain, though it wasn't until they had passed Stratford that it began. It wasn't much more than a light shower to start with, but the closer they got to Chelmsford, the heavier it became, and by the time she stepped off the train, it was hammering down with such force, it was bouncing off the ground.

"Where are you?" she muttered, digging in her bag for her umbrella. She was sure she'd put it in there a couple of weeks ago. Or had she? She should get a larger one, so she could find it quickly when she needed it. She rummaged again, digging her hand in a little deeper, only for her phone to drop out and land with a thud on the ground.

"For crying out loud!"

Several eyes turned in her direction and people gave her a wide berth as they stepped around her. She picked the phone up, wiped the sodden screen and saw the cracks running from corner to corner.

"Perfect. Just perfect."

With the broken phone and the torrential rain came more tears. And these weren't silent ones, like when she'd fallen over and seen Robert. They were heaving, wheezing, embarrassing sobs that she couldn't control, no matter how hard she tried.

"Pull yourself together, Fleur," she said, wiping the screen again to assess just how bad the damage was. Very bad, was the conclusion she came to.

Abandoning all hope of finding the umbrella, she slung her bag over her shoulder and raced as fast as she was able, towards the station exit. Not only was Maldon lacking a train station, but the buses from Chelmsford to home weren't nearly as regular as she would have liked. While the bus and train stations were only two minutes' walk apart, running between them was the only way of ensuring she didn't find herself with a twenty-minute wait. Today, that would have been more than she could take.

She stumbled forwards, only for her ankle to start throbbing with a new intensity, causing her to limp. To make matters worse, she had another set of steps to deal with, and all she could think about was how much steeper they seemed than the previous ones and how much more it would hurt if she fell down these, too. Holding her breath, she grabbed the rail and took them as quickly as she could, only to slow down, feeling that she was going to tumble again. When she reached the pavement, she stared ahead at the bus station. There, waiting at the stop with its bright number 31 illuminated, was her bus.

"Don't go!" she yelled, steeling herself against the pain as she started running again. "Don't go!"

She reached the road, desperate to cross, only to find a constant stream of one-way traffic. She just needed a break in the cars coming towards her, that was all. A little gap and she would dash across and make it. But none came, and as she stood there, with water pouring down her face, she watched her bus departing, confirming the horrendousness of the day. And then, as Sod's Law would have it, just seconds after it had disappeared around the corner, a car stopped to let her cross.

"Perfect, just perfect," she hissed, shaking her head as she waved at the driver, indicating that he should keep going. But instead of driving on, as she'd expected, he tooted his horn and turned his hazard warning lights on. A moment later, the window rolled down.

"Do you want a lift?" Henry asked.

CHAPTER 28

*I*t was a matter of pride and the fact that Fleur no longer felt like she had any. A week ago, she would have refused a lift with Henry anywhere, out of principle. But a fair bit could change in seven days. And if it was a choice of a twenty-five-minute car journey with him or waiting twenty minutes for a bus and having to sit on the hard seats soaking wet next to someone she didn't know, she was just going to have to suck it up. Besides, she hadn't heard anything from Eunice, and it would be good to check how she was doing.

She climbed into his car. The moment he spoke, she wondered if she had made the right choice.

"Are you okay?" he asked. "You look terrible?"

The first thing out of his mouth was rude, of course it was, and she wanted nothing more than to insult him back, to come up with some witty quip that would knock him down a peg or two. But instead, the tears she'd been trying so hard to hold back cascaded down her face. And it wasn't anything to do with her painful knees and hands or the fact that her phone was smashed. It was about life. About Robert and his wife and baby. He had moved on. And she had tried so hard to, but it had been impossible. Why couldn't she be like him? She hadn't even found anyone who liked her enough to go on a date with her, let alone have a baby with. And she wasn't young anymore. What was it they called women her age who got pregnant? That was it. If she was to have a baby now, she'd be a flipping geriatric mother.

"Sorry, I didn't mean … I was just saying …" Henry stumbled over his words, and Fleur wanted to tell him it was okay. It wasn't him who'd upset her. But she was struggling to get a decent breath in, let alone speak.

"I …. I …" She attempted to stem her tears and say something intelligible, but it wasn't happening. She was a blubbering mess.

To say he looked awkward would have been an understatement. He kept his eyes on the road, though they'd occasionally flick towards her, each time a look of concern mingled with trepidation on his face.

"I'm … I'm sorry. It's been a rough day," she managed, eventually.

"I gathered that much," he said. "There are tissues in the glove box."

"There are?"

He nodded and leaned over, flicking it open. There inside were several pocket packets.

"Auntie Eunice insists. She has a thing about always being prepared. I think it comes from her travelling days. There's a first aid kit in there, too."

Noting that there was indeed a red plastic box with a white cross on it, Fleur pulled out a pack of tissues, took one out and blew her nose, noisily. After which, she took another one and wiped her eyes. Given the mass of black smudges that appeared on the paper, she couldn't imagine how much of a mess she must look.

"I'm sorry about that. Bad day," Fleur said, when she'd cleared herself up enough to speak.

"Do you want to talk about it?"

"Trust me, you don't want to hear." Assuming he was only being polite, unusual in itself, she was surprised that, rather than accepting her initial response, he repeated the offer.

"It might do you good to talk about it. Besides, I'm a good listener," he said, with most unexpected genuineness.

"Honestly, you don't want to hear what a mess my life is right now."

"Maybe not," he agreed. "But I do want a drink, and by the looks of things, I think you could do with one, too. Besides, you owe me for the bus fare you've just saved." He paused. "How about when we get to Maldon, we stop off for a quick one? Then, if you feel like telling me what got you in such a state, you can."

Fleur was about to refuse, when something made her stop. Judging from their last two conversations, Henry wasn't quite the villain she'd initially imagined him to be, even if he was somewhat curt. Maybe another argument with him would be just what she needed to push thoughts of Robert and the baby out of her mind. There was no denying she could do with a drink and, as he'd rightly said, he had saved her the fare.

"Okay," she said, despite her better judgement. "A drink sounds good."

CHAPTER 29

*H*enry didn't believe in fate. To him, it was up there with soul mates and true love and the Tooth Fairy. From an early age, he wouldn't accept that anyone or anything was in control of his life, other than himself. As such, he'd refused to read books or watch films which even hinted at any form of *destiny.* But at that moment, it was hard to believe there wasn't some higher force intervening.

Fleur had been playing on his mind all week. He'd thought back to that first meeting in the pharmacy and then the way he'd treated her when Eunice insisted he drove her home from the Book Club. Mainly, though, he'd remembered her reaction to hearing about Eunice's diabetes.

"Why did you say anything? I don't want other people knowing my business," Eunice had scolded when Henry had returned from apologising to Fleur the previous Sunday. "You knew I didn't want her told about that."

"It's not a big deal," he'd replied. "And she wouldn't believe my apology was genuine unless I explained. Besides, you don't need to worry. She's not going to tell anyone else. And I trust her."

And that was it. That was the other reason he couldn't get her out of his mind. Even now, he could recall with perfect clarity that look of deep, unwavering sympathy she had given him. As if she had truly understood the constant worry that afflicted his daily life. She hadn't said anything, but maybe that was why he knew she understood, because she hadn't felt the need to pry or prod or load him with false condolences. Instead, she'd looked at him as though she'd wanted to take his hand, and surprisingly, he had wanted her to. He had actually wanted to take her hand, look into her eyes and promise her he would do better in the future. But before he could even attempt any of that, her sister had returned from the kitchen, and the moment was gone. But since then, he hadn't been able to stop thinking about it.

He was still thinking about that moment, and Fleur, as he was driving home from court when his mind should have been on all the upcoming cases he had to deal with. The traffic down the one-way street past the station was constant, but slow. When she appeared on the pavement, he had to do a double take, concerned he was hallucinating. His heart surged as he saw her standing there, drenched to the bone. She was obviously heading for a bus, and for all he knew, the next one might be about to arrive, but regardless, he couldn't leave her there. As such, he'd stopped and offered her a lift, and now there she was, sitting in his car, sobbing.

"Do you want to talk about it?" he said. Whatever had happened had been enough to shake her up badly, and the dripping wet woman who was currently wiping her nose on one of Eunice's emergency tissues was a long way from the Fleur he'd previously experienced. But as she snivelled and sniffed, he was overcome by the deepest desire to reach over, wrap his arms around her and make all the pain stop.

The thought had come out of nowhere. Shuddering, he attempted to shake off the image of them embracing. Maybe just talking about it would be enough. It had always helped his mum.

"I'm sorry, love," she would always say after one of his parents' fights. "It's over now." And then she would sit on the end of his bed and tell him all the reasons why she and his father had been bickering. She would say how they both still loved him very much and that it was just a rough patch and things would go back to normal soon enough. Apparently, she wasn't aware that, to Henry, the fighting *was* normal. Still, he'd always noted the change in his mother by the time she left his room after one of those chats. As if unburdening herself had somehow been enough to release a little of the pain she kept hidden inside.

So, he tried again. "It might do you good to talk about it. Besides, I'm a good listener."

Fleur's gaze lifted from her lap, and she looked straight at him. For a second, he thought she was about to take him up on the offer, but instead, she shook her head and let out a long sigh.

"Honestly, you don't want to hear about what a mess my life is right now."

A deep throbbing started in his chest. He realised he actually did. That moment in the flat had changed something, and now he wanted nothing more than to listen to her speak, no matter what she was saying. It was how to get her to see this, that he was having difficulty with. For someone who earned a living choosing the right words, he was struggling.

"Maybe not," he said, eventually. "But I do want a drink, and by the looks of things, I think you could do with one, too.

Besides, you owe me for the bus fare you've just saved." He immediately cursed himself. Why the hell had he added that last line? If she hadn't already thought that he was an arrogant arsehole, that must have clinched it.

Horrified at how he was coming across, he was wondering how he could take it back, when he glanced at Fleur and noticed the smile on the corner of her lips. "How about when we get to Maldon, we stop off for a quick one?" he said, needing to strike before the nerves took hold. "Then, if you feel like telling me what got you in such a state, you can."

It felt like forever between him asking and Fleur's answer, and he was fully anticipating her to decline the offer, but she didn't.

"Okay," she said, causing his heart to leap. "A drink sounds good."

CHAPTER 30

The rest of the journey had been notably quiet. Henry had flicked on the heated seats to warm her up, while Fleur gazed out of the window at the winding hedgerows and buzzards circling above the fields. Then before she realised it, they were taking the turning off the roundabout and heading into Maldon. She checked her watch. Had she needed to wait for a bus, she would just be leaving Chelmsford, then trundling around the various housing estates and one-way roads. There was no denying it: she owed Henry a drink.

"The Black Rabbit is just around the corner from you," he said, as they turned onto the High Street. "Do you go there much?"

"Much?" she said. "I've never been there before."

"Really?"

"Really."

"Fair enough. I've never been there, either. And it's not like I live that far away. It's meant to be nice, though. We can park at yours and walk across, if you're all right with that.?

"That's fine by me," she said. Her voice sounded peculiarly detached, as if she wasn't the one speaking.

Two minutes later, Henry had parked up on North Street, just a few doors down from Fleur's flat and was climbing out of the car.

The time spent sitting in the comfy, warm, leather, luxury of Henry's four-by-four had given her knees the opportunity to seize up, and as she stretched out her legs and tried to stand, she winced in pain.

"Are you okay?" he asked, hurrying around to her side.

"I'm fine. Just had a little tumble earlier, that's all."

"Part of the crappy day?"

"Just part of it," she said.

In one hand, he was holding a large umbrella, the type that were so big they inconvenienced anyone else who was sharing the pavement. He stretched out his other hand to Fleur. To stop her knees from hurting more than they already did and to avoid another fall, she took it. The effect was instant. The heat of his fingertips rushed up through her arm, like an electric shock from one of those buzzer games she'd bought Paxton for Christmas.

Henry dropped her hand. "It's just a short distance," he said, then avoiding her gaze, slammed the car door and started walking.

As they made their way towards the High Street, she tried to remember the last time she'd shared an umbrella with someone. She and Robert had, although their heights were so similar that when she'd been wearing heels, she'd needed to be the one carrying it, or he'd manage to catch her hair in the spokes. There wasn't that problem with Henry, though. He had to be at least six feet tall. A good height for holding an umbrella.

When they reached the High Street, they crossed over.

"After you," he said, holding open the pub door.

Before entering, she'd formed an image of what the place would look like. Dark wooden tables, dark wooden wheel-back chairs, dark slate tiled floors. In short, she had expected it to be a traditional, old place. As it happened, she couldn't have got it more wrong. While there were tiles on the floor, they weren't slate, or dark, but had uplifting, light patterns in a style you would expect in a Greek taverna rather than an Essex pub. A feature wall was covered in green foliage and there wasn't a wheel back chair in sight. Instead, a selection of plush, brightly coloured tub chairs surrounded the eclectic mix of tables.

"Why don't you grab a seat?" he said. "I'll get the drinks in."

After a brief deliberation, she made her way to a table in the corner and had just sat down when he arrived with the drinks.

"So, the fall was just one part of the bad day then," he said. "What else happened?"

"It wasn't just any fall," Fleur took a long sip from her wine. "I fell down a set of steps right in front of my ex-husband and his new baby."

"Ouch, that's got to be embarrassing."

"You could say that. Then, in a separate incident, I managed to smash my phone screen and to top it all off, my boss won't let go of the idea of me getting a promotion."

Remaining silent, he lowered his pint glass back to the table and let out a contemplative hum. "Ignoring the fact that you're obviously incredibly clumsy, why did you mention the job opportunity like it's a bad thing? That's what most people want, isn't it?"

"It's not that I wouldn't like the job," she cupped the bowl of the wineglass in her hand. "I don't know much about it, but my line manager thinks it would be right up my alley. And more money."

"And the problem is?"

She took a deep breath. How did she explain this without sounding crazy? There probably wasn't a way, but she suddenly had the desire to try. "My ex-husband — the one I saw with his baby — we broke up because he didn't want to have kids. Clearly, he does now, but that's not why I mention it." Her chest was tightening with memories she had battled to forget. But she wanted to get this out. More than that, she needed to.

"I knew he didn't want children — at least I thought he didn't — but he always said that I didn't either, deep down. We were career people was what he told me, and I'd never want to put mine on the back burner and that it wasn't possible to be a good mother and a highflier at the same time. I suppose I feel that if I go for the promotion, if I start thinking about having a proper career again, then it's like admitting the other thing will never happen."

"You mean having a family?"

She nodded. As painful as telling Henry the truth had been, she'd also found it more cathartic than expected. It was a truth she'd been holding onto for years now, not even discussing it with Annelise. With it all out in the open now, she waited for him to respond, but rather than speaking, he was resting his chin on his knuckles and looking at her. When he finally put his hands down and sat back in his seat, he spoke very succinctly.

"That's bullshit."

"Sorry?"

"That's just an idiotic thing to say. For your ex to say. There are plenty of women in my firm who have children. One is a full partner. I'm not saying it's easy, but then it shouldn't be easy for the dads, either. It should be a split responsibility, assuming that's what you want. I may not know you well, but I've seen enough of you to say that if there's something you want, you can have it. You can have it all."

There was something about the way he spoke, no humour, no pomposity, just factual straight-talking, that struck Fleur right behind the ribs. Like he didn't doubt she really could have it all if she wanted. But what did he know? They'd barely even spoken to each other before last weekend.

"It's all a moot point now, anyway," she said, fighting back the heat that was once again building in her eyes. "Sooner or later, I'm going to have to accept that my childbearing days are over."

"Wow. Wow. Well, there's optimism for you. In fact, I think this is possibly one of the most depressing conversations I've ever had. And that's saying something."

"Hey!" She slapped him lightly on the arm. "You're the one who said you wanted to go for a drink, even though I was a sobbing, snivelling mess."

"You're quite right. But you're not a snivelling mess now, are you? Which confirms what I already knew; I am always right."

With her fingers running up and down the stem of her wineglass, she leaned in closer. "I can't work you out," she said, narrowing her eyes. "There's a part of you that's obviously caring and nice. The way you look after your aunt, the way you helped me tonight. But then there's the other side of you. I know why you got upset at the pharmacy and everything, but it wasn't exactly nice."

Henry picked up his drink, though rather than drinking, his lips twisted tightly together. "I know. And I don't want to make excuses about how I've acted, but yelling and fighting was part of the way I grew up. It was my parents' main form of communication with each other. And with me a lot of the time. And I hate it. I hate that side of me that comes out when something inside just snaps. I hate being like them. But once I've started—" He shuddered.

It was such a small action, but it tugged so deeply on Fleur's heartstrings, it was almost painful. She could see all the demons he was carrying within him. All the burdens he couldn't shake, and another spark of sympathy lit within her. If she wasn't careful, she would find herself liking the guy.

With the noise of the pub around them, she didn't realise that they'd fallen into silence until Henry spoke and broke it.

"You and your sister seem close?" he said, with a notable shift in tone. "That must be nice?"

"It is. It really is. She's frustrating at times. I'm mean, she lives the type of life I could only dream of: two children, part-time job, full-time nanny, tennis buddies and yogilates."

"Yogilates?"

"I think it's a yoga-slash-Pilates type work out. Although I might have misinterpreted it. They might just drink milky coffee whilst in yoga positions."

While Fleur considered this joke fairly weak, it was enough to make Henry throw back his head and laugh; a response she met with mild shock. This was the first time she'd seen him do that, and it changed his entire demeanour. Dimples appeared in his cheeks, and his eyes creased up so tightly they nearly disappeared. It took a second to catch her breath from witnessing the sudden transformation before she could speak.

"What about you? Do you have siblings?" she asked.

"A brother, eight years older. He left home the minute he could, abandoning me to the toxicity of my parents. Needless to say, we're not close. I've got cousins and things, but Auntie Eunice is my main family. My parents ... well, they know I've moved here but they've made no attempt to visit. Not me or Eunice."

That sensation was back again. The one that felt like his words were pulling directly at her heart strings. "If it makes you feel any better, my mother was very disappointed at my divorce," she said, lifting her glass to her lips, only to discover it was already empty.

"Disappointed? Not supportive?"

"No. Well I suppose she did attempt to be. But she didn't think I'd tried hard enough. She loved Robert, which is funny considering how Annelise couldn't stand him. She always thought he was smarmy, which, coming from the circles she moves in, is saying something. But my mother thought he was the bee's knees. Truth be told, I think she wishes she got to keep him after the divorce."

"I don't believe that. Not for one second."

Henry reached across the table and touched Fleur's hand. Just like before, a bolt of electricity shot through her, only this time she didn't move away. As her eyes locked on his, she knew, without a doubt, he had felt it, too, from his dilated pupils, shallowing breathing and slightly parted lips, which she couldn't take her eyes off. The thought of leaning closer and kissing them flashed through her mind.

With a sharp intake of breath, she pulled back her hand and sat up straight, hoping decent posture would erase the thought that had gallingly struck her.

"So, what about you?" she said. "Do you have a girlfriend? Boyfriend? Wife? Husband?"

A slow smile twitched on his lips. Just enough to cause the dimples to reappear.

"No, I am officially terrible at relationships. Besides if I had any of those, I think I'd be in an awful lot of trouble out here with you."

"Why? We're just having a drink." She spoke as casually as she could, trying to ignore the heat that was building.

"I'm glad that policeman never called you back," he said, quietly.

He was staring straight at her, his gaze so deep her pulse ticked higher and higher.

"How do you know he didn't?"

Her heart was drumming now. A nervousness building like a thunderstorm about to break.

"If he had, you would have already told me about it," he replied. "Or at the very least, you would have called him to tell him about your bad day. But you haven't. And like I said, I'm glad."

Fleur wasn't sure when it had happened, but she had somehow shifted closer to him. Their knees were only centimetres away from touching beneath the table, and her hand, that she had previously snatched away from him, was now palm down on the table, their fingertips millimetres apart. There was no denying it; she wanted to kiss him. And the way he was looking at her, he wanted to kiss her, too.

"This would be a very bad idea," she said, feeling herself moving involuntarily further towards him. "A disaster waiting to happen."

"And I do not deal well with disasters."

"I should probably head home."

"Me too."

Neither of them moved.

CHAPTER 31

"What do you mean, you nearly kissed him?"

Fleur was barely in the door before she'd picked up the phone and called Annelise, who'd answered on her second try. "How could you nearly kiss someone you hate?"

"I don't know. I'm not sure I do hate him anymore. Besides, it was a bad day. A really bad day. I saw Robert. And the baby."

"Jeez …" Annelise uttered the word on a breath that reverberated down the line. A pause followed as both sisters figured out what to say next. In the end, it was Annelise who spoke.

"Did you speak to him?"

"Not really," Fleur replied. "I'd just fallen down the steps at the station in front of a ton of people. And he was carrying his baby in a carrier, like he was some househusband or modern dad. How do you go from not wanting to have a child to being a guy who wears one strapped to his chest?" It wasn't a rhetorical question. She must have asked herself it at least a hundred times. Unfortunately, her sister didn't have any answers, either.

"Well, at least you didn't have to listen to him talk about his ultramarathons," Annelise said in an up-beat voice. "I don't know how you stood him rabbiting on about all that stuff. Although, I guess all the training kept him out of the house. That's probably how you managed to stay married to him for so long."

Fleur would have liked to laugh at this, but she couldn't help but wonder if it had been the other way around. If the reason Robert spent so much time outside was because he wanted to be away from her.

Another silence threatened, but before it could take root, Annelise shifted the conversation back to the original reason Fleur had called.

"So, this thing with Henry, do you think it was a rebound from seeing Robert? A moment of insanity?"

"Possibly. Maybe. I don't know. I gave him my telephone number?"

"What? Why?"

"I don't know. He asked for it, and I was too flustered to say no."

This was only a partial lie. She had been flustered. After she'd fought off the desperate urge to kiss him, she'd somehow found the strength to stand up and move away from the table, and he had insisted on leaving with her, given that his car was parked so close to her flat. The rain had finished by this point, and without needing to share the umbrella, she ensured they were walking far enough apart that their fingers couldn't accidentally touch. But that didn't stop her thinking about it or wondering if perhaps he might ask for her phone number. Which he did, in case she got caught out in the rain again, was what he'd said. Though they both knew that wasn't the case.

"I don't expect he'll message," she said, remembering that her sister was still on the line. "He was probably just being polite. I doubt I'll even hear from him."

As it happened, Henry messaged her the very next morning, just as Fleur was fixing her first coffee of the day.

There is a phone place on the High Street. They'll fix your screen for you. I've told them to expect you. They owe me.

It seemed very abrupt, but given how he spoke, she wasn't sure why this surprised her. She also wasn't sure if she was grateful or annoyed. Getting the screen fixed on her phone was on her to-do list for the day, and she didn't need him telling her when and where she should do it. But it was still nice that he thought of her. Wasn't it?

What was equally disconcerting was how early he'd contacted her. At 8 a.m. she was still in her dressing gown and had another hour to go before her first meeting of the day. How he'd sorted out someone to fix her phone when nowhere was even open was a mystery to her. Still, she wasn't going to think about it yet.

The morning was filled with meetings and data entry, followed by more data entry and another meeting. By the time lunchtime rolled around, she was desperate to stretch her legs. Outside, the skies were entirely clear, and a cold, crisp breeze whipped at her as she headed up the High Street. Her aim had been to go to the zero-waste shop first. She had recently fallen in love with their grapefruit body wash and was contemplating trying the charcoal toothpaste tablets. However, before she turned off into the alleyway, she caught sight of the phone shop on the other side of the road. Standing by the traffic lights, she hesitated.

The last thing she wanted was to feel any more beholden to Henry than she already was, and she'd had experience with Eunice of how controlling he could be. But she knew the reason for that now; it came from a place of good intentions. And she would hate to come across as rude or ungrateful.

Thirty minutes later, she was wandering through M&S with a bottle of grapefruit body wash, thirty toothpaste tablets and a mobile with a very sparkly, un-cracked screen.

All fixed she messaged Henry. *What did you do for this guy? No charge and he threw in a new phone case too.*

Unexpectedly, he replied immediately. *Things too dark to mention.*

Fleur chuckled to herself. It was strange understanding now that he did have a sense of humour and hearing it coming across in his words. Not seeing any point in waiting, she fired off a laughing-face emoji, only to have another message ping straight back.

I hope today is going better.

I don't think it could've gone any worse, but yes, thank you.

That felt like an end text. There was no question and no need for him to respond, but it felt too abrupt. She wasn't ready to stop talking to him so quickly.

What about you? How's your day going?

Immediately, she regretted the decision. He didn't seem like the type of guy who wanted to be asked this. And if he did reply, it was almost certainly going to be with a single word such as *Fine*. That was what she thought, until the three dots of an impending message flashed on her screen. With her shopping basket hanging over the crook of her arm and her shoulder getting chillier and chillier from the cold air of the refrigerator beside her, she fixed on the dots and waited for a response.

Currently in discussions as to who gets the dogs versus who gets the children. And they are not arguing the way you would imagine.

She stared at the message. It was definitely the type that

warranted a reply. Smiling to herself, she ambled away from the chilled food and typed.

Are they cute dogs? And horrible teenagers? If it's cute dogs versus moody kids, I completely get wanting the dogs.

And here was me thinking you were so maternal.

I am. It's just my maternal instincts haven't yet reached the level of teenager.

Fair enough. Then he sent a :-) emoji. *Now I need to work. And unless I'm mistaken, you have a job application to write???*

Her hands hovered over the phone as she considered what to send next. She had thought about what he'd said about applying, and Paul had sent through the job description, but so far, she hadn't opened the file. If she really was adamant about not taking the position, then why would reading it matter? In the pit of her stomach, she knew the truth, because if she did, she might find herself wanting it.

She was about to put away the phone when another message came through.

How's this for a deal? When you get the job, I'll take you out for dinner to celebrate.

Her pulse rocketed as she read and re-read his words. Had she got it right? Was the arrogant Mr Pierce genuinely asking her out?

CHAPTER 32

*T*he late afternoon sun glowed a deep burnt umber as, one by one, the men and women in the office abandoned their desks and headed home.

"Bye, Henry." One of the legal secretaries poked her head around the door, offering a short wave. "Don't stay too late, will you? I'm sure you've already done more than enough today."

"Have a good night, Rula," he said, lifting his head briefly from his computer. "Thank you for all your help today."

"That's what I'm here for. Try not to work too hard. See you tomorrow."

She offered another short wave before disappearing down the hallway, leaving him to get on, though as he gazed blearily at his screen, he struggled to remember what he'd been doing. It had been that type of day. A Monday-spent-treading-water day, where every time he'd finished one job, another three would spring up out of nowhere.

Leaning back in his chair, he cracked his knuckles and gazed at his phone, willing it to make a sound. It was no longer the beep of Eunice's glucose monitor he was listening out for. Ever since their drink at the pub, he and Fleur had been sending each other little, light-hearted messages, such as him making derogatory comments about her obscenely colourful shoes and her coming back with equally cutting insults, but it made him smile. In fact, just thinking about her made him smile. But as he stared at her last text, he let out a low groan and his face took on a look of deep-set despondency. *What are you doing here, Henry?* he said to himself, rubbing his temples.

The truth was, it didn't matter how much he liked her or how much her messages amused him, he was leading her on. He knew she was a woman who dived headfirst into love. A hopeless romantic to the very core. And yet here he was, unable to resist replying to her.

The groan that left his lips this time was even louder than the first and he massaged his temples with even more vigour, as if by pressing hard enough, he could erase the images of Fleur that constantly infiltrated his thinking: her standing there, drenched, in the rain; their hands touching; her eyes looking up at him. He was torturing himself. It didn't matter how much he liked her, he couldn't bring her into his life, knowing that she would never be number one. She deserved more than that, especially after the previous idiot she'd been with. She should find someone who would make her their priority, and that was more than he could give. Which raised the question: why did he keep on messaging her?

Deciding to call it a night, he packed up his things, turned off his light and headed out. Like every other weekday he didn't head straight home. Quite a few times since moving to Maldon, he'd wondered whether it was actually worth him renting his own place, given how little he was there. The fully furnished living room was practically untouched, and the only thing the dining chairs had been used for was as a dumping ground for the piles of books he brought home from the office. He hadn't ever used the rolltop bath, for both environmental and time-saving reasons, and the only items in the entire house that had been used regularly were the bed, the coffee machine and the shower. But he couldn't let it go just yet. That was a discussion he and his aunt needed to have first.

"Is that you, Henry?" Eunice called, as he opened her front door and stepped inside. He pulled off his coat, smiling to himself. After all, it was unlikely to be anyone else letting themselves into her house at seven thirty on a Monday evening. Not that he was the only person who had a key.

After her fall last year, he'd arranged for a cleaner to come in three times a week, partially to tidy, but also as preparation. Right now, Eunice was still independent. She regularly went for walks around Maldon on her own — no matter how much he would rather she didn't — and cooking meals for him was a highlight of her day, but a time would come when she'd need more help. Getting her used to having someone around the house would hopefully ease the transition. That was his thinking, at least, although Eunice would probably throw a spanner in the works, knowing her.

"Yes, it's me, Auntie Eunice," he called.

"Fabulous. I've roasted us pork loin for dinner. It's just done."

With his coat hung up and shoes off, he breathed in the aroma of the meat and over-boiled broccoli. *Just done.* The term had a very different meaning to her than to him. Upon entering the kitchen, he went straight to the hob, where a saucepan was boiling away. The water, barely two inches deep, was now more darkly coloured than the vegetables were. He turned the hob off and moved the pan away from the heat, before kissing his aunt on the cheek.

"You know I bought you those bags of veg that can go straight into the microwave," he said. "That way, you don't have to worry about the water boiling over."

"Oh, don't fuss," she said, pushing past him to grab a colander from the cupboard. "I'm perfectly capable of boiling a few greens. Besides, the microwave ones don't cook properly. They're always too hard."

Knowing it wasn't worth arguing over, he grabbed the plates and laid them on the dining table, then fetched cutlery from the drawer.

"So," Eunice said, when the pair of them were both seated. "Have you been up to anything exciting this week?"

Henry was chewing slowly through his pork loin. How a woman could make meat so hard and vegetables so soft was a mystery to him. But she cooked it for him lovingly. Besides, it meant he didn't have to do it himself, so he was hardly going to complain. He offered her a withering look. "Since yesterday? No, just the same old same old."

"Well, I had a lovely start to the week. I went for a walk. Which reminds me, I've arranged to meet Nina at the library tomorrow afternoon, so you don't need to take me to Book Club."

"Oh." The news struck Henry unexpectedly hard. Book Club was going to be his excuse to see Fleur. To drop her home. Maybe walk her to her door this time and ask if she wanted to go for another drink sometime. "Do you want me to pick you up, though?"

The old woman shook her head. "No, it's not a problem. Nina has said she'll drop me back, too."

He speared another piece of meat, knowing there was nothing else he could say without his aunt sensing that something was up. Even now, she was eyeing him suspiciously.

"I thought you'd be pleased. You get the evening to yourself."

"Yes ... Yes, that's good."

"And no more chauffeuring Fleur around, either?" she said, very obviously fishing.

"You're right," he agreed, turning his attention back to his food and avoiding her gaze. He could still feel her eyes boring into him as he dragged his knife through the meat and attempted to swallow the lump that seemed to have got stuck in his throat. This was a good thing. Hadn't he been telling himself all week that he and Fleur were non-starters? That messing around with her like he had been was a bad idea? Not seeing her was exactly what he needed. Now he just had to try and stop messaging her, too.

CHAPTER 33

*F*leur walked down to the riverside, a nervous bubbling going on inside her. This meeting was going to be different for several reasons. It was the first time she had attended one at the café, and the thought of being there in their own private venue, with the door sign saying *Closed* was unexpectedly exciting. And this was going to be the first time she'd seen Eunice since learning about her diabetes. No longer would she buy the line about her phone beeping because of a dodgy battery. Or watch her top up her wine without wondering what number the glucose monitor was reading.

Of course, these were only part of the reason she was unusually nervous; this was the one time in the week she was guaranteed to see Henry.

The recent text message situation had been hard to read, to put it mildly. Last week and through the weekend, they'd been constant, but then on Monday evening, he hadn't replied to her. She'd not thought much of it until Tuesday evening, when she still hadn't heard anything. By yesterday morning, she was sure something was up.

For some reason, the agony of not hearing from him was even worse than it had been with Jack. Even a ten-kilometre run and cleaning the flat from top to bottom hadn't been enough to keep her distracted. Eventually, she found a different way to occupy her mind — filling in the job application for Paul.

It was a spur-of-the-moment decision, and she hadn't put in half as much effort as she probably should have done, but sending it off gave her a sense of relief she hadn't expected; it was out of her hands now. Unfortunately, it still didn't change the issue of Henry not contacting her. She picked up her phone and sent him the only text she could — a single emoji of a ghost. She saw he'd read it almost immediately, but it was an agonising two hours before he replied.

Sorry, crazy family stuff going on.

It was hardly much of an apology, but she knew he wasn't one for going into detail.

Not Eunice, I hope? she replied, with a mixture of genuine concern and a desire to keep the conversation going.

No, she's fine. My cousin's getting married. Too much drama to bother talking about.

Again, his abruptness stung.

Hope it's sorted now, she replied and received a single smiley-faced emoji in response. And that was it. That was all she'd heard from him for the past twenty-four hours. And now she was about to see him again.

As expected, the sign read *Closed*, but the shop door was unlocked.

"Am I late?" she asked, surprised to find she was one of the last ones there.

"No, everyone else is just early," Gemma said. "Sophie and I were about to fix drinks. We've got wine, but I'm happy to make you a chai latte if you'd prefer."

"Wine is fine," she said, taking a seat. Across the table, Eunice was deep in conversation with Nina. She'd talk to her later. Drop Henry into the conversation casually just to see how he was doing. And maybe fish to see if he'd mentioned her at all.

The evening was unusually congenial. For once, everyone agreed the book was a modern classic, even if they couldn't decide whether they liked the film or the book version better.

"Could you imagine going through all that?" Sophie said, practically sobbing. "To discover the reason you'd been raised. To realise you had no value as a human in your own right. For them not to even believe you had a soul."

"It was the teachers that my heart broke for. The ones who really made a bond with them. Honestly, it makes me feel sick thinking about it."

"But I wish they hadn't changed that line in the book. I think it worked far better with Miss Emily saying it."

"Yes, but the book came before the film."

"I think the director made the right choice there."

When they'd discussed the ins and outs of the various chapters, along with the deeper meaning of the book on several conceptual levels, they used one of the bowls from the kitchen to pick their next read. Fleur was undeniably disappointed when a horror book was chosen. This was not her genre of choice. In fact, she couldn't remember when she'd last read one, if ever. But then she'd not initially been keen on tonight's dystopian novel and what was a book club for, if not to widen your horizons?

As discussions drew to a close, she typed the title onto her phone, while her eyes continued to flicker to the window. Henry was almost always early to pick up Eunice, and yet currently there was no sign of him. She was also struggling to decide what she was going to say when he turned up. Given that a footpath ran from the back of North Road down to the promenade, she would be far quicker walking home than getting a lift with him and Eunice. And there was no rain to use as an excuse, either. She could just say hi. Ask if all the family drama was sorted out now. Her mind was still whirring with the possibilities when Nina stood up.

"Are you ready, Eunice?" she asked, looking at the old lady. "I can drive the car closer to the door if you need me to?"

"Of course, I don't," she replied, standing. "I'd be fine to walk home, and you blooming well know it. But yes, I'm ready. Just need to get my coat on."

"Where's Henry?" Fleur asked, trying to sound as nonchalant as possible despite the drumming in her chest. "Is he not picking you up tonight?"

"No, I was with Nina this afternoon, so we arranged to give him the night off. He can't spend all his time ferrying his old aunt around."

"Oh, okay. Yes, that makes sense, I suppose." The disappointment Fleur had felt at him not being more responsive to her texts was nothing compared to this, although she tried to cover it as best she could.

"Did you need him for anything?" Eunice asked. "I'm happy to pass on a message."

"No, it's fine. Honestly. I owe him a drink, that's all. I'm sure I'll make it up to him at some point soon."

Eunice's eyes glinted. "You went for a drink together? He didn't tell me that."

"Oh, it was just a chance meeting," Fleur said, trying to ignore her rising pulse rate. "He gave me a lift home from Chelmsford after I missed my bus."

"He didn't tell me that either," Eunice said, her lips

twitching into a smile. "Well, I'll give him your best. I'm sure he'll be back to dropping me off again in a fortnight. Maybe I'll try persuading him to join us again. Graham could do with a little more male company, and he is very good company, don't you think?"

Fleur could hear the innuendo in her question. The way she was pushing her to get more. After all, from the very first meeting she'd attended, her friend had been trying to get them together.

"Yes, give him my best," Fleur said, deciding on the most neutral response she could muster.

"I will," Eunice replied. "I will."

CHAPTER 34

*T*he weekend was a wonderfully chilled one. On Saturday, Maria and Gemma invited Fleur to join them for a stroll around Heybridge Basin. Though stroll was probably the wrong term, as very little walking was involved. At first, they took a gentle narrow-boat trip up the canal, observing rare water birds and less rare paddle boarders, before they headed to a pub. While the other girls nattered about the feasibility of living on a narrow boat and the work that would undoubtedly go into it, Fleur picked at her cheesy chips, captivated by the lock and the boats that moved between the estuary and the canal. It was a place she planned on coming to again, with its hodgepodge of vessels, from barges to sailboats. Perhaps next time, she thought, she would bring a picnic and do one of the walks marked on the wooden signposts she'd seen.

Sunday was even less eventful. After finding the source of a nasty smell in the kitchen — a mouldy onion, age unknown, that had rolled to the back of a cupboard— she spent the morning cleaning out all the cupboards and drawers, while in the afternoon she dealt with the mammoth pile of clothes that had been consigned to the *chairdrobe*. (This allocated chair in her bedroom had been entirely engulfed with items that, while not dirty enough to need a wash, had been worn and were therefore not in a fit state to be hung up again.)

All the while, she tried to ignore the fact that she hadn't heard from Henry. Again. She wondered if he was cross that she'd mentioned going for a drink with him to Eunice or if this family stuff was still going on. Then again, it wasn't beyond the realms of possibility that he was busy with work. Unfortunately, she was fully aware that there was one much more likely scenario: he had well and truly ghosted her. Men like him were always hypocrites.

By Sunday evening, she'd decided that was the last day she was going to waste any energy thinking about Henry Pierce. That had been the plan, anyway. Everything changed when her phone rang at midday on Monday.

Paul flashed up on her screen, causing an immediate tension in the back of her neck. He didn't ring her mobile. He was all about seeing people face to virtual face so that he could look them in the eye. In fact, she hadn't even been aware that he had her phone number, although in hindsight, it must be on the system somewhere.

Assuming she'd forgotten a meeting and the call was to remind her, she hurriedly picked up.

"Hi Paul, is everything okay?" she said, before he even had time to say hello. "Have I got my times muddled up? I've scheduled us in for a midday meeting on Friday. Did I get that wrong?"

"No, no. You're completely fine. Better than fine, actually."

Better than fine? Fleur had no idea how to respond. As such, she stayed silent and let him carry on.

"As you know, you were shortlisted for the job, along with one external candidate."

"Oh, okay ... yes, the job." Given how she'd only just sent in the application, she hadn't expected to hear about it for several weeks, and the news about there being only one other candidate came as a surprise to her. The tension in her neck spread down to her shoulders. Only one other candidate? That meant a fifty-fifty chance of her not getting it.

"Well, you know you were my favourite from the start," he continued. "But in the interests of fairness, we had to advertise the post widely. Unfortunately, or rather fortunately for you, our HR team has just dug up some rather inappropriate online photographs of the other candidate."

"Oh dear."

"Exactly. And you know how we're all about *living your best life* here at the company. There are some things that we just can't accept. We wouldn't want it coming out that we knew about these pictures and have it bite us on the arse. You understand, don't you?"

"Of course," she replied, although she one hundred percent didn't. She also wasn't that happy to learn that the HR department snooped around on social media, viewing their profiles. Not that there was much to see on hers. There was a nice snap of her with the chickens, a year back, and a selfie taken by the river when she first moved to Maldon. But that was about it.

"The big bosses want the position filled as quickly as possible and they expected to do a full panel interview, but your references were so glowing, they are more than happy to accept me vouching for you. So ... congratulations!"

Fleur didn't reply. Did this mean the job was hers, or was she simply being patted on the back for not having any 'inappropriate' photos online? She cleared her throat, about to ask, when Paul spoke first.

"So, the job's yours. You've got it."

"It's mine? But I didn't interview."

"That's what I just said. Were you not listening to me? It's yours if you want it."

Fleur's stomach flipped with excitement and nervousness. Was she really going to do this? Yes, she realised she was. And not because there was pressure on her to climb the corporate ladder or earn more money or because she was desperate to make her mark on the world. She was going to do it because she wanted to.

"Thank you. Thank you very much, Paul."

"No, thank you. I'll send through all the details this afternoon. Training days, that type of thing. But for now, go celebrate!"

As she hung up the phone, her excitement continued to bubble. She should message the Book Club girls, see if they fancied meeting up for a celebratory drink. But no sooner had the thought entered her head than another one leapfrogged it: Henry. Henry, who had promised to take her out for a meal when she'd got the new job. And he'd said it with so much confidence, as if he'd never doubted it for a second.

Does he really have any right to know about the job? she asked herself, staring at her phone as if it might somehow hold the answer. He obviously wasn't that interested in seeing her again. But she wouldn't have applied for it, if it hadn't been for him. And she didn't have to mention anything about his promise of dinner. She could just let him know she'd been successful. And so, before her courage failed her, she quickly typed *Got the job!* and hit send.

CHAPTER 35

*H*enry had spent most of the weekend ensuring he was up to date on outstanding tasks and emails, so he'd have no nasty surprises waiting for him when he returned to the office on Monday. He had several court dates to schedule and more meetings to book, but beyond that, everything about the first day of the week was entirely predictable ... until he got the message.

Got the job!

He was sitting at his desk, with a fork in a tub of salad, when the ping caught him by surprise. It had taken all his willpower not to message her over the weekend, just to check what she was doing. And this had been tested further by Eunice's constant digging.

"All I'm saying is that I can't remember the last time you went for a drink with a girl. It's nice."

Of course, it wasn't only what she said, but how she said it, with her eyes glinting mischievously.

"I just gave her a lift home."

"I didn't realise she lived over a pub. I thought her flat was by the church."

He'd refused to reply to this. It wasn't like there was anything going on with him and Fleur. And if there had been the possibility of something happening, he knew he'd blown his chances by now. It had been harder than expected not to message her, particularly because of how big a hypocrite ghosting her made him. But on the other hand, it was good that she'd dislike him even more. He needed that. And he was feeling pretty confident he'd now be able to clear his mind of her … and then the message came through.

An unexpected spike of adrenaline flooded through him as he opened the app. This was immediately replaced by a warm sense of pride. Obviously, she'd got the job. It had been clear from the way she'd spoken about it when they were out that she was a shoo-in. As he thought of their conversation in the Black Rabbit, the warmth that had filled him only moments before was doused by the memory of that night. Or more specifically, his offer to take her for a celebration dinner if she was successful.

Sitting back in his chair, he could feel the stress building behind his temples. Was there any way out of it? More importantly, did he want to find one?

Unable to focus on anything else, he looked at the message again, trying to find a hidden subtext in her three words. She hadn't mentioned the meal, and it didn't look as if she was composing a follow-up message, but was that because she wanted *him* to or because she didn't want to go or because she had simply forgotten?

His lunch now forgotten, he kneaded his hands together, the various options swirling around his head. Did he want to take her for dinner? Yes, absolutely. Should he? Probably not.

Was he wasting far too much time thinking about how, or if, he was supposed to reply? Without a doubt.

Taking a deep breath, he picked up the salad again, only to look back at his phone. There was no way he was going to be able to concentrate on anything with this hanging over him. And so, for the sake of his sanity, he fired back a message.

I guess I owe you dinner then. And because he didn't want to lose momentum, added one more word. *Tonight?*

CHAPTER 36

*F*leur arrived at the Mexican restaurant ten minutes before the arranged time of 7 p.m. so she could get a cocktail in before Henry arrived. *If* he arrived, that was. A part of her suspected he was going to cancel last minute. That seemed the type of thing he would do. He'd probably cite work as an excuse. Men like him always did, as if women didn't have to hold down jobs and juggle commitments. Sitting there, sipping her drink, her anger spiked. She should have known better than to think he would turn up, even though he'd been the one to suggest dinner. And that after starting all the text-messaging in the first place before going silent on her.

She took an unfeasibly large gulp of her drink and then reached down for her bag. She might as well pay up and leave, she thought. But as she rummaged for her purse, the bell above the door jangled and there, striding towards her, was Henry Pierce.

"I thought I was early," he said when he reached the table,

before leaning down and kissing her on the cheek in a rather formal manner.

"You are, just," she said, with a glance at her watch. "I was even earlier."

"And it appears you've started without me?" he said, nodding to the empty glass in front of her.

"To be honest, I wasn't sure you were going to turn up."

A deep frown creased his brow. "I probably deserve that. I hope this will go some way towards an apology." He took a seat, then reached into his coat pocket and pulled out a little package, beautifully wrapped in embossed paper and finished with a gold ribbon.

"You bought me a gift?" she said.

"A congratulations-for-the-new-job present. And don't get too excited; it's only small."

Size wise, he wasn't joking. Even wrapped, it was thinner than a phone and narrower too, but that he'd thought to buy her anything was enough to bring a lump to her throat. She couldn't remember the last time a male friend had done that. For the last few years of their marriage, come Christmas or her birthday, Robert had handed her his credit card and told her to buy herself something nice. It hadn't always been that way, though. Back before things had deteriorated, they would go for dinner on Valentine's Day, and she would get him something sentimental like a photo book or an engraved watch, and he would pay for the meal. And on anniversaries and birthdays, they would go away, somewhere pretty like the Cotswolds or Norfolk, when Fleur had been responsible for finding the hotel and the restaurants and booking any activities she thought they would both like. She couldn't remember the last time he'd gone to the trouble of choosing a present she might appreciate.

"I don't know what to say."

"Thank you is fine. Besides, you might not even like it."

"I think I will."

She slowly peeled away the tape, trying to leave the paper intact, to reveal a thin piece of wood, engraved with the letter F.

"A bookmark?"

"Though it's not to be used for romantic books. I need to make that clear."

She ran her finger over the object; the smoothness of the wood was mesmerising. "It's beautiful," she said, then placed her hand on his.

The moment their skin touched, it happened again. That same spark shot through her, leaving her almost breathless.

"Most people would say that this was a romantic gift," she said.

"Well, most people would be wrong. It's purely practical. Suspicion tells me you're the type of monster who dog-ears their books."

"It shows that they're loved!" she laughed, defensively.

"It shows that you're a heathen."

Their eyes met, and her laughter stopped. Neither of them had moved their hands, and now they were staring straight at one another. She wanted to say something, although not as much as she wanted to kiss him. If this had been a date, she would have. But this wasn't that, was it?

"What are we doing?" she said quietly, their hands still together.

She could feel her pulse pounding in her ears, adrenaline rising with every breath. She could do it. She could lean forwards and kiss him. Perhaps his denial of love and romance was simply a pretence he put on to ensure he didn't get hurt. Maybe if she showed him that it was okay to be vulnerable, there could be something between them.

She shifted herself towards him by barely a centimetre, but that was all it took. He snapped back, pulling his hand out from under hers.

"I think we should order some food," he said, "don't you?"

CHAPTER 37

*T*he meal had flown by. Starters, mains and a plate of churros, which they ordered to share. For a while, they spoke about Fleur's new role and Henry's job, but mostly, their conversation was far more light-hearted: favourite childhood films, least favourite chocolate bars, most over-rated actor, that type of thing. Only when the waiter started putting chairs upside down on the surrounding tables and then placed their bill — in a some-what passive-aggressive manner, she thought — on the table in front of them, did they gather up their things and head out into the street. It was the type of night where the moon and stars shone out vividly behind wispy clouds which moved lazily across the sky.

The pavement had never felt more inconveniently sized. It would go from being so narrow that they had to walk in single file, to so wide it felt like they weren't even together. This feeling of separation wasn't helped by the silence that had now fallen. In fact, other than Fleur saying she didn't need a chaperone and Henry insisting she did, they hadn't exchanged a single word since leaving the restaurant. And now they were almost back at her house.

Her head whirred with all the things she wanted to say to him. Like thanking him again for the gift or paying for dinner, but she'd already done both of those more than once, and she didn't want to keep going on about it.

"It's amazing about your aunt's trip to Spain last year," she said, finally landing upon something innocuous. Surprisingly, Eunice hadn't come into the conversation over dinner, and it felt like a safe topic, although the remark was met by a look of confusion.

"What trip?"

"She told us she went to Spain for six weeks. Rented a flat with a view out to sea."

His jaw tightened. "Oh yes. That trip. I'd almost forgotten."

"You sound like you didn't approve?"

He opened his mouth to say something, only to close it again, shake his head and stop in his tracks.

"This is you," he said.

Fleur stopped and turned towards him. Considering how painfully awkward the walk had been, it seemed to have taken them no time at all, and now she was once again wondering what the hell she was doing. Or rather, what Henry was doing.

"What *is* your game?"

"Sorry?"

"What's your game? You say you're not into romance, and yet buy me the most beautiful, romantic gift. You spend half the time acting like you don't want to be anywhere near me, and then you take me out for dinner to celebrate my new job, as if you're my boyfriend. Then you insist on seeing me home, although it's less than a five-minute walk. So why? What is it you want from me?"

He stared at her for a moment, and she briefly thought he

might say something sweet, but instead, he stood back and scoffed.

"You see, that's the problem with being romantic. You believe that just because you want something — someone — and you think about them constantly, you should be able to make it work. But life doesn't operate like that, and feelings don't last. And at some point, maybe not immediately, but eventually, you end up despising the thing you wanted so badly."

So much hurt raged in his eyes, she could have cried.

"It doesn't always end like that," she said, reaching out to take his hand, only for him to back away.

"It ends like that often enough. Believe me; I've seen it. And even if it doesn't, even if you and I are meant to be *soul mates*, or whatever it is you'd call it, real life would get in the way. You could never be number one to me. You'd always come second."

"To Eunice," Fleur said, quietly.

His head dropped. "She's not doing as well as she makes out. Sooner or later, she won't be able to live on her own. And who's going to want to move in with a guy living with an elderly relative?"

"No one, if you don't give them the chance." She stepped forwards and took his hand again, and this time, he didn't pull away from her. "You can't live your life in fear of a future that might never happen and miss out on a present that is here in front of you. To not even try to love is so much sadder than having your heart broken. Trust me, if anyone knows about heartbreak, it's me. But I'm still standing up for love, Henry, and I always will. I hope that, someday, you'll let yourself open up to it, too."

She planned on walking away at this point and turned, preparing to grab her keys and head inside, but she'd barely taken a step when his grip on her hand tightened, and he pulled her around and back towards him. If she'd had the opportunity, she might well have shouted out in shock, but there wasn't a chance for that. The moment she looked up, he was there, his face only inches from hers, so close that she could feel the heat of his breath on her skin. Her heart started pounding as she struggled to draw in a deep breath.

"Is this what you actually want?" she asked, subconsciously pushing herself up onto her tiptoes as he tilted his head down to hers. They were close enough now. Close enough to kiss.

"I don't remember ever wanting anything more," he said.

CHAPTER 38

"You kissed him? You *kissed* him? But you *hated* him?"

"Hate is a pretty strong word," Fleur said into her phone. She was slumped on the sofa, clasping a pillow to her chest as she filled her sister in on the night's events, despite the fact that it was nearly midnight. "I just didn't understand him, that's all. He's scared. He's scared of love, and he's worried about his aunt. He's terrified he won't be able to cope with a relationship and everything else he has going on in his life."

"He sounds like way too much work," Annelise said, not pulling any punches, as usual. "Besides, what happened then? You still haven't told me what followed, after you kissed him."

An involuntary sigh blew from Fleur's lips. Wistful and dreamy, it caused the butterflies — which she'd only just got under control — to re-emerge.

"That was it. We just kissed. And technically, he kissed me."

It seemed unfair to dismiss what she'd experienced as *just kissing*. It was an earth-moving, bone-trembling, this-is-my-whole-life-changing event. Henry's hands had run through her hair as he pulled her body as close to his as physically possible. The urgency. The fervour. This was what they wrote about in romantic books. Not that she was going to tell her sister all that.

"And what then? Did you arrange to meet again? Has he texted you? Are you two a thing now?"

Fleur shrugged and cast a glance at the bookmark on the coffee table. "I don't know what happens next. I suppose I'll message him, then see him at Book Club next Thursday."

"Next Thursday? But that's over a week away!" Annelise exclaimed, as if Fleur wasn't aware of this. "Is that the plan? Not to see him until then?"

"I don't know."

"You sound okay about it."

"I am. I'm okay. It's going to work out; I can feel it. Anyway, I'd better go. Late night and everything. And I was hoping to read through the details of the new job, but that's probably going to have to wait until the morning."

"New job. New man. Would this be a good time to bring up your fortieth birthday party?"

No matter how much she wanted to throttle her sister, Fleur couldn't help but laugh. "Nice try. I'm still not having one. I'll speak to you tomorrow. Give my love to the children."

"Will do."

She hung up the phone and dropped back with a sigh. If nothing else, Book Club was going to be interesting. Given how frequently she and Henry had messaged each other immediately after the previous drink, she'd expected to hear from him that evening. Then again, he had walked her home, so it wasn't like he needed to check that she had got back okay.

When she woke up the next morning, there was a whole

stream of texts. Unfortunately, they were all from members of the Club and not a single one from Henry. By lunch time, paranoia had started to raise its ugly head again.

There was no chance she had mis-read the signals this time. After all, *he* was the one who had kissed *her*. And it wasn't like he'd broken away immediately, the way someone would if they didn't like a kiss. In fact, when she'd attempted to, he'd pulled her back to kiss her again and again. It didn't make any sense at all.

By the time evening arrived, she was going crazy. Needing a way to blow off steam, she headed out for a run, although she didn't take any of her normal routes. This time, she headed up into the centre of town and then down again towards the canal, coming out right by Henry's office.

This is getting close to stalking, she said to herself as she slowed her pace enough to look up at the windows. She didn't know which floor he worked on, though several of them still had their lights on. Not that it mattered. Even if she'd known where his office was, it was not like she could go up there and demand he explain why he hadn't texted her yet. And after all, she hadn't messaged him either. But after his last trick with ghosting, it was absolutely his turn to make contact first.

"Maybe he's waiting for *me* to text," she said to Annelise, when she got home. "Do you think that's it?"

"I think he's already proved himself to be a — Paxton, do not hit your sister with her Switch!" She cleared her throat before continuing. "Okay, I'll be honest with you. I think you're wasting too much time thinking about him. And it's not as if anything will come of this."

These words felt like a knife to her stomach. "Sorry .... what do you mean by that?"

"This has been the pattern since you and Robert split up, hasn't it? The married man in the last place you lived, the policeman and now a guy who has categorically said he's sworn off relationships. He told you himself it would never happen."

"Yes, and then he kissed me. Did you miss that part?"

Annelise's sigh reverberated down the line. "You must see what's going on. You're picking men who are inherently unavailable. All I'm saying is, maybe you should take the fact that he's gone cold again as a definite sign this time. You know I don't mean this unkindly. I just don't want to see you get hurt again. And that guy has heartbreaker written all over him."

Of all the things her sister could have said to her, this was something she'd never imagined coming out of her mouth. Sure, Annelise had made her feelings about Robert perfectly clear from the get-go, but Fleur had been young when she fell for him. She wasn't the same person anymore. She didn't need her big sister judging her and being overprotective.

"Well, thank you for your support," she snapped.

"I do support you. I supported you going for this new job. I supported you moving to a different town. I supported you trying to reinvent yourself and step away from the corporate rat-race. But I don't support you getting into a situation where it's blatantly obvious you are going to get your heart broken. I just can't do that."

Every hint of hope and optimism Fleur had felt disappeared. "Thank you for your input, but I think I need to go to bed," she said, sharply, then hung up the phone.

For a second, she stared at the screen. As sisters, they bickered a lot, but it was an unspoken rule that, when it came to the big things, they had each other's backs. But this didn't feel like that. This felt as if she'd been trying to put her down, and when she thought back on it, Annelise would realise just how out of order she had been.

Placing her phone on the arm of the chair, Fleur picked up her book and turned it to the page marked perfectly with Henry's gift. Less than a chapter in and her phone buzzed. A smug feeling of satisfaction rolled through her. Her sister normally took a bit of time to come back with an apology, but this quick response just proved how in the wrong she had been. Only the message wasn't from her but from Henry. Without pausing for breath, she opened it up.

If Annelise's words had felt like a knife to her stomach, then the text from Henry was a twist of the blade. Only five words long, yet that was all it took to floor her.

I'm sorry. It can't work.

CHAPTER 39

*H*e was an arse. A grade A arse, and he knew it. But it was better this way, Henry told himself. Better to cut things off now, before either of them got too hurt.

The minute he'd arrived home after their dinner, he'd realised what an absolute mess he'd made of everything. But that kiss. It had made him almost believe romance really did exist. That everything written in the bloody books was true. But you couldn't base a relationship on one kiss even if he couldn't get out of his head how laughing with her had caused his cheeks to ache or that, even before the starters had arrived, he'd wanted to whip her out of the restaurant and have her all to himself. No. None of that counted. She wanted a future he couldn't give her, and no matter how much fun they might have in the short term, he couldn't lead her on. She was too special for that.

"You need to get outside more. All you do is work."

His head snapped from his phone to where his aunt was standing on tiptoes, trying to reach a top cupboard. "What are you doing?" He dropped his mobile and jumped to his feet. "What are you looking for? Let me get it for you."

Still on tiptoes, Eunice waved away his offer of help. "Don't be ridiculous; I don't need you fussing."

"I'm not fussing. I'm helping."

"You're fussing, and you know it."

He drew in a long breath and forced himself to be patient. There wasn't a single person in the entire world he loved more than Eunice, and there wasn't anyone who drove him more insane, either. "Can you please remember what the doctor said? You need to slow down."

"He's been saying that to me for the last ten years."

"Please, Eunice. I'm just thinking about you. That's all." He paused, debating whether he should say the next thing that was on the tip of his tongue. In the end, he decided there was nothing to lose. "I know you told Fleur about your *trip to Spain.*"

Eunice finally dropped from her tiptoes. "So, what if I did? And when were you talking to her about this, exactly? Have you seen her again? Are you finally dating?"

"Don't change the subject. This is not about me. You tell me all the time how these people are your friends, how they watch out for you. But you don't want to tell them the truth about having a fall. Making up some ridiculous story about a sea-view apartment abroad rather than letting them know you were on crutches the whole time and couldn't go anywhere."

He didn't need to see her face to know that she was seething. That was another annoying trait of hers. She hated anyone calling her out on anything.

Fleur's comment about the *holiday* had been the final nail in the coffin. They hadn't even been properly dating, and yet he was already having to choose sides and decide whether to tell her the truth or keep his promise to his aunt and not let any of her friends know about the fall. There was no way he could maintain a relationship like that, no matter what he thought of Fleur or the kiss or the way his entire body would light up when he saw a message from her ping onto his screen. But he wasn't going to think about that now. It was done and dusted, and it was for the best. He would have to drop Eunice off early next week though, so that he wouldn't risk bumping into her. His resolve might not hold.

He was still thinking about Fleur when his phone beeped. It wasn't a message, though. This was the alarm that caused him to jump every time it sounded and would even wake him from a deep sleep with its piercing noise.

"Auntie Eunice, your blood sugar is low. Will you please eat something?"

"You know, it's time you stopped worrying about me and thought about yourself instead," she replied.

But they both knew that wasn't possible. There was only enough room for one woman in his life, and he had already decided which.

CHAPTER 40

*A*fter Robert, Fleur had wallowed in grief and self-doubt. Day in and day out, she would do nothing but analyse their life together, wondering if she had done things differently, then he wouldn't have left her. But that was the old Fleur. The new one wasn't going to waste energy on a man like Henry Pierce. She was going to use it all on something more reliable.

The new job was exactly the distraction she needed, and despite not officially starting for another week, she got stuck straight in, throwing herself into every task Paul sent her way, whilst still covering her old job, just as she would have done fifteen years ago. Of course, juggling both positions meant there was no time for herself, and she spent her entire weekend in her dressing gown, typing away at her computer. But that was okay. She was doing what needed to be done.

However, one thing she wasn't currently doing was picking up the phone to Annelise.

Will you please call me back? I'm getting worried. Her sister had sent several variations on the same theme since Fleur had told her about the text from Henry, but she didn't know what to say to her. *Congratulations for thinking I'm going to be single forever. Turns out you were right?* No, she didn't need that right now. Instead, she'd fired off a simple *Sorry, really busy with the new job* message that she knew her sister wouldn't believe but hoped it might keep her placated for a while.

It was with mixed feelings that Fleur approached the Book Club meeting the following week. She was looking forward to seeing everyone, having declined the offer to go for drinks with Gemma and company at the weekend. The WhatsApp chat group had been abuzz with plans for a trip to the cinema in Chelmsford, and she'd sign herself up to go even though she'd not heard of the film. She was also anticipating talking about the current book and picking the next one, too. What she was not looking forward to was seeing Henry.

As Thursday approached, Fleur played out a thousand different scenarios of how the evening might go. He would probably try to talk to her when he picked Eunice up. That would be less awkward than when he was dropping her off. And she would be perfectly polite. So polite, in fact, that he would think she wasn't at all fazed by seeing him. Maybe she would give him a playful thump on the arm, in a completely platonic, buddy-like manner. Or perhaps she would just carry on chatting with one of the girls, as if she hadn't even noticed him.

Yet, no matter how much she tried to convince herself otherwise, she did want to see him. Badly. She wanted him to look her in the eye and say it wouldn't work, rather than getting away with sending a cowardly text message. Which was why she arrived at Maria's ten minutes early. However, that turned out to be not early enough.

"Eunice, I didn't expect to see you here already," she said, taking a seat beside her. Maria was busy in the kitchen, swearing at the oven, and for now, it was just the three of them in the house.

"I thought *I* was early. Is everything all right?" she continued, as casually as possible. She wanted to say more. She wanted to ask if Henry had dropped her off or if he had mentioned her at all, but she stayed silent and waited for the old lady to reply.

"Henry's had a busy week," she said, as if reading her thoughts, "and been in a grump for days now. Had to drop me off early for some reason." Then, with a twinkle in her eye added, "While there's no one else here, Fleur, I wondered if I might ask you something?"

From the way she was looking at her so intently, Fleur assumed this would be something to do with her diabetes. Just like Henry, she found the idea of keeping it a secret ridiculous, but she was hardly going to object if it was her wish. However, this turned out to be the furthest thing from her mind.

"I wondered if you would like to join me on Saturday. I'm going to a do at my cousin's niece's in Danbury. Lots of lovely girls like yourself will be there, and I wanted to repay you for the bubbles and cake the other week."

Fleur went to smile, then stopped. Was this a pity invite? Something she did every time Henry was an arse to one of the young women she befriended? The idea made her stomach turn.

"You don't have to do that. Besides, it was Annelise who paid for everything."

"Please, dear, it would make my weekend, and it would be lovely to have a familiar face there amongst all the strangers. There'll be free wine, too. And dancing."

Fleur was tempted to ask what sort of party didn't have free wine. "I've got a new job," she started to explain, but Eunice simply clapped her hands excitedly.

"Well, that's just perfect. We can celebrate. And Danbury's beautiful. Have you been?"

Danbury woods had been on Fleur's list of places to visit since she'd moved, but she hadn't yet found the time, and she could tell that Eunice wasn't going to take no for an answer.

"Are any of the others from the Club going to be there?" she asked. If they were, then maybe she could show her face for a short while and then head off for a walk.

Eunice let out a sigh. "I did ask, but you know what it's like. Work commitments. Family obligations. I was a bit late getting the invites out if I'm honest. But it would be so nice if you could join me. I talk about you Book Club girls so much, I'm sure if it wasn't for Henry they'd think you didn't exist. It would show them I'm not completely batty."

Fleur had to smile at this. It wasn't as if she didn't deserve a weekend off after all the work she'd been doing recently.

"Okay, that sounds lovely. Where should I meet you?"

With a small shriek of glee, Eunice clasped her hands. "Come to mine for ten. I've already got a taxi booked."

She was about to ask if there was a dress code when the doorbell rang in perfect synchronicity with a string of expletives from Maria in the kitchen.

"I'll get that!" she called, jumping up. It seemed like Maria had already got enough on her plate.

After that, the lounge started filling up, and it wasn't long before they were in full flow, discussing various tropes and evil characters. For the first time since their date, Henry was all but gone from Fleur's mind, until Eunice brought him up during supper.

"Gemma, dear," she said, dunking a wedge of garlic bread into the homemade lasagne. "I forgot to ask earlier, but Henry's caught up with work tonight. Any chance you could drop me home?"

"Absolutely," Gemma replied, through a mouthful of pasta. "That's no problem at all."

"Fabulous."

Despite being on opposite sides of the dining table, Fleur could have sworn Eunice's eyes flickered towards her as she spoke, as if looking for a reaction. Gripping her cutlery, she took another mouthful of food and fixed her smile as best she could. No surprise he wasn't coming. He was every bit the coward she knew him to be.

An hour later, standing at Maria's front door ready to leave, Eunice accosted her.

"Fleur, dear, I should have said. About the party this weekend, you might want to wear something nice. These girls like to do dressy."

"Dressy?"

"You know, just a pretty dress. A smart one. Anyway, I'll send you my address when I'm home. I'm looking forward to it. Very much."

"Me too," Fleur replied, though she couldn't help but feel her friend was up to something. Whatever it was, she would find out soon enough.

CHAPTER 41

*a*fter trawling through her wardrobe for a smart, dressy dress, Fleur decided the best thing to do was go shopping. And so, after work on Friday, she took herself into town to look for something appropriate to wear. While Maldon didn't have a great variety of big retailers, one thing it was not short of was charity shops. From one end of the High Street to the other, umpteen stores were filled with other people's unwanted items.

A few years ago, when living in London, she would have turned her nose up at second-hand clothes. Or at least Robert had, and she always felt the need to follow his lead.

"Why on earth would you want someone's castoffs?" he'd said.

But after she'd taken a big drop in pay and tried them out, she'd discovered that they were, in many cases, blooming fantastic.

"How much?" she asked herself, eyes widening in disbelief at the price tag attached to a second-hand designer jacket. She was sure that Annelise had one almost identical to it and was tempted to buy it just to show her. But she would have to come back for it. Because right now, she was on a mission.

"A dressy dress," she muttered, as she searched along the rails. There was no shortage of options, from full-on ball-gowns — several of which had the original price tags on — to shorter cocktail dresses, strapless numbers and lace garments, too.

"This looks good," she said, pulling one out and holding it up in front of her. The shimmering dress was covered in sequins which graduated in colour from black at the top to red at the bottom. It was something she could imagine being worn by one of the cast of The Great Gatsby. And it was most definitely dressy. After checking the size and paying for it, she headed home for an early night.

Early nights were good, Fleur had discovered after Robert. The less hours awake and thinking, the better. Although back then, she had struggled to sleep unless she took the tablets the doctor had given her. And then she had struggled to wake up and be productive the next morning. At least Henry hadn't done that to her. No, she outright refused to lose any rest over him. But it was difficult to forget about him entirely.

You know I'm your sister, right? The message came through on Saturday morning, after several missed calls on the Friday night. *You know you can't ignore me forever? I'm sorry if I get a little overprotective, but I love you. You're my baby sister. You deserve someone who's going to treat you like a princess, and I know they're out there somewhere for you. Please forgive me?*

Fleur groaned as she stared at the words. She should have known she wouldn't be able to stay mad at Annelise forever. She never could. The last two weeks of radio silence had probably been a record. Maybe she would ring her when she got back from the party. Put her on speakerphone as she tidied her bedroom. She'd neglected the flat lately and it certainly needed a thorough clean through. She must get on top of things again.

By nine thirty, she was wearing her sequined dress, complete with silver shoes and a headband that bordered on Gatsby fancy dress but looked awesome, regardless. She gave her makeup one last check, grabbed her coat and headed outside.

As promised, Eunice had messaged her address, though as she stepped onto the street and typed it into her phone, she stopped and frowned. It didn't make sense. She'd said that Fleur's flat was on the way home to her house, which was why she'd insisted on Henry giving her a lift. But that wasn't the case at all. Wellington Road was all the way on the other side of the High Street, meaning Henry would have needed to do a U-turn and drive back the way they'd come after he'd dropped her home. No wonder he'd been grumpy about it. Still, she followed the directions she'd been given and banished all thoughts of him from her mind.

The house was a beautiful, red-brick semi, with large, bay windows and wooden eaves. After pushing through the garden gate, Fleur picked her way across the pavers and rang the doorbell.

"Just coming!" came a call from inside. A moment later the door creaked open, and Eunice's hand flew to her mouth. "Oh my, you look incredible! Perfect, absolutely perfect."

Before she'd left, she'd been worried she was overdressed, but judging by Eunice's outfit, she had pitched it just right. The old lady looked fabulous in a calf-length, red dress with a shimmering, gold bolero and a deep-green fascinator. It reminded her of Christmas but in the best possible way.

"Come in, come in. You're right on time. Our lift will be here any minute. We've just got time for a quick glass of bubbly."

Fleur recalled the last time they'd drunk Prosecco together. "Are you okay to be drinking at this time of day?" She hated feeling she was criticising her friend, but she would have hated it even more if something bad happened.

"Don't you start fussing. I'm perfectly capable of judging my own alcohol consumption. Now, if you could just fetch us a couple of glasses; they're on the top shelf over there."

Following her directions, she reached up and took two flutes out of the cabinet.

"If you could do the honours," Eunice said, handing her the bottle. "My fingers aren't quite what they used to be. And try not to smash any of my photographs."

It was then Fleur noticed all the frames dotted around the kitchen, containing photos of people. Family, she assumed. Her eyes were strangely drawn to those which included Henry. In some, he was on his own. In others, he was with Eunice or standing amongst a group of people his own age, who she could only assume were other cousins or relatives. Mostly, however, the photos were of Eunice and a striking man she presumed to be her husband.

"He was very handsome, wasn't he?" the old lady said, sidling up to her.

The chill of the bottle was seeping into Fleur's hand, yet she was finding it impossible to draw her eyes away from the pictures.

"You both look stunning," she said, her gaze travelling from one to another. "Was that one taken in Italy? How old were you there?"

"That one?" Eunice reached up and took down the frame. "We went to Italy a few times in the 80s. I think this was on one of the first trips, though. I suppose we'd have been around forty." Rather than replacing the photo, she continued to gaze wistfully at it, as if her mind was running away with a thousand memories. "He was very dashing, wasn't he? My Stanley. He'd aged a bit here, but he never lost it. An old-fashioned gentleman, you know the type. When we were walking out together, he'd always see me home. And always pay for a meal."

Always lead you on and then dump you Fleur wanted to say, as Eunice's words brought an image of Henry to her mind. "He does sound like he was perfect," she said, instead.

Given how much she'd already gushed about her late husband, Fleur was a little surprised when, rather than agreeing with her, Eunice threw back her head and laughed. So much so, that her fascinator nearly fell off.

"Oh, he was definitely not perfect. No. He was as a stubborn as a mule. God help the man or woman who tried to interfere with something he was doing. We could butt heads like you wouldn't believe. But it came from a place of love, and that's what mattered. He always wanted to do the right thing, and at the end of the day, he would have walked through fire for me."

Fleur's heart ached as she tried to imagine anyone who would do that for her. Robert had been a man who'd pushed her. Who'd had expectations she'd constantly tried to live up to. But walk-through fire for her? No.

"I should open this," she said, with a nod to the bottle. She'd barely peeled the foil from the cap when she heard a key in the front door.

"Sorry, I'm late. Are you ready? We need to get a move on. The taxi's outside."

There was no mistaking the voice, with its gravelly timbre and ridiculous ability to turn Fleur's knees to jelly.

"Eunice?" she said, her stomach twisting into a series of knots. "What's Henry doing here? You said we were heading out for a girly day."

"Well, there'll be lots of girls there, too. Plenty of them."

"Please tell me he's just making sure you get in the taxi okay?"

Whether Eunice was going to reply to that she didn't find out, for at that moment Henry stepped into the kitchen, and the tension in her stomach reached an entirely new level. She'd known, from the first time she'd witnessed him being rude in the pharmacy, that he was an objectively handsome man. But this was totally different to every other time she'd seen him. Not a hint of stubble on his cheeks, his hair was fixed with wax, and he had an aroma of expensive aftershave about him. He was wearing an unbuttoned waistcoat over a dark-blue shirt and a deep-red cravat around his neck.

He was, unequivocally, gorgeous.

"What are you doing here?" he asked, his eyes boring into her with such force she could feel her body about to fold in on itself. Mustering all the strength she could, she stood up straight, attempting to match his height.

"Eunice invited me. To join her at the party. Her niece's party."

At this, the tell-tale vein on Henry's forehead reappeared.

"It's not a party we're going to," he said. "It's a wedding."

CHAPTER 42

*H*enry stood rooted to the spot, unable to move. The fact he'd managed to get a single word out was a miracle, although it would have been difficult for an onlooker to tell who was more stunned, him or Fleur. Of all the tricks for his aunt to pull, this was one he'd never seen coming. To invite Fleur to his cousin's wedding. An event that had been years in the planning. A celebration that had been the cause of so many family arguments, from the guest list to the seating plan to the selection of aperitifs.

What was even more annoying was that he hadn't even considered his aunt would pull a stunt like this. That, and the fact he could not draw his eyes away from Fleur. Her outfit should have been totally ridiculous. The dress, the shoes, the headband. On anyone else it would have looked like fancy dress, but on her, it looked magnificent. As though she had been transported into his aunt's kitchen straight from another era, and it took every bit of willpower he had not to reach out, grab her wrist and pull her in for a kiss, the way he had outside her flat less than two weeks ago.

"There's obviously been some kind of misunderstanding," she said, putting the bottle down. "I should be going. Let you get to your family wedding."

"I think that's a good idea." He didn't mean that to come out as it did. It was just his default tone when stressed. A way to distance and detach himself from a difficult situation. In other circumstances, it wouldn't have mattered. But he saw the sharpness of his words strike Fleur and a feeling of guilt corkscrewed within him. "I'm sorry about the misunderstanding."

She nodded, catching his eye as she did so, and in that moment, his heart felt as if it was going to break clean out of his ribs. It had been bad enough not messaging her, but seeing her now, like this, it was impossible not to admit he'd missed her. And he wanted to tell her that. He wanted to say that he'd missed their silly text conversations and how her smile was enough to lighten the weight of responsibility he continuously felt. He wanted to tell her how he thought of her so much that he physically ached and couldn't sleep because he felt sick about how badly he'd treated her. But before he could manage anything even close to that, she was moving to leave.

"She can't go," Eunice said, stepping to the side and blocking her path. "Hazel is expecting her. I've told her she's my plus one. Her name is on the seating plan and everything."

"What? You can't be serious?" he said, fighting the urge to shout at his aunt with Fleur present. Despite her age, Eunice pulled off the butter-wouldn't-melt-in-my-mouth look to pure perfection, although she should have known better than to try and use it on him.

"I thought it might be nice for Fleur to see a little more of the area," she said, her doe eyes sparkling. "To meet some different people. There are going to be lots of women her age attending, after all. Hazel and Pippa have been together for such a long time. We're ever so happy they're finally tying the knot."

He clicked his jaw from side to side. He could already feel the vein on his forehead pulsing, hopefully not enough for Fleur to notice.

"This is not okay, Auntie Eunice. This is meddling."

"What nonsense. I wanted to have one of my friends with me, that's all. It's been a long time since I've been able to bring a plus one to something."

During this heated exchange, he'd almost forgotten Fleur was still there, until she cleared her throat and stepped forwards.

"I'm really sorry about this. I honestly didn't know."

This caught him by surprise. If there was one person who didn't need to apologise to him, it was Fleur.

"I don't blame you at all," he said softly. "This is not your fault. And you look beautiful, by the way." Where had that come from? Not that it wasn't true, he just hadn't expected to say it.

"Thank you. Look, I'll go. Just say I came down with a sickness bug. I'm sure no one will notice one empty seat."

That would be a way out of the mess, he thought, and probably the most sensible option, but she had clearly made a big effort to look nice, and given how she'd been willing to give up her Saturday to spend it with an old woman, it hardly seemed fair to agree. He would just have to make sure he wasn't sitting next to her. Hopefully, the seating plan would be such that he wouldn't even see her all night, but he certainly wouldn't be drinking, or he wouldn't be able to trust himself around her.

With a sharp intake of breath, he responded. "No, no, it's all been paid for. And Eunice is right, it will be fun for you to meet new people. Besides, the crazy great-aunt bringing a random woman as a plus one to a wedding is hardly the most outrageous thing she's done. You should come. It'll be easier if you do."

Time was ticking by, and he could see the conflict in the furrowed lines of Fleur's brow. She was going to say no, he thought, that it would be better if she didn't join them, but he didn't want that. Now he'd seen her, he needed her to come, for his sake as much as Eunice's. Which was why he turned on his heel.

"The taxi is waiting. We should go now," he said, marching towards the front door, while praying with every fibre in his body that she would follow.

CHAPTER 43

The journey to Danbury was surprisingly bearable, mainly because Henry was in the front seat and their driver would not stop talking. Before this, he'd been a removal man and insisted on telling them all the sordid tales of the various jobs he'd done over the years. Fleur suspected that most of it was made up, but it passed the time and meant that they weren't forced to sit in awkward silence as they probably would have done otherwise. Thankfully, in less than fifteen minutes, they were driving up a long, gravel entrance.

"Wow, this is stunning," she said, as they made their way from the taxi to the barn, where the wedding was taking place. *Rustic* was how she imagined a magazine would describe it but in the best possible way. As they stepped inside, her breath was stolen by the natural beauty of it all. Raw oak beams were wrapped with white lights, while garlands of dried flowers spiralled up the pillars.

A deep ache spread across her chest. Even after all the years, it was difficult to go to any wedding without thinking of hers. Held in a swanky, London venue, the drinks had been obscenely expensive, and every little extra, from flowers on the back of the chairs to candles on the dining table, had been meticulously counted and charged. And Fleur had had it all. The wedding favours. The gifts for the bridesmaids, who she rarely even spoke to now. Monogrammed handkerchiefs and handmade cufflinks for the groomsmen. Centre pieces with enough flowers to fill a greenhouse. And what difference had it made at the end of the day? Zero.

This then led her to think about Robert's recent marriage, too. Had there been no expense spared once again? Had they ticked every box on the wedding planner's list? Or had they gone the other way and booked a registry office, followed by dinner in a pub with a few close friends? She had looked down on that type of wedding once, assuming you'd only choose that option because of a limited budget, as opposed to wanting simplicity. What she wouldn't give for that now. Someone who would commit to her without the need for pomp and ceremony. Who simply wanted to say *I do* to her, for life, regardless of the setting.

"Oh look, there's Pippa. I'm going to go and say hello," Eunice said, shuffling away and leaving Henry and Fleur alone for the first time that day.

A minute passed, during which Fleur turned in a small circle, as if she were taking in the setting and not aware of the fact that Henry was looking straight at her.

"Is everything all right?" he asked, quietly.

Her throat tightened as she stopped and faced him. "I'm sorry about this. I really had no idea."

"I know you didn't. Believe me, I realise this was nothing to do with you. This is all about Eunice. She always thinks she knows best."

"That reminds me of someone." She didn't know why she'd said this, but now it was out there, she couldn't take it back.

There was a tension in the air that seemed to be trying to pull them closer together. Why did she want him to take her hand so much? And why did she think that was what he wanted, too? And why on earth had she imagined that attending this wedding was the right thing to do? It was a totally ridiculous idea. She should have gone home. But she was here now, and to leave straight after arriving would be rude.

"Right, you two," Eunice said, appearing at their side out of nowhere. "The girls have made sure I have a place at the front, but that's just for me, I'm afraid. Old person's privilege. You two will have to find somewhere to sit together, I'm afraid."

"How very convenient," Henry said, with a huff before turning to Fleur. "I guess we should take our seats, then."

The wedding was beautiful. Both brides wore white, lace dresses, although the styles were completely different. One had a fitted bodice with a strapless, sweetheart neckline, while the other was far floatier with long sleeves and a plunge back.

More than once, Fleur found her eyes sliding up towards Henry's. Did people think they were a couple? she wondered. More than likely. It was a wedding, and they were sitting together, like couples did.

When the brides said *I do*, her eyes wandered up yet again. This time, she found he was staring at her.

"Beautiful," he whispered, before turning back to the service.

After the ceremony, the photographer bustled the brides outside for a series of poses, while trays of drinks were brought around for the other guests.

"They're only doing a twenty-minute photo session, apparently," another guest said to Fleur as they both took a glass of Pimm's from the same tray. "I'm so glad. I hate it when you're standing around for an hour and a half. I always end up famished."

"Yes," she smiled, tightly. "Me too."

"Who do you know? Pippa or Hazel?"

"Oh, I'm here as a plus one," she replied, not sure whether she should add any more.

There was no doubt that Eunice was enjoying all the attention of her relatives fussing around her. By contrast, Henry was glued to his phone, only occasionally allowing himself brief conversations with those same relations. Had Fleur not known the situation, this would have made her angry, but the likelihood was that he was busy monitoring how the Champagne was affecting his aunt.

Just as the guest had told her, twenty minutes later, a fork was clinked against a glass, calling the room to silence.

"Ladies and gentlemen, if you would like to proceed to the dining room, the wedding brunch will shortly be served."

The woman beside her turned and smiled. "Well, I guess I should check where I'm sitting."

"Oh, I should do that, too," Fleur replied.

Given how many times Eunice had explicitly said that she was her plus one and that she'd called her niece to ensure they would be sitting together, she assumed that she would be placed on a table next to her. But when she looked at the seating plan, displayed on an A-frame next to the dining hall door, she quickly found Eunice's name near the top table. However, hers was nowhere to be seen.

A mixture of panic and relief coursed through her. If she wasn't on the list, it meant that she had just gatecrashed a wedding she wasn't invited to. But it also meant that she could leave straight away and wouldn't have to sit there and explain to other guests that she didn't know either of the brides and was simply accompanying a member of her Book Club, who was on a different table.

Ready to walk away, she quickly scanned the plan once again, only to finally spot her name there in the perfect, pink calligraphy. It wasn't anywhere close to Eunice but was on a table near the doorway. But that wasn't what hit her. It was the name of the person placed next to hers. Henry Pierce.

CHAPTER 44

*S*omething about the way Fleur was standing in front of the table plan alerted Henry to the situation. He hadn't been able to keep his eyes off her all day and now he noted that her arms were fixed by her side, as though she had turned rigid with shock. Another minute passed, and she was still standing there, in the exact same position, not moving.

"Excuse me," he said to the distant relative talking to him. "I need to check on something." With Fleur fixed in his sights, he picked his way through the crowd and slid in next to her. He very quickly saw what the issue was. And he didn't know whether to laugh or cry.

"I think it's fair to say this is definitely a set up," he said. It wasn't just the fact that he was sitting next to her. It was all the other people on the table, too. Everyone else was seventy-plus and most had been friends for nearly half a century. He could see it all now, the way they would wax lyrical about the good old days, completely ignoring him and Fleur, leaving them with only each other for company.

"I guess we should sit down, then?" she said, moving away

from the board. She wasn't even able to meet his eye. Without so much as a backward glance in his direction, she moved through the double doors that led into the dining area, leaving Henry to stare transfixed.

"Henry, long time no see old man."

His attention was pulled away from Fleur by the voice of his second cousin, Archie. They were the same age, although that was where he liked to think any similarity ended. Growing up, Archie had been the epitome of a spoiled brat, with his parents indulging his every whim, be it a horse to get into eventing or a go-kart with the hope of one day becoming a racing driver. Henry wasn't even sure what he did now. Banking probably. The last time they'd spoken had been at another wedding, four years earlier, and he had no desire to make their meetings any more frequent than that.

"Yes indeed, long time no see, Archie," he said, moving away from the table plan, only for his cousin to follow him.

"I haven't seen your brother here. He's okay, I assume?"

"I expect so," Henry replied. "He's probably in Geneva. He took a job there a couple of years ago."

"Is that so?"

He hoped this would be where the conversation ended, but as he strode into the dining room, Archie remained hot on his heels.

"So, what about you? Are you getting any closer to one of these things?"

"A wedding?" Henry laughed. "Absolutely not."

"Why does that not surprise me? We all heard about the plus one Eunice set you up with. Absolutely love it. You know things must be really desperate when your old aunt is trying to get you laid!"

Henry could feel his teeth grinding together. He may not have seen that much of Archie, but he knew him well enough to know he wasn't going to like whatever was coming next.

"Look," he continued, gesturing towards Fleur. "If you're not planning on showing her a good time tonight, mind if I give it a go? I reckon I could teach her a thing or two, if you get my drift."

This was more than Henry could stand. His hands were clenched into fists at his side, and it took every bit of strength he had not to grab Archie by his skinny tie and lift him a foot in the air. He leaned in close. "You do not go near her, understand?" he hissed. "Fleur is off limits. Or you will be learning a very uncomfortable lesson. Do I make myself clear?"

Archie's lips twitched into a smirk, although it didn't disguise how pale he'd turned.

"Okay. I hear you. Off limits. Interesting. Well, it's been nice chatting to you." And with that, he turned away and scampered off, leaving Henry to find his seat.

No one else had arrived at the table yet, and Fleur was sitting entirely on her own. Henry couldn't help but envisage her in one of those romantic novels she defended so fiercely. His heart was pounding, partly from the sight of her and partly from what Archie had just said. Taking a deep breath, he prepared himself for an evening of cordial, yet restrained conversation and headed towards her.

Reaching their table, he took his phone out of an inside pocket, pulled off his jacket and hung it over the back of his chair. Then, out of habit more than anything, he tapped the screen and viewed the number it displayed.

"Is she okay?" Fleur asked. "Do we need to do anything?"

The question caught him by surprise. He was so used to dealing with Eunice on his own, he would never even mention it to anyone else unless it was absolutely necessary, in an emergency. The concern in her voice was genuine, although it was her use of the word *we* that struck him the most. As if she would do anything she could to help, which, he suspected, was true.

Ignoring the building heat he was experiencing, he nodded. "Yes, she's fine. There's no chance she'd risk messing things up here. Not with everyone around her. It's just a habit I've got into, always checking on her."

She pressed her lips together. The same lips he had kissed, he thought. Just thinking about that night was enough to make him doubt his decision to cut ties with her.

"I know the situation between us is …" Fleur took her time choosing the right word to finish the sentence. "… tricky. But I want you to know that I really admire how you look after your aunt. What you do is incredible, and I don't know if you get told that often enough."

The heat was intensifying, making it near impossible for him to breathe properly. Why did she have to look at him like that? And speak like she understood? And make him want her even more?

In the centre of the table, eight bottles of wine were sitting unopened. He reached across and grabbed a bottle of white in one hand and a red in the other.

"Which do you want?" he said. There was no way he was going to get through this without it.

CHAPTER 45

Fleur had lost count of how much she'd drunk. She knew she'd had at least one glass with each of the courses and more Champagne with the speeches, but there had been top ups, too, some by Henry, some by the wait staff and probably, a couple of times, she'd done it herself, but she couldn't quite remember. Other than very brief introductions, no one on the table other than Henry had spoken to her, but at least they had been generous with the wine and not hogged the bottles. Then again, maybe it would have been better if they had.

"Why didn't you tell me that Eunice lived in the opposite direction from me?" she asked him. "You did a complete detour to drop me off each time?" She'd assumed the conversation would stagnate, that after everything that had passed between them, they would struggle to find anything to say. But she couldn't have been more wrong. After a few minutes of bizarre cordiality from Henry, conversation had started to flow, and soon it felt as if they were picking up where they'd left off on their first drink together.

"Either I dropped you home, or I'd be forced to listen to Eunice drone on about how ungentlemanly I was, and how if I just showed nice girls the same attention I gave her, they'd be lining up for me."

"Is that right?" she laughed. "And I thought women liked the bad boys."

"Do they?"

Fleur's heart rate took an upward trajectory, and she found herself unsure how to reply. Silence descended on them, as the sound of laughter and chatter drifted across from the other tables.

"I'm sorry about the way I handled things," he said, eventually. "I'm not very good at this kind of stuff."

"Dumping people, you mean?"

He lowered his gaze and chewed on his bottom lip. At times like this, he was so damn cute Fleur wanted to scream, though given their current situation, it didn't seem appropriate. How was it possible this was the same man who had ended things with a text message?

Their knees touched under the table, prompting a reaction that she was now well accustomed to. Trying to appear casual, she placed her hand on the table, only for Henry to mirror the action, resulting in their fingertips ending up only millimetres apart. It would be so easy to make a move, she thought. She could tuck an invisible strand of hair behind his ear or run her hand across the top of his arm. He would reciprocate; she could feel it. But why on earth would she think about starting anything with a guy who'd made it abundantly clear that he didn't want any type of relationship with her? But if he wasn't interested, why was he still sitting there talking to her, not off chatting with his family?

"There you two are. It seems like you've had lots of fun."

Fleur's hand shot back onto her lap, her pulse spiking even higher than before.

"Is everything all right?" Henry said, standing up and checking his phone. "Are your levels okay? Do you need me to get you something?"

"I'm fine, perfectly fine," Eunice said, waving away his concern. "I'm also perfectly capable of sorting myself out. I'm just letting you know that I'm going to head back to Maldon with Val."

"Val? I didn't think she was staying there?"

Fleur sat silently, listening to their conversation. Given the size of Eunice's family there, she assumed Val was another member. One Henry had probably ignored all evening.

"One of her kids is feeling funny, and there's an issue with her hotel room, so I told her that she and children can stay with me tonight. To be honest, I don't know why I didn't think of it before."

"Okay then," he said, and before Fleur realised what was happening, he was on his feet and retrieving his jacket from the back of his chair. "Just give me a minute to say goodbye and congratulations to Hazel and Pippa."

Sensing that she should probably do the same — particularly as she was attending a wedding where she only knew two people — Fleur also stood up.

"What do you think you're doing?" Eunice frowned.

"What do *you* think I'm doing?" Henry replied. "If you're leaving, I'm coming too."

"And I've probably outstayed my welcome," Fleur said, feeling she should say something too.

Eunice's frown disappeared as she planted her hands firmly on her hips. "Don't be ridiculous. I don't need you two ending your night early and coming back with me."

"It's fine," Fleur insisted.

But Eunice was having none of it. "I absolutely refuse. Anyway, there's not enough room for both of you in her car, and we've already got the taxi booked for later. You two stay; carry on enjoying yourselves."

Fleur suddenly realised just how much fun she'd been having. The flirting, the easy laughter, the wine. She could happily stay on until the end of the night. But it wasn't her decision. She glanced at Henry, waiting, as his gaze lingered on Eunice. She was certain he was about to refuse, but instead, he nodded.

"Okay, then. But let me walk you to the car."

"No, thank you. I've got plenty of help as it is. Besides, they're all waiting for me."

She nodded to the other side of the hall, where a group of two adults and two children was looking in their direction.

"Fine then," he said, offering them a small wave which was immediately returned. "But you'll ring me when you get home?"

"Which one of us is the old person here?"

"And make sure you check your levels properly before you go to bed. And leave your phone on your nightstand, just in case they drop while you're asleep."

"Goodnight, Henry," Eunice said, firmly, then kissed him before turning to Fleur. "Have fun, my dear."

As Fleur could have predicted, Henry's eyes didn't leave his aunt as she crossed the room to meet up with the others, at which point she offered him one last wave before they headed outside. Only then did he turn back to Fleur.

"Well, I guess it's just you and me then."

"Apart from the hundreds of relatives you've got here."

"Apart from them," he smiled.

It was the same smile he'd offered her once before when they'd been on their own. The dimpled one that lit up his whole face and turned her insides to jelly. But that was just a reaction to a man making her a compliment. Wasn't that what Annelise had told her? Nothing to do with Henry. He wasn't interested in her. He'd told her as much. Still, those dimples were holding fast, and she found it near impossible to look away. When he spoke again, butterflies swarmed inside her.

"Why don't you and I dance?"

CHAPTER 46

*H*enry Pierce did not know what the hell he was doing, and that was something he didn't often admit. Even when he'd done seemingly ridiculous things, like heading to a university three hundred miles from his family home or moved across the country to be there for his elderly aunt, they'd been conscious, planned decisions. When he'd given up a great job at a law firm where he was a shoo-in for partner, it was because he'd picked a new one where he knew, with a bit of effort, he could make himself indispensable. And he'd been right, making junior partner in under two years. He could stand in an office or boardroom or courtroom and feel perfectly confident that he was doing the right thing.

But when it came to Fleur, he lost sight completely of what that was. Being next to her was like having the world suddenly start spinning in the wrong direction. Everything looked the same, but he knew it wasn't. He couldn't keep his balance like normal, and it didn't even stop when she wasn't there, because she occupied his thoughts all of the time.

"Why don't you and I dance?" he'd said, standing up and offering her his hand before he could second guess himself. Though rather than immediately accepting, as he'd hoped she would, a deep furrow formed between her brows.

"It's a slow song," she said.

He chewed his bottom lip. Of course, it was. That was why he'd waited until now to ask her. He hardly wanted her to join him in a rendition of the Macarena.

"I hadn't noticed," he said, dryly.

He continued to hold his hand out towards her, feeling more and more conspicuous the longer he waited. Given how he'd treated her, it shouldn't have come as a surprise that she didn't immediately accept, but there was a limit to how long he could stand there for.

"I didn't think you were the type of man to like dancing?" she said, looking up at him from under her eyelashes.

God, she was going to make him work for it. Though there was nothing else he'd rather do, especially as it was a choice between Fleur and the cousins he'd been doing everything in his power to avoid.

"There are lots of things you don't know about me," he said, stretching out his arm a little further. "Now, would you like to dance?"

Without replying, she pressed her lips together, drawing his eyes to them. What he wouldn't give to kiss them again. To kiss her and not have to stop. He was still lost in his imagination, picturing that moment, when she finally placed her hand in his.

"This is purely because I'm intrigued to see your dance skills."

"I hope I don't disappoint you."

Their hands fitted perfectly together and when he pulled her up onto her feet, he was amazed how effortlessly their fingers intertwined. He'd always gone for tall women before. Or rather tall women had gravitated towards him and his six-foot-four frame. But Fleur's petite stature gave him an overwhelming urge to wrap his arms around her.

Several pairs of eyes watched as they weaved through the tables together. No doubt family chat would be alive with gossip about them in the morning. If Uncle Ted's drunken escapades didn't take precedence.

As they slipped onto the dance floor, he deliberated where he should place his hands. Walking together had been easy, but slow dancing was an entirely different matter. He suddenly felt as if he were back at a school dance and had to decide whether it was better to put his hands around the girl's waist, where he could hold her as close as possible, or around her neck so that he could kiss her, should the opportunity arise.

"You don't make this easy for me," he said, settling on her waist, and their bodies started rocking gently from side to side. His hands felt so natural sitting there above the curve of her hips.

"You were the one who asked me to dance," she replied.

"I forgot. I seem to forget a lot of things around you. Like why exactly I shouldn't kiss you right now."

Her bottom lip disappeared beneath her top teeth in an infuriatingly gorgeous manner. Unable to stop himself, he lifted a hand and pushed a strand of hair gently behind her ear, an ensuing shiver affecting them both.

"I wasn't the one who thought we should stop, remember?" she said, gently. "You were the one who decided it couldn't work."

"And now I'm having a great deal of trouble remembering why."

She shifted her stance a fraction, so that she was just far

enough away that he couldn't lean in and kiss her. "I think I should probably go home," she said, looking straight at him. "It's getting late."

He nodded, butterflies swarming inside him. "I understand. Would you like some company?"

CHAPTER 47

"Is this a good idea?"

"This is definitely a good idea," Fleur said, as she kissed a line down Henry's neck.

"But I don't want you to think I'm taking advantage of you."

"You are definitely not," she said, feeling like a teenager again, although she'd never behaved like this at that age.

Once in the taxi, they'd barely been able to keep their hands off each other, and every kiss made her desperate for the next.

"Fleur, I know I messed up before. But I really think—"

"It's fine," she said, wishing he'd stop talking so that they could carry on kissing.

"Where in Maldon are we going?" the taxi driver asked, keeping his eyes on the road. Thankfully, it wasn't the same man as before, and this one didn't seem bothered about making small talk.

"Are we going to your place, or mine?" she asked Henry, her stomach performing multiple somersaults.

"Yours," he immediately replied. "Your flat. Your bed. I want to be surrounded by everything you. Besides, I've case files all over my floor."

"Hmm, case files. I don't think I've ever heard anyone make them sound sexy before."

"Divorce case files," he reminded her.

"Wow, you really know how to sell it," she laughed, before turning to the driver. "North Street, please. At the bottom of the High Street."

"North Street it is." The driver turned up the volume on the radio, leaving Fleur and Henry to get back to their kissing.

It felt like they'd barely driven off, when the taxi drew to a stop.

"North Street. This is you, isn't it?"

"This is us," Fleur said, unbuckling her belt while simultaneously opening the door. It had been a long time since she'd felt like this: that insatiable urge to hold a person and not let go. And she knew for certain it was reciprocated. Yet when she took Henry's hand to pull him out behind her, he didn't budge.

"What are you doing?" she said, stepping back onto the pavement to give him more room to get out. But still he didn't move.

"I don't know if this is a good idea."

She ached at the sight of so much tension on display. How was it possible for someone to survive being like that all the time? There again, if anyone was to answer that, it should be her. She remembered so well the constant desire to be perfect. To hold everything together. If only he could see how much easier it would all be if he allowed the weight to slide off his shoulders and let himself go.

"Henry, the meter's still running. Whatever you want to do, it's up to you, but I'm going inside."

She swivelled on the ball of her foot and turned to the front door, refusing to look back over her shoulder. She wasn't going to beg. A minute later, she heard the taxi drive away and felt the soft skin of his lips on her neck.

"You are a terrible influence," he whispered, and then they were kissing again and practically falling into one another.

"I need to find my keys." Fleur broke away just long enough to delve into her handbag. When she'd found them, it took her three times longer than normal to get the key into the lock than it should have done. She stumbled up the stairs and into the living room, Henry close behind.

"You have no idea how much I kept thinking about that first kiss," he said, as he pulled her towards him for yet another. "How much I kept thinking about you and how I wanted to kiss every single part of you. Can I do that? Can I lay you down on your bed and kiss all of you?"

"My bed?" Dropping his hands, she jumped back. "Are you okay to wait here for a moment?" She edged back towards the door.

"Wait here?"

"Yes. I just need to go into my bedroom for a second."

His eyes narrowed. "If this is one of those things where you get changed into something you think I'll find more attractive, believe me, it's totally unnecessary. You are absolutely incredible as you are." He moved towards her, but she placed her hands squarely on his chest and pushed him back towards the sofa.

"I'll just be two minutes." She rushed to the door, only to turn around and say, "There's wine in the fridge. Why don't you pour yourself a glass? Pour us both a glass. Big ones."

A second later, she slammed the door and dropped to her knees. "Crap! Crap! Crap! Crap!" She scrambled to pick up as many things as she could in one go. Why, of all weeks, hadn't she done any tidying up? "Get in! Get in!" she seethed, trying to shove a dress into an already over filled drawer. It didn't help that she'd tried on almost every accessory she possessed before she'd headed out. Necklaces and scarves, along with a variety of underwear, were littered all over the place. And this wasn't attractive underwear. This was the big, suck-it-in-from-every-angle type with more elastic than a bungee rope.

"Is everything all right in there?" he called through from the living room.

"Oh yes! Yes! Everything's fine! I'm just freshening up!" She picked up a packet of tissues and shoved it in another drawer.

"I've poured the wine! Do you want me to bring it in?"

"No! No! I'll just be a minute!" With a pair of striped tights in her hands, she attempted to steady her breathing, while desperately trying not to think about Henry's bedroom. Knowing him, he probably even ironed his underwear. If he saw this, he'd bolt straight out the door.

In a last-ditch manoeuvre, she pushed as much as she could beneath the bed. T-shirts, her yoga mat, even a plate and some cutlery went under.

"Okay, I don't know what's going on in there, but I'm coming in!" he called.

"One second! One second!" Panting, she combed her fingers through her hair before adjusting her top and then quickly fetching a candle. She was busy lighting it when he stepped into the room, holding two glasses of wine, although rather than offering her one, he placed them both down on the dresser she had only just finished clearing.

"Now, remind me," he said. "Where were we?"

CHAPTER 48

*F*leur rolled over, trying to fight her internal body clock. She needed more rest. A couple more hours sleep. Proper sleep.

It was trickier than she remembered, having someone in bed with her. At least the sleeping part had been. The movies always made it look so romantic. One head resting exactly in the dip of the other person's shoulder, a blissful synchronisation of their breaths rising and falling. But as much as the bit before had been incredible, the sleeping part had not been.

Even when their conversation had fallen silent and she knew Henry was asleep, she'd been unable to settle. After tossing and turning, she'd given up and headed out into the living room, then the kitchen, clearing up as quietly as she could, so it would be slightly more presentable when they got up. She'd come back and tidied a little more in the bedroom, too, although that was harder, given that she didn't want to turn the light on and disturb him. She'd taken his jacket from where he'd dropped it on the floor and hung it up in the hallway closet, then folded his trousers and placed them over the back of a chair. After which, she'd found herself an attractive nightgown for when he woke up.

But her late-night cleaning session was only half due to difficulty sleeping. The other issue was Henry. There was no denying this was a man used to having the entire bed to himself. He was lying stretched out like a starfish, while she had only a sliver of mattress. And as for the duvet, he'd somehow looped his feet around both the bottom corners, leaving hers to freeze. The next time he stayed over, there would have to be a serious duvet-hogging conversation. And perhaps she would place a pillow down the centre of the bed to mark out the halfway point and ensure she got her fair share, although how cuddling would work like that, she wasn't exactly sure. But despite this, she knew she'd do it all again in a heartbeat.

It felt as though she'd barely got back into bed and closed her eyes when the cawing of seagulls drifted through the window, announcing the morning. Knowing there was no point fighting it any longer, Fleur blinked slowly awake and then again, until her eyes were finally wide open, when they landed on Henry's sleeping form. A cascade of excitement filled her as she recalled the previous night. How could it have only been one night they'd spent together? The wedding felt so long ago. The taxi ride back a hazy memory.

His chest moved up and down and a slight whistling noise came from his lips. No doubt all the drinks he'd had were responsible for him still sleeping, although considering the amount of wine she'd drunk, she was feeling decidedly clear headed. She smacked her lips together, finding that while her head was fine, her tongue was dry and furry. She needed a glass of water, but she really didn't want to move. It would mean taking his arm off her, and she desperately didn't want to wake him. She lay there for a couple of minutes, wondering if he might move his arm of his own accord or wake up, but when that didn't happen, she lifted it as gently as she could and slid out from underneath.

"Is everything all right?" he asked, his voice groggy with sleep. It somehow made him sound even more attractive.

"Sorry. I didn't mean to disturb you. I was just going to get some water. Would you like some?"

With a low growl, he stretched out, somehow managing to take up even more room in the bed. A standard double had seemed perfectly adequate when she'd bought it; a king-size now appeared to be a must for anyone in a relationship, at least with someone as tall as Henry.

"What's the time?"

"The time?" She picked up her watch and squinted at it. "Just gone ten. But it's a Sunday, remember? No work today."

She lay back down, ready to snuggle up with him again and possibly continue where they'd left off, but he sat bolt upright, all drowsiness gone.

"Ten? Are you sure?"

"Yes, I'm sure." She was about to make a joke about finding him doubting her ability to tell the time insulting, but he was already on the move.

"My phone? Have you seen my phone?" He swung his feet off the bed and picked up his trousers, shaking out the pockets.

"I don't think I've seen it. Did you have it in the lounge?" She stood up and crossed the room, to where he was now picking up her clothes and shaking them, too.

"Henry, it's fine. It can't have gone far."

His head snapped round to her. "It is not fine. It is not fine at all."

His words hit her like a blow, and she backed away, flinching. It reminded her of the Henry she'd met that first time, in the pharmacy all those weeks ago. A Henry she'd thought was well behind them.

"I'm sure if we just calm down and look, there can't be that many places it can be," she said, trying to steady her own nerves, too. She knew why he was reacting this way. She knew it wasn't personal. He was worried about Eunice.

"I don't understand where it can have gone," he said, marching into the living room and starting to toss cushions off the sofa.

"My jacket," he said, stopping in his tracks. "Where's my jacket?"

Fleur considered the question for a second before recalling her late-night activities.

"Oh, it's in the closet in the hall. I put it away. I didn't want it to get all creased."

Without bothering to respond, he disappeared into the hallway, returning a moment later with the phone in his hand. Fleur's relief was short-lived.

"It's out of battery. It's out of battery." His breathing was visibly staggered as he grabbed his shoes and battled with the laces.

All the while, the ache in Fleur's chest grew deeper. As gently as she could, she stepped forwards and took hold of his arm.

"Eunice is an adult, Henry. She's an adult and she is not your responsibility."

His head came up, his jaw locked, and that one vein bulged more fiercely than she had ever seen it.

"I should've known you'd never understand," he said.

She shook her head. Tears stung her eyes, but she wasn't going to let him do this. She wasn't going to let him push her away again.

"Henry, please, you—"

But he didn't let her finish. After opening the door, he turned around. "This was a mistake," he said, looking her dead in the eye. "This was my mistake."

CHAPTER 49

*H*enry was still buttoning up his shirt as he flew down the stairs and raced out onto the road. Of all the stupid things to do, how could he have let his phone battery run down? How could he not have thought to put it near the bed or plugged it into the power bank he kept with it, in case Eunice needed him in the middle of the night?

Mornings were always the worst time for her. Her glucose levels would drop overnight and given that she didn't show the same fastidiousness when it came to keeping her phone charged as he did, he'd lost count how often he'd had to race over, armed with jelly babies or something else sugary. And it didn't end there. More than once, she'd tucked into the jelly babies while he was busy in another room, and then needed a shot of insulin to bring her levels back down again. But he always got it sorted. Normally, that was.

His fast walk up the hill turned into a jog as he passed Mrs. Salisbury's pink walls. Why had he let himself get distracted like that? And why had Fleur taken his jacket and put it in the hall cupboard, miles away from him. And why hadn't he noticed when she had? Anxiety clawed beneath his ribs. He would never forgive himself if something had happened.

When he reached the top of the hill, he switched up the pace again, to a sprint. A thousand images were running through his head. Hopefully, if Eunice had been feeling light-headed, she would have taken herself to sit down even if she hadn't fixed herself a snack. She might have gone back upstairs for a lie down. But those were both best-case scenarios. If she hadn't realised her blood sugar was low, she could have passed out in the kitchen or the bathroom, where she could have hit her head on anything. And by now, she could have been lying there on her own for hours.

"Eunice!" Henry shouted, fumbling with his keys, struggling to find the one he needed. When he finally got it into the lock, he opened the door with such force, he practically fell inside.

"Eunice!" He raced into the kitchen, only to find it empty and the living room, too.

Please be okay. Please, please be okay, he kept repeating to himself as he took the stairs two at a time. When he reached the landing, he checked the bathroom first. It was with a mixture of relief and confusion that he found it empty. The bathroom and kitchen would be the two worst places for her to fall and hurt herself, but the fact she still wasn't answering him was enough to kick his adrenaline into overdrive.

"Eunice! Where are you?" His panic only deepened when he pushed open her bedroom door and found she wasn't there, either. "Eunice! Eunice!"

He went to the bedroom where he'd spent more nights than he cared to remember, and then on to the third, which was always ready for guests, though used far less frequently than she would have liked. With still no sign of his aunt, he began to get seriously desperate. Back in the bathroom, he checked behind the shower curtain and then in the bath itself, before returning to her bedroom and opening the wardrobe door. Of course, she wasn't in the wardrobe. But where the hell was she? If only he could ring her.

With a sudden burst of clarity, he bolted downstairs to the kitchen again, where a charger was plugged in above the countertop. He attached his phone and waited for it to light up.

"Just hurry up, will you?" he said. Why the hell was it taking so long to come to life? Did it normally? He couldn't remember the last time he'd let it run completely dead. Was it broken? Perhaps something had happened to it. Maybe he'd banged it without noticing or Fleur had dropped it and not wanted to tell him.

A tiny white shape flickered on the screen, and a surge of relief flooded through him. He picked the phone up, ready to hit dial, when a sound caught his attention: the click of a key in the lock, followed by talking.

"You're right. I should. It's lovely at this time of the morning."

Abandoning the phone, he dashed into the hallway. There, fully dressed and standing beside his cousin Val, was Eunice, happily chatting away.

"Henry, this is a surprise. I didn't expect to see you this morning?" she said, walking across and kissing him on the cheek. "You look rather flushed, dear. Is everything all right?"

"I ... I ... Where have you been?"

"We took the children out for breakfast. I sent you a message, so you wouldn't worry. Did you not see it?"

The adrenaline that had been coursing through him was quickly dropping away, leaving him in a state of near exhaustion.

"My battery died," he mumbled.

"Oh, well. We went to the Driftwood restaurant, and then Johnathon took the children to the park. Have you been there? The Driftwood, that is. They do a fabulous poached egg."

"No, I've not." As Eunice hung up her coat and sauntered into the kitchen without a care in the world, he wasn't sure if he wanted to laugh or cry.

"I would definitely recommend it. You could take Fleur there for the evening — I think they do dinners — you seemed to be getting on so well yesterday."

Fleur. All the relief he'd felt at discovering his aunt safe and well, evaporated and was replaced by a lead weight in the pit of his stomach. What the hell must she think of him? He'd been awful. Worse than he'd ever behaved before, and that was saying something. His heart was close to breaking as he recalled how incredible the previous night had been. Now he had ruined all that without giving it a second thought. There was something about her that made him loosen up and feel like there could be more to life beyond work and his aunt.

But that was exactly the point. All his fears about dating her had just been proved correct. Being with Fleur risked him not looking after Eunice properly. And he wouldn't need reminding twice.

CHAPTER 50

"*I*'m coming down now," Annelise said. "Just let me throw a few things together."

"You can't do that. It's Sunday. It will take you hours. I'm not even sure if the buses run."

"I'll drive. Honestly, it's fine."

"You don't have to do that."

"I do. But trust me, if he makes an appearance, I will not be able to hold my tongue."

Despite all the tears she'd shed that morning, Fleur had to smile. No matter how insane her sister drove her, she knew she was lucky to have her.

"He was worried about his aunt," she said, feeling the need to defend Henry's actions. "It's not easy for him."

"Showing consideration isn't easy? Nope. You don't treat someone like that. You don't slam the door on them without even saying goodbye after you've just spent your first night together. That's just downright wrong."

She knew her sister was right. He'd made her feel as if not keeping track of his phone had been her fault, which she guessed in a way it was, moving his jacket. But she'd done it in all innocence. Surely he knew her well enough by now to realise she'd never do anything to put Eunice at risk.

Shock at him storming off had hit first. Pure, undiluted shock. After which it had taken a full fifteen minutes to realise the extent of her hurt and for the tears to start. And when the floodgates had opened, and she knew she wouldn't be able to stop them on her own, she had called Annelise.

"I'll be a couple of hours, tops," her sister said. "I just need to sort out the school run for the children tomorrow and send a couple of emails saying I won't be able to attend a seminar."

"You really don't have to do that. I don't want you missing out on anything for me."

"And I don't want you falling back into a bad place because of Henry Pierce. But will you do me a favour before I come."

"Okay?"

"Get out of that flat and go for a walk. Or a run. Or grab us something nice for dinner. I'm not having you sitting indoors for hours moping 'til I arrive."

Fleur looked down at the soft, oversize, fleece hoody she was wearing. Covered with a pink-and-purple-teddy-bear pattern, she'd shoved it under her bed the previous night. It hadn't seemed like something he would approve of. But it was so soft and comfortable, basically a fitted duvet. The thought of having to take it off, let alone get dressed, made her want to start crying all over again. But if her sister was rearranging her entire life at the drop of a hat to make sure she was okay, it was the least she could do.

"Okay, I'll go for a walk."

"Good. I'll be there soon."

When she hung up the phone, she was tempted to ignore her promise. After all, Annelise would be at least two hours. Probably nearer three. She was always one to underestimate how long things would take her. There was definitely another hour and a half before she needed to think about leaving the flat, or she could get dressed and pretend she'd just returned. Then again, Annelise would know. She had a way of reading things.

"Let's start with a shower," she said to herself.

As she stood under the running water, Fleur found it difficult not to think about Robert. Or, rather, the aftermath of Robert. There had been a period when she'd found it hard to even get out of bed and clean her teeth. There'd seemed no point. Who would she be doing it for?

Then she had started to call in sick to work; something she'd never done before. It was only an odd day here and there at first, but then the absences had started getting longer and longer and they had begun asking questions. The doctor had suggested that the way she was feeling ran a little deeper than just the blues. Perhaps it was something she needed to take more seriously. He'd recommended medication to help ease the numbness that was overpowering her. She'd resisted at first and made a little more effort to get up each day and do something, but it was harder than it should have been. That was when Annelise had stepped in and made her understand the doctor was right. She needn't be ashamed about it. She'd just needed a little extra help at the minute. That was all.

Little by little, Fleur had managed to see that *she* was the person she needed to get out of bed for each day. *She* was the one for whom she must clean her teeth and get out into the world. Even if she was going to be on her own forever, she owed it to herself, she finally realised.

The last thing she was going to do was let Henry Pierce have the power to take that away from her again.

Once dried, she dressed in her brightest, most over-the-top, flowery clothes, and she didn't stop there. With her outfit sorted, she worked on her hair, arranging it in fifties-style ringlets, before applying mascara, blusher and a final slick, bright-orange lipstick. As she looked in the mirror, she fixed a smile on her face, only for it to slip almost immediately. Her image blurred and began to distort as tears welled up in her eyes again.

"No!" she said aloud, wiping her nose and dabbing her eyes to ensure her makeup stayed in place. She wasn't doing this. She wasn't going to accept being treated like crap. She deserved better. It had taken her years to finally see that she was worth better than that, and she wasn't going to let an arrogant divorce lawyer take that away from her. No one was ever going to do that to her again.

CHAPTER 51

*B*y the time Annelise showed up, Fleur had been out, but the walk had been far from uplifting. She'd reached the corner of the road, and spied the Black Rabbit, where she'd gone with Henry for their very first drink. She'd steeled herself against the pain and headed up the High Street, until her heels made it necessary to pause. It was only when she noticed a man waving at her through the adjacent window that she realised she'd stopped directly in front of the phone shop where Henry had arranged for her cracked screen to be mended. How was it possible, she thought, that she could have so many memories associated with a man she had only been on one official date with? Everywhere she went seemed to evoke them.

When she'd finally walked back through her front door, she was in just as much of a state as before she'd left, if not worse. And as much as she tried, Annelise did not help matters.

Her sister meant well but Fleur didn't want to listen to upbeat music or have living room dance sessions. And she didn't want to watch cringeworthy comedies featuring drunken escapades. (Annelise had decided that any form of romantic film was out, meaning that the only ones they could watch involved people in such mortifying situations that she hid behind her cushion in sympathetic embarrassment.) What she would have really liked to do was watch a horror film, with a Chinese takeaway and then maybe do a little bit of yoga, if she wasn't too full.

"You should take a rest. Call in sick," Annelise said on Monday morning when she came into the living room to find Fleur already sitting at her laptop, working.

"I've just started a new job. I can't call in sick already."

"What about a working lunch, then?"

Fleur was now hitting the keys harder, though the change was too subtle for Annelise to notice.

"You know, I was thinking, you need a distraction from all this Henry drama. It's not too late to plan a party. It might be just the thing you need to keep your mind off him and, you know, the other one."

"My mind is already busy enough not to worry about Henry ... or Robert," she replied, unsure why Annelise would no longer mention her ex-husband's name. "In fact, if my mind could do with anything, it's a little more hush, so that I can focus."

Now she felt crappy for speaking to her sister like that, especially given how she'd travelled all that way to see her, and expected a retort to follow. She deserved it. But instead, Annelise stepped forwards and kissed the top of her head.

"Well, as it happens, the school has just messaged. Apparently, someone in Margot's class has head lice and there's no way I can let the nanny deal with that. If she doesn't do it properly, we'll all end up riddled with them, so I need to head off after lunch, anyway. Which should give you all the quiet you need."

Feeling even more guilty, Fleur got up from her computer and wrapped her arms around her sister.

"Thank you," she said.

"I'm just at the end of the phone, remember," Annelise replied, unable to disguise the worry that filled her eyes.

As CONCERNED as Annelise had been that she would slip back into old habits, Fleur found her line about being too busy to think about Henry turned out to be pretty accurate.

"We're extremely impressed by the visuals you sent in," Paul said in their Friday one-to-one meeting, "I was hoping you might come up to London next week. There are a few things we want to discuss and several of the managers are in next Thursday. It would be ideal if you could join us."

"That would be great. Thursday works really well for me," she replied.

She'd worked in business long enough to know that when your manager suggested you attend a meeting, there really was no option, so it worked better to seem enthusiastic. But Thursday really was perfect. It meant she couldn't attend Book Club, which she didn't want to do anyway. No matter how much she was loving the psychological thriller they were reading that fortnight, she couldn't bear the thought of facing Eunice. Or any of them, really. She imagined how quickly the news of her stupid dalliance with Henry would have worked its way through the group. Besides, there was the added issue of him dropping his aunt off, and there was no way she could face him.

Since he'd bolted out of her flat, she'd received only one

message from him. *Eunice is fine. Apologies.* That was it. No explanation. No real apology where he took responsibility for his actions or the fact that his behaviour must have left her feeling like crap. And she had waited, staring at her phone, expecting the three dots of an impending follow-up message to appear, where he would write that he understood how he had hurt her. But there was nothing more.

"So that time works for you?" Paul's pixilated face was looking at her, expectantly.

"Sorry, you just cut out for a second," she lied, to cover how she'd just slipped off into a world of her own. "What time did you say?"

"Eleven?"

"Yes, of course. Eleven is fine. I'll see you then."

With her last meeting of the day over, she put down her phone, collapsed back into the sofa and picked up the TV remote beside her. Given how sunny it was outside, it would be perfect weather for a run. But she didn't fancy it just yet. For now, she wanted to chill out and forget everything, which proved trickier than she'd hoped.

As she flicked through the channels and decided on a home-makeover programme, her phone buzzed.

Girly drinks on Wednesday? came through from Gemma. *It's been too long since the last one.*

Fleur didn't hesitate before replying, *Sorry. Crazy at work. Won't make book club this week either.*

A series of sad face emojis pinged up, immediately followed by another message.

We'll miss you. Don't work too hard.

As she stared at the screen, a pang of sadness hit her. Strange as it was, considering she'd only known these people a few months, she'd miss them, too. But that was the way it had to be.

CHAPTER 52

*H*enry stared at the piece of paper on the desk in front of him. He'd got as far as the first line, but that was it. He couldn't work out how he was supposed to continue. *Dear Fleur,* but where did he go from there?

Like most people would, he'd considered telephoning or text messaging his apology, but somehow that didn't feel enough. And she hadn't replied to his last message. He needed to say more. But what? He was really, really, *really* sorry? She knew what the situation was. He'd never made any pretence about Eunice always coming first. He thought it would have been easier than this to cut the ties, yet nearly two weeks had passed, and she was still the first thing he thought of when he woke up and the final image that flickered in his mind before he fell asleep.

Hence the letter. He thought if he wrote down everything he needed to say to her, it would help get her out of his system.

"Fleur wasn't at Book Club last night," Eunice said, walking into the kitchen and flicking on the kettle.

He hurriedly folded the paper and put it back in his pocket. He'd been carrying it around for days in the hope that inspiration would strike, and he'd suddenly know the exact words to say, but so far that hadn't happened. Besides, given how much Eunice liked to stick her nose in, it didn't feel like the right place to work on it.

"Gemma's rather worried about her. Says she's been very quiet lately. Not even wanting to meet up for drinks. I don't suppose you know anything about that?"

"No, I haven't heard from her at all," he replied, before quickly changing the subject. "Remember I'm in court today, so I won't have my phone switched on. I should be done by three, but you know how these things can run over."

"You won't? You've never mentioned that before." Eunice's voice dripped with sarcasm.

"If I knew you actually listened to me, I wouldn't have to repeat myself so much," he said, sounding more like a parent than a younger relative.

"I listened. You're in court in Chelmsford. Divorce case. Can't have your phone on. Should finish at three but might run on late. Does that sound about right?"

He wrinkled his nose. There was no doubt which side of the family his know-it-all attitude came from. "Fine, but can you humour me, please? I've already set out meals in the fridge, with their carb values on. Please make sure you're measuring everything properly. Your glucose is still quite low."

Eunice pursed her lips, her nostrils flattening as she sucked in a deep breath.

"Henry, darling, how many years have you been in Maldon, trying to help me monitor my diabetes?"

He paused. He was almost certain he was walking into a

trap, but he answered the question all the same. "Just under three."

"Just under three. And how many years did I take care of it myself before you arrived? No, wait; don't answer that. I'll tell you. Over seventy. Will you please stop fussing? Two minor hiccups in over half a decade is hardly worth worrying about, in the grand scheme of things."

Henry also took a deep breath in. There were several responses he wanted to give, like how he didn't consider collapsing and ending up in hospital with a broken bone a *little hiccup*. But he knew there was no getting through to her, and he didn't want to waste energy arguing. Not when that was what he was about to spend his day doing in court.

"Just promise me you won't go on any long walks. And make sure your phone is in your pocket, not at the bottom of your handbag. You know you don't always hear it when it beeps."

"So now you're telling me I'm deaf, as well?" Eunice scowled. "Aren't you a charmer?"

Aware that time was getting on, he glanced at his watch. Parking outside the courthouse could be a nightmare, and the last thing he wanted was to have to use the multistorey where the spaces left barely enough room for him to open his door. This battle would have to wait.

Walking over to his aunt, he bent over and kissed her on the top of the head. "Please, just take care of yourself. That's all I'm asking."

"I always do," she replied, and he wished with all his heart he could believe her.

CHAPTER 53

*F*leur had actually woken up feeling good, which hadn't happened for at least a week. Perhaps it was the fact she'd cut all caffeine from her diet. Or maybe it was a left-over high from the work meeting the previous day, when the big boss mentioned her and said how her work was at the level they should all be aspiring to. Then again, it could just have been because it was a perfectly sunny day.

Had she still been in her old job, she might have delayed starting work and headed out immediately for a run, but there were a few tasks she needed to get on with first. And so, it was nearly midday when she finally got her trainers on, deciding that there wasn't anything so important left in her inbox that it couldn't wait for another hour or so. As tended to be the case now, she double checked she'd got her keys and phone before closing her front door and heading out.

At first the plan was for a four-kilometre loop, which involved heading down to the seawall, then weaving back and forth through the little foot paths and around the duck pond until she got back home. But three quarters of the way through the run, when her legs still showed no sign of tiring, she decided to extend it, cutting through the houses until she hit Fambridge Road, then heading past the secondary school and up to the top of town. Next, she took a left into the White Horse carpark, which ran behind the main shops. She hadn't decided where she was going from there. It would be an easy downhill run home, but considering how good she was feeling, she ruled out heading down Market Hill.

She was still debating which was her best option, when she noticed a cluster of people at the entrance to the arcade. There was something about the way the group was standing that made her slow her pace. They were mainly adults, but there was a couple of teenagers there too, and together they'd formed a rough semi-circle with each of them looking down towards the centre.

"We need to get an ambulance," she heard a voice say. "Someone call 999."

With her pace still slowing, she considered what to do. There were already plenty of people present, and one more might just get in the way rather than help the situation, and that was the last thing she wanted to do. Deciding she should leave them to it, she was about to jog on, when she noticed one of the teenagers taking her mobile out of her pocket and start filming.

You have to be joking! she said to herself and immediately switched back up to a sprint.

"Put that thing away!" she ordered, slapping her hand on the front of the girl's phone.

"Hey, what are you doing?" she protested. Dressed in school uniform, with her tie dangling loose around her neck, the girl was probably no older than fifteen, although it was difficult to tell beneath the layers of makeup which had been far more expertly applied than Fleur could have managed.

Now that the casualty was no longer being filmed, she took her time to speak again. "You heard me. Get away from here. Before I call the police."

The girl sneered. "What for? This is a free country. I can video who I want."

"Wow," Fleur muttered under her breath. She'd seen teenagers like this one depicted on television. Entitled, angry and generally rude. She'd always assumed they were an exaggeration of the day's youth. But apparently that wasn't the case.

"Turn your phone off before it ends up broken," she replied, enunciating each word clearly.

"Are you threatening me? 'Cos I'm a minor, and you could go to prison for that."

Fleur was near dumbstruck. At that age, she'd have scarpered the minute an adult challenged her. She straightened her back, making the most of her five-foot-two frame.

"Well, you might be a minor, but I'm a lawyer, and I'm willing to bet my knowledge of what you're doing is better than yours." Fleur couldn't believe what she was saying. It was outright lying. But it felt good and even better when she watched the angry, red face in front of her turn pale. "I'm happy to call this straight into the office," she continued. "What about you? Do you have any idea how much it would cost you to take me to court? A lot more than this phone of yours is worth, that's for sure."

That was all it took. Dropping her hand, the girl grabbed her friend. "Whatever," she said petulantly, offering Fleur one more attempt at a withering glare. "It isn't interesting now, anyway. The old woman's sitting up."

Only at these words did Fleur remember that there was someone in trouble there. An old lady, it appeared.

"The ambulance will be here in forty minutes," someone said.

"Forty minutes? That's ridiculous."

"Did anyone see what happened?"

Once again, she considered turning around and walking away. She'd done her civic duty, stopping the recording, and there were obviously people on top of the situation with the ambulance. But something made her stop. Unable to explain why, she pushed up onto her tiptoes to try and take a look at the person collapsed on the ground.

"Eunice!"

CHAPTER 54

wo women were crouching by her friend, who was sitting propped up against the wall. Only she didn't look like the Eunice she knew. She was too pale, too frail. Far too old. One woman had her phone pressed to her ear, while the other was currently adjusting the old lady's head to place a jumper behind it as a pillow.

"What happened?" Fleur asked, pushing forwards and dropping onto the ground next to them. "Did anyone see what happened? Eunice? Can you hear me, Eunice?"

She gently shook her by the shoulder, but her eyes remained closed. Her body limp.

"I was walking towards her when I noticed she looked a bit wobbly," said the woman with the phone. "Then she suddenly leant against the wall, and before I could ask her whether she was okay, she was on the ground. Do you know her?"

"Yes, she's in my book club."

Fleur tried to rouse her again, this time pinching an ear lobe. It was something she'd been told to do on a first aid course years ago. She remembered the instructor telling them it was one of the most painful places to squeeze. She wasn't holding out that much hope, yet Eunice's eyes flickered.

"Eunice, I'm here. I'm here. It's Fleur. I'm with you."

It was impossible to tell whether she could understand what was being said to her or not. Her eyes were once again closed, although a low groan rose from the bottom of her throat, as if she was trying to say something.

"She's diabetic," Fleur said to the women. "Type One. This might be to do with her blood sugars."

She tried to steady her thoughts and recall everything Henry had told her that time he'd come over to apologise. If it was too low, she could fix it with sugar, but if she had extra sugar when it was already too high, it would make things even worse, catastrophic even, and she couldn't risk that. She racked her brain, trying to think as logically as she could. But there was too much noise going on. There were people chattering, talking about the ambulance. Others trying to find something to keep her warm. And then there was that incessant beeping, like a distant car alarm. Only it didn't sound that far away. In fact, it sounded remarkably close.

"Her phone!" Fleur jumped to her feet. "We need to find her phone. That'll tell us if her blood sugar is too high or too low."

She scanned up and down Eunice's jacket, patting her down, then digging her hands into her pockets, but found nothing. Still, the beeping continued. She turned around. "Her bag? Has someone got her bag?"

The eyes of the woman who'd used her jumper as a pillow widened. "Oh, yes. Sorry. She was lying on it when we sat her up. It's here. I've got it here." She handed Fleur the bag.

The moment Fleur unzipped the top, the volume of the beeping increased. She delved in, rummaging around until her fingers hit the hard plastic case. When she pulled out the phone, the screen was flashing red.

"Low. It says it's low." She held it up for the others to see.

"What does that mean?"

"It means we need to get her to eat some sugar?"

"How? Can she even eat anything?"

There were so many questions firing off around her, she couldn't make sense of them all. "Someone Google it. Search what to do for a low-blood-sugar diabetic," Fleur instructed. She wasn't sure if she'd remembered the words accurately but was confident it would be close enough to give her an answer.

"It's okay," she said, leaning in and stroking Eunice's hair. "It's fine. Don't worry; we can fix this. We can sort this out." Even as she spoke, she wasn't sure it was true.

"What does it say?" she called out.

"Sugar. She needs fast-acting sugar."

"Like a sugary drink," someone else added.

That's when it struck her. How many times had she listened to Robert going on about *hacking his macros* to ensure he performed at his physical peak in those damn races he used to do? And how many times had he bragged at dinner parties about getting so exhausted that he'd needed to take fast-acting glucose that you could only get from a pharmacy?

"Someone needs to run to the chemist," Fleur was back on her feet. "Ask for fast-acting glucose gel. Say it's for a diabetic."

"I'll go!"

As the woman who'd donated her jumper bolted towards the High Street, Fleur knelt on the ground next to Eunice, closed her eyes and offered up every prayer she could think of. "You're going to be fine," she said. "You've just got to be."

The woman arrived back with the glucose only minutes later, her face as bright red and sweat-covered as Fleur's had been during her run. How she'd managed to get to the pharmacy, ask for what she needed, pay and get back so quickly was a mystery, but she wasn't going to worry about that now.

"Is this what she needs?" The woman asked, handing her the packet.

"I think so."

Eunice was making noises again, attempting to speak, but Fleur couldn't decipher it. "Eunice, I've got some glucose for you. Is that what you need? Can you tell me? Is that right?"

Most of the crowd had dissipated now, leaving just Fleur and the two women, along with an elderly gentleman who was standing at the edge of the pavement, ready to wave down the ambulance.

"Can you hear me, Eunice? Is this right?"

Slowly, the old woman's chin dipped in a nod.

"It's right? Okay, great."

Fleur's heart was racing faster than she could ever recall, as she pulled the cap off the tube and pushed it gently between the old lady's lips.

Now, all they could do was wait.

CHAPTER 55

"*T*hat was impressively quick thinking there," the paramedic said, when Fleur handed him the empty packaging to show what she'd given Eunice. "And you say her blood sugar's already going up?"

"According to the app on her phone." Fleur held it out for him to see. "I don't know if it's going up fast enough, though. Or too fast."

"Don't worry, we'll take it from here. You're a friend of the patient, is that correct? Do you want to ride in the ambulance with her?"

"Ambulance? Don't be ridiculous. I'm fine. I don't need to go in an ambulance."

In the last couple of minutes, Eunice had regained her voice and, with it, her stubbornness.

"Yes, I will. Thank you," Fleur said, before turning to Eunice. "Don't fight me on this; you will lose. You're going to the hospital and letting the doctor check you over. He might want to keep you in for the night."

Eunice scoffed. "That's ridiculous. I'm fine now. I just walked a little too far, that's all. I'm perfectly all right."

"Well, why don't we let the doctor decide about that."

Eunice's scowl deepened, but there was no real determination behind it. "You're as stubborn as I am. No wonder my nephew likes you so much."

Fleur bit down on her lip and stayed quiet. Three times she'd tried to call Henry from her phone and another three from Eunice's, just in case it was her calls he wasn't picking up. She'd been going to try a fourth time, but quickly realised there was no point. The fact he hadn't seen his aunt's low blood sugar himself was all the evidence she needed to know he didn't have his phone switched on. She sent him a message instead, letting him know they were heading to the hospital.

By the time they reached A&E, Eunice was back to normal. "I do not need you hanging around here, wasting your day. You've got far better things you can be doing."

"I'm not going to leave you," Fleur insisted.

"Please, you're making me feel terrible. I've already taken up far too much of your time."

"Eunice, I am not going anywhere."

"It will take hours for me to be seen. Please go."

"Sorry." Fleur placed her hand on Eunice's shoulder. "That's not going to happen, so you might as well just deal with it."

Despite Eunice's scepticism, the doctor was quick to see her.

"I can go in with you," Fleur said, standing up the instant Eunice's name was called, although as she should have expected, she was none too taken by the offer.

"Absolutely not. I would like to maintain what little of my dignity remains, please. I am perfectly capable of seeing a doctor by myself." And with that, she walked slowly off towards him.

Fleur was looking for something to read among the magazines on offer, searching through the gossip ones for something a bit deeper, when a voice stopped her.

"Eunice Osbourne? I'm looking for Eunice Osbourne. I was told they'd brought her here."

"Henry!" Fleur hurried across to him. She knew exactly how he acted when he was worried about his aunt, and the last thing this poor receptionist needed after a long shift was to face the brunt of that. "Henry, it's fine. She's in with the doctor now."

As he stepped away from the counter, his brow wrinkled in confusion. "Fleur, what are you doing here? What happened? Where's Eunice?"

"It's fine. Honestly. She's seeing the doctor now," she repeated. "But she's okay. Her blood sugar is normal again. It corrected pretty quickly. It was on the rise even before the ambulance arrived. They said I could come with her, and I didn't want to leave her on her own." She stopped talking to see if he was following what she was saying, judging by the frown lines etched on his forehead, he was having difficulty.

"How did you get here?" he said.

"In the ambulance, like I just said, and I texted you. I told you I was coming in with her."

"Sorry. I didn't read the messages. I saw all the missed calls from Eunice and then heard the voicemail saying she was here. That was you?"

"That was me."

He turned away, pressing his fingers against the bridge of his nose, and took a deep breath, almost as though he was trying to reset the moment. Fleur wanted so much to reach out and take his hand. To lower his head onto her shoulder and tell him it was going to be all right. And perhaps she would have done, had he not turned to her with his shoulders pushed back and a hard expression on his face.

"I'm here now," he said. "You can go."

She hadn't expected any great accolades for doing what any decent person would have done, but given that she was the one who had kept him in the loop, she didn't think a thank you would have been out of place. Besides, given what she'd just been through with Eunice, she sure as hell wasn't going to be dismissed like that.

"I'll wait for Eunice to come back from the doctor. I want to make sure she's okay," she said, fixing her own posture a little straighter, as if she could somehow match his height.

"It's okay. You don't need to stay. I'm here."

"I know I don't need to. I want to."

"Fine," he said, dropping onto one of the plastic chairs and picking up the gossip magazine beside him. "Stay then."

CHAPTER 56

It was no wonder so many people at work thought him an arrogant arse. The Iceman, that was what they called him. As if he had no emotions. Of course, they said it like it was a good thing. After all, that was what made them so much money. But hearing himself talking to Fleur like she was nothing, was enough to make him hate himself even more than he already did. He needed to apologise. For this and everything else. After all, if she hadn't contacted him, who knows when he would have learned where his aunt was.

"I came as soon as I could. I was working in Chelmsford," he said, only to want to punch himself. That wasn't an apology. It sounded like he wanted congratulating for turning up.

"I assumed it must have been something important for you not to have your phone switched on. You were in court, I take it."

"Yes, and the case ran over. It's all sorted now though. I won."

"Well done you," she replied, dryly. Why the hell was he

talking about winning court cases at a time like this? It was even worse than when he'd accused her of scrounging lifts.

As he swallowed back a mixture of guilt and self-loathing, he glanced around the waiting area. Considering they were in A&E, it was quieter than he would have expected, but then perhaps mid-afternoon wasn't their busiest time.

"Fleur, about the other week, the wedding, I need to explain."

"There's nothing to explain. I'm a grown-up, Henry."

"That's not what I meant. When I left, it was all about Eunice. Without my phone, I didn't know what her glucose levels were like."

"I know. I assumed that's why you reacted the way you did. Why you wouldn't at least have had the decency to call me afterwards is another matter entirely."

He watched her purse her lips then. Lips he desperately wanted to kiss. "Fleur, I … I …" He stopped.

Why did he have such difficulty admitting he was wrong? It came from his parents. He knew that much. They could be at loggerheads for hours, sometimes even days, neither of them prepared to acknowledge they were in the wrong. In his family, it was better not to speak at all than to admit you had messed up, even if it was true. As a child, he could remember thinking how he was never going to let himself get like that and be in a relationship where he couldn't put his hands up and say he was sorry, he'd been mistaken. Unfortunately, the only way he'd made good on that promise was by not being in a relationship. And he didn't want that anymore. He didn't want to be lonely. He wanted to be able to fight and make up. To own up to his errors. He wanted to live his life with someone who knew how important Eunice was, too. Who would be prepared to spend an entire day in a hospital for her.

"Henry, what are you doing here?"

He turned his head to the doorway, the sight of his aunt stealing his words and his breath as he fought back tears. Sometimes, catching her like this, seeing how old she'd become, would cause an unbelievable grief to well up inside him. She had been so energetic when he was young, taking him on trips like drive-through safari parks, where they would enjoy an hour getting lost in a maze. Or else spending the day together dressing up, so she could take a role in a play he'd written to perform to the family. And then he would see her like this. Walking so slowly, it was as if the weight of her body was too much for her legs to handle. And every time, it would break his heart anew.

Bringing himself back to the moment, he rushed across to her.

"What do you mean? You were unconscious."

"Hardly. I was just a little woozy, that's all."

There was no point getting into it with her. Not now. She would just keep battling until he relented anyway.

"Well, I've got the all-clear. I guess we should go home. Fleur dearest, you'll need a lift."

That was a statement, not a question, and Henry's eyes went straight to Fleur. He was sure she was about to decline, and he didn't know if this would please him or not. But then she patted herself down, and a flush of pink rose from her neck.

"I would get a taxi, but I don't seem to have any money on me …"

"Well, we're not going to leave you here. You're coming with us. Isn't she Henry?"

Being together in the car would remind him of when he couldn't take his eyes, or lips, off her on the way home from the wedding. The thought of her so close but not able to touch her, was nearly unbearable. He could offer her the cash for a taxi and say it would be quicker than waiting for him to find his car and bring it around, which might well be true.

He glanced at Eunice and saw her wide eyes glaring up at him. Who was he kidding? There was only one answer he could give.

CHAPTER 57

*T*he music coming from the radio was the only sound. Once again, Eunice had insisted Fleur sat in the front next to Henry. But unlike all the other times, there was no awkward small talk. No inane conversation which would end in mild, or sometimes not-so-mild, insults. Fleur didn't know Henry's reason for not speaking, but she knew hers; she was exhausted. She hadn't realised until she'd sat on the soft leather just how worn out she was. Part of it was down to the extra-long run and the fact it was the end of the week, but all the time panicking about Eunice and feeling responsible for her had taken its toll on her body. There was no adrenaline left now to keep her going. No reason to stay alert and on top of things. As such, they were barely out of the hospital carpark when she closed her eyes and fell asleep.

When she woke up, a hand was gently rocking her.

"Fleur, we're back. You're home now."

As she slowly opened her eyes, Henry's face appeared only inches from hers. For a split second, she forgot everything that had happened in the last fortnight. It was as if she was back in bed, with him there beside her, his lips ready to kiss her again. A blink, and it all came rushing back. Eunice. The hospital. Sitting up, she glanced out of the window and saw her front door.

"Thank you." She fumbled to release her seatbelt. "Sorry, I didn't mean to drop off."

"You've nothing to apologise for. I'm the one who should be doing that," Eunice said, from the back seat. "Henry, be a gentleman and walk Fleur to the door."

She finally managed to undo her belt. "Really, I'm fine."

Henry had opened his car door and was walking around to hers. He pulled it open and offered his hand to help her get down, but she didn't take it. Instead, she twisted around and poked her head into the back of the car.

"I'm glad you're better Eunice," she said. "Please take care of yourself. I don't think I could cope with another scare like that."

"I'll be on my best behaviour from now on. And I'll see you at the next book club?"

"I'll try my hardest."

Eunice nodded, and Fleur was about to step out of the car when something about the old woman's demeanour made her stop. "Eunice, are you sure you're okay?"

She pressed her lips together and stared intently at Fleur. "I know I shouldn't ask you this … but would you mind not mentioning today to anyone at the Book Club? They'll just worry; that's all."

"Of course; I won't tell any of them," Fleur reassured her. Then she got out, sidestepping neatly to avoid Henry.

"I'll just be a minute," he told his aunt, promptly closing the door.

It was only half-a-dozen steps to the door, but each of them was excruciating. Fleur had hoped that as he'd decided to accompany her, he might say something. But instead, he just trailed behind. She pulled her key out of her pocket, but rather than putting it in the lock, she spun around to face him.

"I get it, you know."

"Get what?" He frowned at her.

"The stress. The constant tension. I got it straight away, or at least I thought I had, but I couldn't fully understand until today. I was only there with her for a few hours and my nerves were shot, wondering if I'd done something wrong. Whether there was more I could have done."

"What you did to help her was incredible. I should have said that already."

He stepped towards her, but she shook her head and stopped him in his tracks.

"I'm not seeking validation. I did what any decent person would do. What I'm saying is that I can't imagine what it's like to spend your entire life feeling responsible, analysing every action you take. It must wear you down. It has worn you down."

As she looked up, she met his gaze for the first time that day, and the moment their eyes locked, it became impossible to turn away.

"I know how hard it must be, Henry, but she's her own woman. And she wants you to lead your own life, just as she wants to lead hers. You can't be blind to the reason she's constantly pushing us together? It's for your sake. Because she's worried about you being lonely. Because she won't be here forever. And when she's gone, you'll have pushed everyone else in your life so far away that this act you play, of pretending to be fine on your own, is all you're going to be left with."

She looked at him a second more, before turning and stepping through her door. She'd said what she needed to say.

CHAPTER 58

*D*espite it being a Saturday, Fleur spent her morning responding to emails she'd missed the previous afternoon. She'd messaged Paul in the ambulance, simply stating that she was on her way to the hospital in an emergency. Just as she'd expected, he'd told her not to worry and hoped it was nothing critical. But she was still new to the job, and the last thing she wanted was for them to think she'd started slacking.

Given how much work she wanted to finish, the last thing she needed was a distraction, which was exactly what she got when, at ten a.m., her doorbell buzzed.

"What are you doing here?" she said, through the video intercom.

"Don't ask." Annelise shuffled to the side, and there behind her, were Fleur's niece and nephew, Margot and Paxton.

"I swear they plan these things just to mess with our lives," she said, stepping into the flat and taking off her coat. "Two inset days in one week. We did everything fun we could think of on the first day, then had a pyjama day on the second, and so I thought, why not come and see you? Go watch your tablets, kids. Just five more minutes while I talk to Auntie Fleur. Then she'll take you to the park or something."

Following their mother's orders, the children collapsed onto the sofa, while Annelise went and dropped onto one of the dining chairs.

"Honestly, it's not that I don't love them. You know I do. But the nanny's been off sick this week, and obviously Jude has work, and it's damn tough when it's just me and them. And then I realised it doesn't have to be like that; I can bring them here."

Fleur looked through to the living room, where the children were slumped in front of their screens. "As happy as Auntie Fleur is to see them, I've got work to do."

"On a Saturday? I thought the entire reason you moved here was to have a better *work-life-balance?*"

"I did. And I do. But I was off all day yesterday, so I need to catch up."

"Why were you off?"

She didn't want to get into it, mostly because she didn't want to talk about Henry, but if she didn't say what had happened, then Annelise would think she was just making up an excuse not to see her and the children, when in fact, an afternoon with her niece and nephew at the play park felt like much more fun than the mundane email responses she had planned.

"Eunice had an issue. She needed taking to hospital."

Annelise's eyes bulged. "Eunice, as in Henry's aunt? Why couldn't he take her? I thought that was why he was so anti-commitment. Because he always had to be there for her."

"I know, but she was out in Maldon when she collapsed, and I was there, and he was in court, meaning that I couldn't reach him. He got to the hospital eventually, though. And she's fine. They let her go once her glucose level was sorted."

"Wow, sounds like it was full on."

"It was," she admitted. "It really was."

With a long sigh, Annelise placed her hands firmly on the table in front of her.

"Well, even more reason to take a proper break. You should go for a walk with the children to that pirate-ship thing you keep telling me is so amazing. They'd love it."

"Yes, but I could have done with a bit of warning. You know you could walk them there. It's not that far, straight down towards the river. It's not like you can get lost."

Annelise's pout told her an excuse was well on the way. Her sister adored her children. She would have taken a bullet for them without a second's hesitation. But sometimes Fleur wondered if she'd take a bullet to get out of joining in any form of imaginative play, too.

"I've got a bit of a headache, if I'm honest, from the car journey here. You know what it's like, with children in the back."

Fleur actually didn't. She glanced to where her nephew and niece were sitting silently with their headphones on, staring at their tablets, probably the same way they had all morning.

"Okay, I've got two more emails I need to write now," she said, verbalising her thoughts as she tried to figure out the logistics of her new day. "That will take about fifteen minutes. After that, I can walk them down to the park for half an hour. Then we could all meet up for lunch?"

"Perfect. We can do some party planning then, too. I can't believe it's only a week away, and nothing's sorted."

"That's because I don't want to get anything sorted."

"You're just saying that to be awkward. Anyway, finish your work. I'll just put my feet up on your bed, if that's okay?"

Twenty minutes later, Fleur was heading out to the river, with a niece and nephew in each hand, while Annelise now lay on the sofa, meditation music softly playing in the background.

"How the other half live," she'd muttered, as she'd shut her front door.

CHAPTER 59

*H*enry straightened the duvet on his bed, flattening it down and giving it another tug to ensure it was completely smooth. Given that it wasn't his room, it was certainly starting to look like it. He had a suit in the wardrobe, along with two spare shirts, while the underwear drawer was basically full, although that was mainly because Eunice insisted on buying him multipacks of socks and pants for both birthday and Christmas every year. His drawers at home were overflowing.

After the previous day's events, he'd spent the night at her house, and for once, she hadn't protested. Though he knew she'd never admit it, the collapse and trip to hospital had shaken her up. Having checked that everything was in impeccable order, he gave a long, drawn-out sigh. Sooner or later, they would have to face the inevitable, and this room would become his, permanently.

The size of his aunt's home was a source of mixed emotions. Eunice and Stanley had bought it when they were first married. Airy and bright and with a large back garden, it had been the perfect house for raising a family. But children had never come. Or at least not in the form of their own. Henry had many fond memories of staying there for weekends with his cousins. Not to mention all the times he'd visited on his own. He'd once stayed for three months, solid. It was during his A-levels and studying in his own home had been near impossible, with his parents constantly shouting at each other. He'd done another stint there soon after, when the exams finished, and then again after law school, while he was applying for jobs. Which was why, when she'd needed someone to come and live closer, on a permanent basis, he hadn't hesitated to offer. After all she had done for him.

"Henry, breakfast is ready!" Eunice's voice called from downstairs, alerting him to the aroma of food. Normally, the thought of a bacon sandwich would be the exact thing to raise his spirits on a Saturday morning, but that day, it did the exact opposite.

"What are you doing up?" he asked, marching into the kitchen to discover it wasn't as simple as a mere sandwich. A full English breakfast was laid out on the table, with sausages, fried eggs, mushrooms, the lot. "You shouldn't be cooking. You were meant to stay in bed and have a lie in. Rest."

"I'll have plenty of time to lie down and rest when I'm dead," she replied. "There's nothing wrong with me. Now eat up, or it'll get cold."

Not wanting to start the day with another argument, he did as he was told, scraping a layer of black off the sausages before he started.

"Right, tell me; what are your plans for today?" she continued, as she picked at her own miniature fry-up.

"Plans?" They'd previously been to head into the office or take his laptop to a café and clear a few tasks there, but now he had no intention of leaving her alone. "I've got a few bits of work I need to get finished. I thought I'd bring them around here to do. Your house is a much nicer temperature than mine."

She fixed him with her most withering stare. "You mean so you can keep an eye on me?"

He popped a forkful of mushroom into his mouth, using the chewing time to figure out how to respond. There was no point in lying when she'd see straight through it. So instead, he used one of her favourite tactics and turned the moment back to her.

"How are you feeling this morning? Truthfully?"

"Truthfully? Good enough to know that you're mollycoddling me. That's how I'm feeling."

"When will you accept that, sometimes, it's just what you need?" he said, rolling his eyes almost by reflex.

Eunice pounced. "Don't you go rolling your eyes at me," she said, dropping her cutlery onto her plate with a clatter. "I made a mistake, that was all. I didn't realise I'd taken one of those damn sugar-free biscuits you keep getting me from the tin, instead of one of the proper ones."

He didn't know if this was true or not, and he certainly wouldn't put it past her to lie, but it caused a surge of guilt to flood through him. Guilt that displayed itself as anger.

"What were they doing in a tin? I've told you; you need to leave them all in their packets, so you can see how much sugar is in them."

"Who leaves them in packets? They belong in a tin."

He gritted his teeth. This argument wasn't just about biscuits, and they both knew it, but he wasn't going to drop it yet. "Well, if you insist on doing that, even though both the doctor and I have told you it's not sensible, perhaps we should get two tins, then. One for sugar-free and one for regular biscuits?" He waited for her to offer some ridiculous reason why that wouldn't be possible, but surprisingly, she didn't.

"I suppose that might be a sensible thing to do," she said, instead.

Henry was nearly floored. Of the countless suggestions he'd made to his aunt about how she could make her life easier, he knew exactly how many she'd taken on board. One. Accepting lifts to and from the Book Club.

"You will?"

"I will. I'll get an extra tin, just for sugar-free biscuits. If you tell Fleur how you really feel about her."

"Eunice, stop." He shook his head, as annoyed at himself for walking into the trap as he was at her for suggesting it. "There is nothing between us."

"No, not anymore. Because you're too stubborn to admit you messed up. Several times, in fact, I believe."

He was still shaking his head, although it had now turned into a movement of resignation rather than disagreement. "Fleur and I missed the boat. If there was such a thing."

"Tosh. I saw the way you looked at her when she was asleep in the car last night. I'm amazed you didn't crash, you were so gooey-eyed."

"I was not gooey-eyed."

"I know what I saw. Besides, she's a good one. Genuine. And they don't come along like that very often. Ones that will stand up to you. And not that I was in any real danger yesterday, but she ... she did well, Henry."

Silence settled over them. He didn't know what to say to that. Every word she'd said was true. He'd barely been able to keep his eyes off her as she lay with her head against the window, and more than once, he'd found himself desperate to slip his hand off the gear stick and take hers. But any hope he'd had that she would forgive him disappeared the moment she'd walked into her house without a glance back.

"It's too late," he said. "If there was any chance of anything happening, I've messed it up too many times now. It's too late."

"Oh, Henry darling, if this is real love, which I think it could be, then it's never too late."

CHAPTER 60

*H*enry's breakfast was turning cold. Now that Eunice had spoken about Fleur, all he could think of was her asleep in his car and the dozen scenarios that had run through his head at the time. He'd imagined that they weren't coming back from the hospital but instead a dinner out with friends, and she'd fallen asleep after one-too-many glasses of wine. Or they'd been on a trip to the theatre. Or had just left the airport heading back to Maldon after a city break to Europe. He now imagined what it would have been like not to have left her on the doorstep, but to have gone in with her, like he'd done that night before he'd screwed it all up the first time.

"She won't forgive me," he said, picking up his cutlery and starting on a rasher of bacon.

"You don't know that. Men have done worse and been forgiven."

"Possibly, but I doubt they messed up as many times. And if they had, then they probably shouldn't have been forgiven anyway." His eyes went back to his plate, but he could see his aunt wave her hand dismissively from the corner of his eye.

"Henry, you are not a bad guy. Sometimes you can't see the wood for the trees, that's your trouble."

He wanted to agree with her, but he was a lawyer, and all evidence was to the contrary.

"Think about it this way," she continued, determined not to let it go. "If you go out there, and offer her your heart, what's the worst that'll happen? You'll get an earful. And let's be honest, it's no less than you deserve. You know, your great-uncle and I didn't have the perfect start to our relationship. He was two-timing me behind my back."

"What?"

Eunice had said plenty of things to astound Henry during their recent times together, but never in reference to her marriage. She had only ever spoken about Stanley with complete adoration. And it had been the same when he'd been alive. They'd doted on each other, often sickeningly so. The fact that they'd been anything other than completely in love since they first laid eyes on one another, was completely unfathomable.

"You've never said anything about that before," he said, still trying to recover from the shock of discovering the most perfect couple he'd ever known was perhaps not so perfect after all.

"Of course, I haven't. It's hardly something you brag about. Janice Cooper, that was her name. They were working at the pub together, and she asked him to give her a lift to the cinema. She said she was meeting a bunch of friends there and she'd pay for his ticket if he'd drive. Well, what do you know? They got there, and no one else turned up."

"Sneaky."

"Absolutely. And she knew he had a girlfriend and every-thing — nasty piece of work, if you ask me."

"Well, what happened?" He was now desperate to know more about this part of her relationship with his great-uncle she'd never spoken about.

"Well, they went into the cinema, and she tried to take his hand in the dark, but he didn't let her."

"So, he went to the cinema with her, but he didn't actually do anything?" he said, realising there wasn't going to be the dramatic revelation he'd been expecting.

"Will you let me finish? Nothing occurred at the cinema, but then he drove her home to her parents' house and that's when it happened. They kissed."

"Kissed?"

Eunice nodded. "Now, I don't doubt she was the one who instigated it— he said it caught him by surprise — but it takes two to tango."

While it wasn't the two-timing, affair-level scandal he'd been expecting after her initial comment, this was still a surprise. "What about you and him?" He felt ridiculous needing to ask. After all, they'd obviously sorted everything out.

"Well, he came back and told me the next day, and I wasn't having any of that. I told him to sling his hook."

"You did?"

"Damn right, I did. I wasn't being treated like that."

That wasn't the answer he'd expected, either.

"Then what happened?"

"Well, the following day, he turned up with a ring and went to see my father."

"You're serious?" It was difficult to understand why this wasn't something she'd brought up before. After all, they'd clearly put all their differences behind them, and it would make a great dinner party story. "And you then said yes, of course?"

"I did not. You don't trust a man who kisses another girl one day and asks you to marry him the next."

Henry rubbed his temples. "I don't understand. You obviously forgave him eventually."

"It took a year and thirteen more proposals before I finally gave in and agreed."

"You turned him down thirteen times?"

"I needed to know he was serious, didn't I? Besides, I was too young to get married when he first asked. It seemed like a sensible thing to string it out a bit. Make sure he didn't stray again. And he didn't. Thirty-six years and I wouldn't have had it any other way."

A faint wisp of a smile graced her lips and crinkled the lines around her eyes as they drifted off into the distance, only for her gaze to come back to Henry with deadly seriousness.

"It's not too late. If you think she's the one. You just need to show her. Prove it."

He nodded. If his aunt and uncle could get through all that, then maybe there was a chance Fleur could forgive him, after all.

"Okay, you're right. I'm going to see her," he said, standing up, only to realise his plate was still half full.

"Go," she said. "I'll see to the washing up."

CHAPTER 61

*H*enry was torn. As much as he wanted Fleur to be home, if she was out, he wouldn't have to face his fears and tell her how he truly felt. Maybe he should finish the letter he'd tried writing and post it through her letterbox instead. But he knew that wouldn't be enough. He needed her to look into his eyes and know he wasn't lying. He wasn't going to mess it up again. He couldn't.

His pulse was racing as he tried to decide what to say. He could start with the story about Eunice and Stanley and the fourteen marriage proposals. Although he should probably apologise first. But where he would start with all the things he needed to ask her forgiveness for, he had no idea.

His heart was lodged all the way up in his throat as he turned up North Road, trying to work out how to begin. He would need to ask to go up to her flat, to start with. The last thing he wanted was to have the entire conversation via the damn video phone. His heart rate rose. What was to say she'd even let him in the front door? If he was her, the minute his face came up on the little screen, he would run downstairs and double bolt the door. It was nothing less than he deserved. But if Stanley could cope with the humiliation of thirteen rejections, then he could deal with Fleur not wanting to see him that day.

As he reached the house, he wiped his palms on the seat of his trousers. Even before his biggest court cases, he never felt this nervous. Maybe that was because he knew how things would play out there. Now, he had no idea what might happen.

Taking a deep breath, he pressed the button. A loud buzz followed, then nothing. He waited a few seconds, then pressed again.

"Fleur, for pity's sake, just answer," he muttered. Butterflies accosted his insides, making it impossible for him to stand still. He pressed yet again, holding the button down even longer. Then, admitting defeat, he dropped his head, turned around and trudged back towards his car, just as an answering buzz sounded.

"Hello?"

In one leap, he was back in front of the intercom.

"Fleur?" It hadn't actually sounded like her. But people always came across tinny and distant on these things. "It's me. I'm sorry. I need to speak to you. I *really* need to speak to you."

"Henry? It is Henry, isn't it?"

For a second, he assumed she was mocking him, but it still didn't sound like her, and the uncertainty in the voice seemed genuine.

"Who is this?" he asked, only to put two and two together. "Annelise? Annelise, is Fleur there? I just need to speak to her."

Any doubt that he was speaking to her sister was erased when she spoke again.

"Even if she was here, do you really think I'd let you in? Haven't you already done enough?"

His palms were once against slick with sweat. How on earth his uncle had kept going before he finally got his yes was a mystery. While he knew he wanted to be with Fleur more than anything, he wasn't sure he could take another thirteen of these. Particularly if each one involved an angry gatekeeper.

`

"I just wanted to speak to her … I need to … I want to …" he stammered. He couldn't get the words out. Not to Annelise at least. "It doesn't matter. It's fine. I'll come back later." Maybe this was for the best. Maybe his aunt was wrong about him being a good guy, and it was better he left now, rather than mess it all up, yet again. Resigned, he turned back around only to hear the door swing open behind him.

"Where do you think you're going?" Annelise was standing with her arms crossed, glaring at him.

"I'm sorry. I didn't mean to intrude. I just wanted to see Fleur, that's all."

"Why?"

He sucked in a deep breath, which he slowly released. "I need to tell her something." He'd been terrified enough working out what he was going to say to Fleur. There was no way he could explain it to Annelise. "Can you tell her I popped over?"

He expected her to say Yes, of course or No sling your hook! But instead, the scary sister continued to look at him, with a disturbingly penetrating gaze.

"You do like her, don't you?" she said. "*Like* like her?"

"What are we, children? *Like* like?"

"You know what I mean. Do you like her, like she likes you?"

"Does she? Does she still *like* like me?" Henry's heart fluttered. He'd thought it impossible that a single bone in Fleur's body could feel positively towards him. And yet, as Annelise stood there, a small smile touched the corners of her lips.

"I think you and I ought to have a conversation," she said.

CHAPTER 62

There had been several birthdays through the years when Fleur hadn't felt like celebrating. Her fourteenth had come the day after she'd had train tracks fitted. She could barely smile, let alone eat cake and had spent most of the time applying Bonjela to her gums, to the extent that she couldn't stop dribbling. That was one birthday to remember.

Then there was the one after Robert had told her he couldn't ever imagine having children and the one, the following year, after the divorce had gone through. She hadn't felt particularly celebratory for either of those. They'd happened at the obscure ages of thirty-seven and thirty-eight and no one cared about those milestones. But this year was the big four-zero. The one people always made a massive fuss over.

Thankfully, after seemingly endless badgering, Annelise had given up. Since her visit with the children, she'd finally dropped the idea and accepted that her little sister simply wouldn't agree to a big celebration. A dinner with her and the Book Club girls would be the height of it. Unfortunately,

Gemma, Nina and Maria already had plans, and they'd agreed to do something together, later in the month.

"So, it's just me and a fabulous meal," Annelise had said on the phone the day before. "Let's be honest, with my company, why would you even need anyone else?"

"My thoughts exactly."

The Big Day arrived, and Annelise appeared on her doorstep at 9 a.m., entirely alone, as promised, Fleur should have been happy. There was only one minor issue.

"You know I have to work today, don't you? It is a weekday."

Annelise smiled the type of smile Fleur recognised from their childhood, and it didn't make her feel good.

"Did you know that Jude went to university with your line manager, Paul? Crazy coincidence, right? Anyway, it turned out he didn't know today is the big four-zero. But he does now, so he's not expecting you to be attending any meetings. Which is good, because I've booked us in for a spa day. Massage, facial, mani-pedi, the entire works."

"Annelise …" Fleur tried her hardest not to sound cross.

"What? You said no big party; this is exactly that. Besides, I want you to look good for our meal out."

"We are literally going over the road."

"So? Grab your swimsuit. We need to get cracking."

THE SPA WAS A DREAM. The hot tub, sauna and steam room on their own would have been enough, but Annelise hadn't been joking when she'd said she'd organised an entire package. For five hours, Fleur was pampered with a full body scrub, facial, hot stone massage, a manicure and a pedicure. Not to mention half an hour in a sensory-deprivation, flotation tank that she had expected to be horrendous but turned out to be incredible.

"I've booked the table at the pub for seven, but it shouldn't matter if we're there a bit later," she told Annelise when they arrived back home. Her entire wardrobe had been emptied onto the bed as, apparently, the outfit she'd picked for herself wasn't suitable. Still, it made Annelise happy, and that was worth it, given everything her sister did for her.

"Oh, about that," Annelise said, handing her a red, peplum dress Fleur thought was far too dressy for Maldon and therefore hadn't worn at all since moving there. "I looked at the menu online and decided I wasn't really in the mood for pub grub. I hope you don't mind. I cancelled and booked the little tapas restaurant right at the top of the hill."

"Tapas?" Fleur was still looking at the dress. It was excessively over the top, but she only turned forty once. "Okay, that sounds good."

"Fantastic. Now get that on. I'm going to do your hair. And we don't want to be late for the reservation."

Along with seeing to her hair, Annelise also adjusted her makeup and picked out the right jacket. But Fleur drew the line at footwear. No-one chose her shoes for her, not even her sister.

As they walked up the hill, their arms interlinked, Fleur chatted about the smell of the facial moisturiser the spa had used and whether she could arrange a trip there with the Book Club girls. Annelise was unusually quiet and seemed to be more concerned with her phone than talking.

"Is everything okay?" Fleur asked.

"What? Oh sorry, yes. Just checking on the children. I tried to get them to send you a birthday video, but Margot's at a funny stage, refusing to put her face on camera."

"That's all right; you don't need to make them do anything

for me," Fleur replied, but Annelise continued to stare at her phone.

When they were halfway up the hill, she suddenly stopped. "Oh, look, a cocktail bar. We should have a drink first."

"I thought you said we had to hurry because of the reservation."

"I was probably just being dramatic. Look, everything is pink. We must go in. I'll message the tapas place we might be a tad late."

"I think that would be a good idea." Fleur hadn't been to the restaurant before, but she knew from the outside it was fairly small. Not turning up on time could well mean they'd lose their table.

"Okay, you head inside and order us drinks. I'll stay out here and ring them. And get me something with bubbles in, please. Lots of bubbles."

Everything inside really was pink. The seating was pink. The lighting was pink, and there were even large, pink feathers decorating the bar. It therefore shouldn't have come as a surprise when both their drinks arrived pink, too.

"My God, this is delicious," Annelise said, and took another sip through the paper straw.

"I know. These are far too drinkable. If I have another one, I might not make it up the rest of the hill." Fleur sipped hers slowly. If this was what turning forty involved, it really wasn't that bad after all.

But no sooner had she relaxed into her seat than Annelise spoke again. "Talking about the hill, I think we should get going now." And abandoning the straw, she brought the glass up to her lips and emptied it.

"We've only just sat down. And you rang the restaurant, didn't you?"

"I couldn't get through. And we don't want to lose our

table." Standing up, she removed her coat from the back of her chair.

Fleur, drink in hand, remained seated. "What have you done, Annelise?"

"What do you mean?"

"I know you. You're up to something. What have you done?"

Her sister was trying to look casual, but the tell-tale twitch of an eyebrow was more than enough to confirm her suspicions. "I'm not budging from here until you tell me what you've done."

Dropping her hands like a toddler about to have a tantrum, Annelise let out a long groan. "You make it sound like it's a bad thing. It's not, I promise. The kids felt sad that you weren't having a proper birthday party, so Jude brought them over this afternoon. I had to wait for them to get to the restaurant before us. Sorry."

"The kids wanted to be here for my birthday?" A prickling heat came to her eyes.

"Of course, they did. You're their favourite auntie."

"I'm their only auntie."

"Now you're just splitting hairs. So, can you at least pretend to act surprised for them? They're really excited."

"Of course, I will," Fleur replied, an unexpected warmth flooding her. Perhaps there was something to a party, after all.

"Great, so we need to get going. They're a nightmare if they don't eat soon enough."

As they reached the restaurant, Annelise took hold of Fleur's hand and squeezed it tightly. "Now, it's time to see how good your surprised face is."

Fleur stole a quick glance through the window as they walked towards the door. "Are you sure it's open? It looks closed to me."

"Oh, it's definitely open." Annelise pushed her forwards. "You go in first. They said there's a table for us in the back."

Despite knowing the surprise was coming, Fleur couldn't help but feel a flicker of excitement and prepared her best *I didn't have a clue* face. But as she stepped inside, her jaw fell open.

"Surprise!!!!"

CHAPTER 63

*S*he was too stunned to move. There, in the centre of the room, were Paxton and Margot, along with Annelise's husband, Jude.

"Happy birthday, Auntie Fleur," they yelled, although she could barely hear them for all the other people who were yelling, too.

Eunice, Graham, Gemma, every single member of the Club was there.

"But … but how?" She struggled for words. The girls had said they couldn't make her birthday meal, so how on earth could Annelise have pulled this off without having met any of them — other than Eunice that one time at the Continental — was beyond her.

"I don't understand?" she said, turning to her sister. "How did you do this?"

Fleur was smiling, but her sister was beaming. Positively glowing with satisfaction.

"Well, as much as I love to take credit for everything, I

should probably confess that I had a substantial amount of help arranging this."

"From whom?" Fleur looked around the room, only for a voice to come from directly behind her.

"Happy birthday, Fleur."

Her stomach performed a triple somersault as she turned around to face him.

"You? How? Why?"

"Henry and I happened to bump into each other," Annelise said, from beside her. "Turns out he's an *actions-speak-louder-than-words* type man. One I might have judged a little too quickly."

Fleur could hardly hear her sister speaking; her heart was drumming so hard in her chest. She knew there were many other people looking at her, waiting to wish her happy birthday, but she was only able to see one.

"Why? Why did you do this?"

Henry tipped his head, and locked eyes with her. "Let's be honest, this is only a fraction of what you deserve. Fleur, I know how badly I've messed things up, repeatedly. And I know helping throw one little party will not make up for that. But I would like to try. Fleur, I want to throw you a party every year for as many years as we have on the planet, if you're okay with that? And before you speak, you need to know that if you turn me down now, I'm not going to give up. You could turn me down thirteen times, and I would still come back for more."

"Thirteen? That's very specific."

A smile played on his lips. "I'll explain it to you some other time."

"That would be nice."

He took her hands in his and moved his head ever so slightly, as if he was going to kiss her, not even caring who else was there. She closed her eyes and waited for the moment.

"Are we having cake yet, Auntie Fleur? Mummy said there'd be cake?"

She stepped away from Henry, a matching blush tinting both their cheeks.

"Perhaps we should do this later?" he said.

"Sounds good to me."

"So, do I throw a good party?" Annelise cornered Fleur at the end of the evening. "Admit it; I do."

"You did a very good job." Fleur hugged her sister as tight as she could. "Thank you."

"You are most welcome. Jude and I need to get going, though. The kids are shattered, and they get unusually cuddly when they're this tired, so I intend making the most of it."

Fleur offered her sister one last squeeze. "Thank you again."

"No problem. But you know I'm not the only one who needs thanking."

Since discovering what Henry had done, there hadn't been a minute to speak to him alone. After the children had accosted her for cake, she'd had to blow out her candles and then there were all the people in the Book Club to thank, after which the food arrived, and music started. Although Fleur had caught his eye several times across the crowded room, it was only when everyone was saying goodbye and half the people had filtered out, that she finally got to talk to him again.

"Happy birthday, Fleur," he said, taking her hand. "I hope it's been a good one."

"It has. It really has."

Then he was looking at her again, in a way that made her want to push up onto her toes and kiss him. But Eunice was gathering her things, and she knew the only way to make this work was slowly. One step at a time.

"Maybe I could give you a call tomorrow?" she said.

"That would be good. I'd like that very much."

Then she did go on tiptoes. After all, it was her birthday and what better way to start the next decade of her life than kissing her man? With their lips only an inch away, Eunice's voice caused them to jerk apart again.

"Right, you two. Gemma is giving me a lift back now."

Henry stiffened. "What about—" He stopped and clamped his mouth shut.

Fleur couldn't help but smile. "I don't mind waiting here," she said. "Why don't you give Eunice a lift home, then you could come back and walk me to my flat." She watched as he considered her suggestion, but when he spoke, he didn't give the answer she expected.

"Actually, I think Gemma has got this. Right Gemma?"

"Absolutely."

Then, before Fleur had a chance to question whether he was truly okay with that arrangement, Eunice and Gemma were kissing her goodbye. Five minutes later, she and Henry were the only ones left.

She looked at her phone for the first time all evening. "Wow, its's got late."

"I think there's still time to get one last drink here?" Henry directed the comment to the waiter, who nodded, at which point he ordered a bottle of wine.

They sat at a small table, their fingers entwined.

"Thank you—"

"I'm sorry—"

They both said at the exact same moment, causing them to

respond in unison, too.

"You go."

"You go."

After a moment's pause, it was Henry who continued.

"Fleur, I am so sorry for everything. The day after the hospital incident, I came to your flat to apologise and to tell you how I felt, but you weren't there."

"And Annelise was …" The answer to how he and her sister had pulled off the surprise party finally dawned. "So that's when she badgered you into doing this?"

"She can be very forceful." He was smiling nervously, now.

She desperately wanted him to know there was nothing to be nervous about, but before she could speak again, he was standing up.

"I almost forgot. Your birthday present."

"I don't need a present. You arranged all this."

"You do. Besides, it's kind of a present for me, too."

"What does that mean?"

"You'll see."

He disappeared into the cloakroom, appearing a moment later with an unexpectedly large parcel which, judging by the way he was holding it, was heavy, too.

"What is this?" Fleur's curiosity was genuinely piqued. She couldn't possibly imagine what he would have got her in a box that size.

"Open it up and see."

It was wrapped in brown paper but with a dark-blue ribbon around it. She pulled on the bow before slipping a finger under the tape and tearing it open.

"Books," she said.

Books and not just one or two, but dozens. Some were classics, like Pride and Prejudice and Jane Eyre, others were newer. The Fault in our Stars. The Time Traveller's Wife. As she flicked through them, the theme struck.

"They are all romance books?" she said, with a chuckle.

"They are."

She continued to lift them out, one by one. Several of them were hardbacks, and some of the classics were cloth bound, too. When she had a dozen spread out on the table, and the box was still half full, she picked up another and frowned.

"The Time Traveller's Wife, again?" she said, only to see that it wasn't the only one in duplicate. In fact, by the looks of things, all of them were.

"You've put two of each in?"

He took the book from her and placed it with the others, so that he could hold her hands in his.

"I'm not saying I'm going to come to Book Club. In fact, I will definitely leave that to you. But I thought it might be nice for us to read these together. That way, I can see what all the fuss is about."

A smile refused to shift from her lips, even as she leaned forwards to kiss him.

"Yes, you don't get romance at all, do you, Henry Pierce?"

So, it appears Fleur and Henry have made a match, but just how will they be doing five years down the line? As a special treat, why not find out with this cheeky Five Years On Epilogue.

SCAN QR CODE FOR SECRET
EPILOGUE

MORE FROM THE LONELY HEARTS BOOK CLUB

LESSONS IN LOVE

Meet Jules, a single mom juggling a demanding job at an exclusive prep-school and raising her 11-year-old son. She's got no time for love, but all of that changes when she meets Nate.

Nate is charming, funny, and seemingly perfect, that is until the first parent-teacher conference of the year. Jules is faced with a difficult decision: risk her job and security for a chance at love, or play it safe and miss out on a once-in-a-lifetime connection.

As sparks fly between Jules and Nate, their resolve will be put to the test. Will Jules take a leap of faith and follow her heart, or will she let her fears hold her back? Don't miss out on this captivating romantic comedy that will leave you laughing, swooning, and cheering for the ultimate happy ending.

NOTE FROM HANNAH

First off, thank you for taking the time to read **It's Never Too Late**.

If you leave a review for **It's Never Too Late** on Amazon, Goodreads, or even your own blog or social media, I would love to read it. You can email me the link at Hannah@hannahlynnauthor.com

Don't forget, you can stay up-to-date on upcoming releases and sales by joining my newsletter, following my social media pages or visiting my website www.hannahlynnauthor.com

ABOUT THE AUTHOR

Hannah Lynn is an award-winning novelist. Publishing her first book, *Amendments* – a dark, dystopian speculative fiction novel, in 2015, she has since gone on to write *The Afterlife of Walter Augustus* – a contemporary fiction novel with a supernatural twist – which won the 2018 Kindle Storyteller Award and Gold Medal for Best Adult Fiction Ebook at the IPPY Awards, as well as the delightfully funny and poignant *Peas and Carrots series*.

While she freely moves between genres, her novels are recognisable for their character driven stories and wonderfully vivid description.

Born in 1984, Hannah grew up in the Cotswolds, UK. After graduating from university, she spent ten years as a teacher of physics, first in the UK, then in Thailand, Malaysia, Austria and Jordan. It was during this time, inspired by the imaginations of the young people she taught, she began writing short stories for children, before moving on to adult fiction.

Nowadays you will most likely find her busy writing at home with her husband and daughter, surrounded by a clowder of cats.